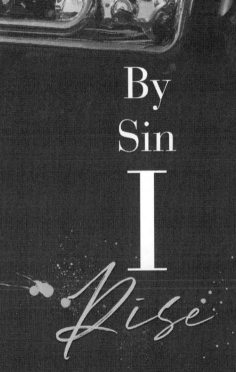

By
Sin
I
Rise

PART ONE

USA Today Bestselling Author
Cora Reilly

Maddox—Mad Dog—White hates everything the name Vitiello stands for after he witnessed his father and his men getting butchered by the Capo of the Italian mob in their territory. Raised by his uncle, the president of the Tartarus MC, Maddox is destined to follow in his footsteps. Now their chapter is on the rise again, but for their ultimate triumph, they need to destroy the Vitiello empire. And what better way to do it than to steal the spoiled Vitiello princess and break her piece by piece until her father begs for mercy.

Known as the spoiled princess of New York, Marcella Vitiello grew up in a golden cage. If your father is the most feared man in New York, people gift you with reverence.

Destined to marry the man approved by her father, Marcella is sick of being treated like an untouchable porcelain doll.

She resents the life forced upon her by her family until everything she took for granted is ripped from her. Where she is now, her name doesn't bring awe, only pain and humiliation.

If you've grown up in a high castle, the fall is all the farther down.

Sins of the fathers have a way of catching up... who's going to bleed for them?

By Sin

I

Rise

Prologue

Marcella

SOME THINGS RUN IN YOUR BLOOD. THEY CAN'T BE SHAKEN, can't be changed, can't be lost, but they can be forgotten. From an early age, I had a foolproof instinct when it came to danger or sniffing out a person who couldn't be trusted. And I listened, always paused before I acted to glimpse deep inside of me for that gut feeling, to double-check.

Until I stopped listening, until I got used to others taking care of my safety, until I trusted their judgment over mine. I handed over my life to others, to capable bodyguards, to *men* who were so much more equipped to protect me than I—a mere girl, and later woman—was. If I had listened to my gut feeling, to the tingling at the back of my neck that first night, and later when they took me, I would have been safe. But I'd learned to be deaf to my inner voice, to an instinct inherited by my father, because I was meant to be oblivious to the dangers of our life.

Little children quickly learn that closing your eyes from evil doesn't protect you. It took me far too long to grasp that lesson.

Maddox

From the very first moment I spotted Snow White, she'd burned herself into my brain. Every fucking night, the image of her naked body tortured me in maddening detail.

Sometimes I woke with the remnants of her taste in my mouth, half convinced I'd actually buried my tongue in her undoubtedly pretty pussy. Fuck, I hadn't seen an inch of that legendary body yet, much less touched her. Oh, but I would, even if it took a poisoned apple.

A guy like me would never be allowed near Snow White. I wasn't a fuckin' loser, far from it. I was going to become the president of the Tartarus MC, following in my uncle's footsteps, the current prez. Of course, that made me the lowest scum on earth if you asked Snow White and her fuckin' father, Luca Vitiello, the Capo of the Italian mob on the East Coast. I was a little boy, barely five years old, when the life I knew was ripped from me. As the son of the president of the New Jersey chapter of the Tartarus motorcycle club, I had watched many disturbing things at my young age. Club brothers getting it on with whores in the middle of the clubhouse in broad daylight, brutal fights, shootings… but nothing had left quite a mark like the night the Capo of the Famiglia brutally killed my father and his men.

The murderous bastard had slaughtered an entire chapter of our club—alone.

Strike that.

Not alone—with a fuckin' ax and a skinning knife. The screams of my dying club family still haunted my nights, an echo of a memory I couldn't shake unless I drank enough booze to kill an elephant. Those images were the fuel for my hunger for revenge.

And revenge I would finally get, with the help of the spoiled princess of New York: Marcella Vitiello.

Chapter
One

Maddox
Five years old

I HUDDLED ON THE FLOOR OF THE CLUBHOUSE AND SPUN AN empty beer bottle around. My palms were sticky from it. When I brought my fingers to my mouth for a taste, my lips pulled into a grimace. A bitter, rotten flavor exploded on my tongue, clinging to my gums and throat. I spit it out, but the foul taste didn't disappear.

The room was filled with smoke from the cigars and cigarettes, making my nose itch a little and sometimes my snot even had dots of black in it.

I kept spinning the bottle. I didn't have any other toys here. My toys were all with Mom, but Dad had picked me up there yesterday and they had screamed at each other like they always did. Dad had slapped Mom, creating a red handprint on her cheek, and he'd been in a foul mood ever since. I always stayed out of his way when he was like that. Right now, he was yelling at someone on the phone.

Pop, his second in command, usually played games with me, but he sat at the bar with a blonde woman and was kissing her. The other bikers huddled around the table and played cards. They didn't really want me to annoy them. One of them had pushed me away, so I fell on my bum when I'd asked if I could watch them. My tailbone still ached where it hit the floor.

Steps thundered closer. The door to the clubhouse swung open and one of the prospects stumbled inside, eyes wide. "Black limousine!"

Everyone jumped up as if the words were a secret code. My head swiveled to Dad who barked out orders, spittle flying from his mouth. I didn't understand what was so bad about a black car. A cry sounded, high-pitched, then gurgling. I looked back to the door and the prospect fell forward, an ax in the back of his head, parted like a ripe watermelon. I dropped the bottle, my eyes going wide. The body fell to the ground and blood splattered everywhere as the ax toppled out of his head, leaving a deep gash in his skull so I could see bits and pieces of his brain. Just like a watermelon, I thought again.

Dad rushed over to me and grabbed my arm in a painful grip. "Hide under the couch and don't come out! You hear me?"

"Yes, sir."

He shoved me toward the old gray couch and I dropped to my knees and crawled under it. It had been a while since I'd tried to squeeze under the couch and I barely fit anymore, but eventually I lay on my belly, facing the entrance door and the room.

A huge man with wild eyes stormed inside, a knife and an ax in his hand. I held my breath as he came in with a roar like a mad bear. He hurtled his knife at Dad's treasurer, who'd reached for his gun. Too late. He fell forward, right before the sofa. His huge eyes stared at me as blood pooled under his head.

I scooted back a few inches but froze abruptly, worried my feet would stick out. The screaming got louder and louder until I pressed my palms over my ears, trying to block them out. But I couldn't look away from what was going on. The madman had grabbed his knife and threw it at Pop. He hit him square in the chest and Pop toppled backward as if he'd had one too many drinks. Dad dashed behind the bar with two prospects. I wanted to hide there with him, wanted him to console me even if that wasn't something he did. The madman shot another club brother in the hand when he reached for a dropped gun. I could hear shots even through the palms over my ears, dulled bangs that had me flinch every time.

The madman kept shooting at the bar, but eventually everything turned silent. Had Dad and the prospects run out of ammunition?

My eyes moved to the armory at the end of the corridor. One of the prospects jumped out from behind the bar, but the man chased him and swung the ax at his back. I squeezed my eyes shut, taking a few shuddering breaths, before I dared to open them again. The blood of the treasurer slowly spread closer and began to soak my sleeves, but this time, I didn't dare move. Not even when it soaked my clothes and covered my small fingers. Two more of Dad's men came in, trying to help. But this madman was like an angry bear. I was motionless as I listened to screams of agony and rage as I watched one dead body after the other drop to the ground. There was so much blood everywhere.

Dad cried out as the man dragged him out from behind the bar. I lurched forward, wanting to help him, but his eyes cut to me and warned me to stay where I was. The bad man's eyes followed Dad's gaze. His face was like that of a monster, covered in blood and twisted with rage. I ducked my head, terrified that he'd seen me. But he kept dragging Dad toward a chair.

I knew better than to disobey my father's orders and so I remained motionless for what felt like days, but were probably only minutes. The bad man began hurting Dad and the prospect who was still alive. I couldn't watch anymore and so I closed my eyes so tightly my temples throbbed. I pressed my forehead to my arms. My chest and arms were warm with blood and my pants were warm where I'd peed myself. Everything stank of pee and blood, and I held my breath, but my chest hurt and so I had to suck in a breath. I started counting the seconds, tried to think of ice cream and fried bacon and Mom's Key Lime Pie, but the screams were too loud. They pushed all the memories out of my head.

Eventually silence settled around me, and I dared lifting my head. My eyes watered as I looked around. There was red pooled and splattered everywhere with pieces of flesh. I shuddered and threw up, bile making my throat feel all raw, then froze, terrified the bad man was around to kill me as well. I didn't want to die. I began to cry but quickly wiped the tears away. Dad hated tears. For a while, I listened to the pounding of my heart that rang in my ears and vibrated in my bones until I felt calmer and my vision became clear.

Finally, I looked around for the man, but he was nowhere. The front door was open, yet I still waited a long time before I finally crawled out from under the sofa. Despite my clothes being dirtied with pee and blood, and my body screaming for food and water, I didn't leave. I stood in the middle of the torn-apart bodies of men I'd known all my life, men who had been the closest thing to a normal family I'd ever had. I hardly recognized any of them. They were too disfigured.

Dad's body was the worst. I didn't recognize his face. Only his tattoo on his neck—a skull spitting fire—told me it was him. I wanted to say goodbye to him, but I didn't dare go closer to what was left of his body. He looked terrifying. I finally stormed outside and didn't stop running until I reached the house of an Old Lady. She was the treasurer's property. I had visited her a few times before when she'd baked cookies for me. When she saw me covered in blood, she immediately knew something was horribly wrong.

"They are dead," I whispered. "All dead."

She tried to call the phone of her old man, then that of Dad and other brothers from the club but no one answered. Eventually, she called my mother for me and cleaned me while I waited to be picked up.

When Mom finally arrived, she looked white as a sheet. "Come on, we have to leave."

She took my hand.

"What about Dad?"

"We can't do anything for him anymore. New York isn't safe for us anymore. We have to leave, Maddox, and we can't ever come back." She dragged me toward our old Ford Mustang and sat me down in the passenger seat. The car was stuffed so high with bags that I couldn't look through the rear window.

"Are we leaving?" I asked, confused.

She turned the key in the ignition. "Didn't you listen? We have to leave forever. This isn't Tartarus territory anymore. We're going to live with your uncle in Texas now. It'll be your new home."

My mother immediately called my Uncle Earl, asking for help. She didn't have any money, which Dad had always given her even though they always fought and didn't live together anymore. Earl took us in and so we moved to Texas, and eventually Mom became Earl's old lady and they had my brother Gray.

Texas became my temporary home, but my heart always called to return to my birthplace, to claim my birthright and seek revenge.

I didn't return to New Jersey for many years, but when I finally did, it was with one purpose in mind: kill Luca Vitiello.

Marcella
Five years old

I perched on the edge of my bed, my legs bouncing up and down. My gaze was glued to the door, waiting for it to open. It was already seven.

Mom always woke me at that time. The clock turned to 7:01, and I began to slide off the bed. Would Mom be late *today?*

I couldn't wait anymore.

The door handle moved down and I froze, sitting back on the mattress and watched as Mom poked her head in. Upon spotting me, her face lit up and she laughed. "How long have you been awake?"

I shrugged and hopped off the bed.

Mom met me halfway and hugged me tightly. "Happy birthday, honey."

I squirmed in her hold, desperate to go downstairs. Pulling away, I asked, "Can we go down now? Is there a party?"

Mom laughed again. "Not yet, Marci. The party is later today. Right now, it's only us. Come now, let's look at your presents."

After a brief moment of disappointment, I took Mom's hand and followed her downstairs. I wore my favorite frilly, pink nightgown which made me feel like a princess. Dad waited in the foyer when we walked down the stairs and picked me up before I reached the last step and kissed my cheek. "Happy birthday, princess." He lifted me up over his head and carried me into the living room. It was decorated with pink and blush colored balloons, a garland that said happy birthday, and a golden crown sat on the table beside a huge pink cake with a unicorn. On another table, a big pile of presents waited, all wrapped in pink and golden wrapping paper. I rushed toward it.

"Happy birthday!" Amo screamed as he raced around the table, trying to steal the show.

"They are from us, and your aunts and uncle," Mom said, but I only half listened as I began unwrapping everything eagerly.

I got almost everything I asked for. Almost.

Dad stroked my head. "You'll get more presents at the party today."

I nodded and smiled. "I'll be the princess."

"You always are."

Mom gave Dad a look I didn't understand.

A few hours later, the house was filled with friends and family, and men who worked for Dad. Everyone had come to celebrate with me. I wore a princess dress and a crown, loving how everyone brought me presents and congratulated me and sang happy birthday for me. The present tower was three times my size. Late that night, when my eyes kept falling shut, Dad carried me up into my room.

"We need to put on your nightgown," he murmured as he put me down on my bed.

I held on to his neck and shook my head vigorously. "No, I want to wear my princess dress. And my crown," I added after a yawn.

Dad chuckled. "You can wear the gown but the crown is too uncomfortable." He gently took it off and put it down on my nightstand.

"Am I still a princess without a crown?"

"You'll always be my princess, Marci."

I smiled. "Cuddle me to sleep?"

Dad nodded and awkwardly stretched out beside me, his legs dangling off the too-short bed. He wrapped an arm around me and I leaned my cheek against his chest, closing my eyes. My dad was the best dad in the world.

"I love you, Dad. I won't ever leave you. I'll live with you and Mom forever."

Dad kissed my temple. "And I love you, princess."

Chapter
Two

Marcella

THE SOFT SWINGING OF THE HAMMOCK LULLED ME INTO A half-slumber as I watched the frothy waves lap at our jetty and beach. The hammock in our mansion in the Hamptons was my favorite place on a sunny day, and there had been weeks of sunny, hot summer days since the beginning of June, but I hadn't had much time for leisure.

I wiggled my toes, releasing a sigh. The last few days had been tiring and so a few days to relax were sorely needed. The organization of my nineteenth birthday party had meant weeks of intense preparation with cake and menu tasting, clothes shopping, guest list corrections, and many more tasks. Even an event planner had hardly reduced my workload. Everything needed to be perfect. My birthdays were always one of the most important social events of the year.

After the big party two days ago, Mom had taken me, and my younger brothers, Amo and Valerio, to the Hamptons for a week of much needed relaxation. Of course, Valerio didn't understand the meaning of relaxation. He was out on the waves, water-skiing while one of our bodyguards steered the boat in risky maneuvers to satisfy him. I doubt I ever had as much energy as that kid, not even at eight.

Mom read a book on a lounge chair in the shade, her blonde hair framing her face in messy beach waves. My hair was always straight, even a day at the beach didn't change that. Of course, my hair was coal-black and not angelic blonde like Mom's.

Black as your soul, Amo tended to joke. My eyes cut to him. He had set up a CrossFit parkour in a less needed part of our property and was doing the Workout of the Day. It looked like self-inflicted torture judging from his expression. I preferred Aunt Gianna's Pilates courses. Of course, Amo's dedication let him look like Hulk at age fifteen.

The sliding door opened and our maid, Lora, stepped out with a tray. I swung my legs out of the hammock and smiled when I saw she had prepared our favorite strawberry fresca. That drink cooled me down even on the hottest summer days. She poured me a glass and handed it to me.

"Thanks," I said, shivering in satisfaction as I sipped at it.

She put down a bowl with iced pineapple pieces on the side table.

"The pineapple isn't as good as last time."

I popped a piece into my mouth. It was a bit too tart. I sighed. "It's so difficult to get good produce."

Amo jogged over to us, sweat flying everywhere from his glistening upper body.

"Don't get sweat on my food," I warned.

He made a show out of shaking himself like a wet dog and I jumped up from the hammock, taking a few steps back to save my fresca. Sibling love only went so far…

He ate a few of my pineapple pieces, not even apologetic about it.

"Why don't you get your own?"

I motioned at Lora who was currently serving Mom her fresca and fruit.

He nodded at the book of Marketing Analytics on the side table. "It's summer. Do you really have to take homework with you? You're best in class anyway."

"I'm best in class because I take my homework with me," I muttered. "Everyone's waiting for me to slip. I won't give them the satisfaction."

Amo shrugged. "I don't get why you care. You can't always be perfect, Marci. They'll always find something they don't like about you. Even if you organize the birthday party of the century, someone's still going to complain that the scallops weren't glassy."

I tensed. "I told the chef several times to take extra care with the scallops because…" I trailed off when I saw Amo's grin. He was pulling my leg. "Idiot."

"Just chill for God's sake."

"I am chill," I said.

Amo gave me a look that said I was most definitely not a chilled person.

"So were the scallops glassy or not?"

Amo groaned. "They were perfect, don't get your panties in a bunch. And you know what? Most people will still not like you even if the scallops were out of this world."

"I don't want them to like me," I said firmly. "I want them to respect me."

Amo shrugged. "They do. You're a Vitiello." He jogged after Lora to get his hands on more pineapple and fresca. For him, the discussion was over. Amo was going to be Capo, and yet he didn't feel the pressure as I did. As the oldest Vitiello and a girl, expectations were sky high. I could only fail. I had to be beautiful and morally impeccable, pure as the snow but at the same time progressive enough to represent the new generation of the Famiglia. Amo got bad grades, slept around, and went out in sweats, and everyone just said he was a boy and would grow out of it. If I ever did either of those things, I'd be socially dead.

My phone beeped with a message from Giovanni.

I miss you. If I didn't have so much work, I'd come over.

My fingers hovered over my screen but then I pulled back. I was glad that his internship in the law firm of our Famiglia lawyer, Francesco, kept him busy. I needed a few days away from him after our almost argument on my birthday. If I didn't manage to get rid of my annoyance before our official engagement party, I'd have trouble keeping up a puppy-love expression.

I turned the sound off and put my phone screen down on the table and grabbed my book. I was immersed in a particularly dragging part when a shadow fell over me.

I looked up to find Dad towering over me. He had stayed in New York for urgent business—with the Bratva.

"Hard-working as always, my princess," he said and bent down to kiss the crown of my head.

"How was business?" I asked curiously, putting the book down.

Dad smiled tightly. "Nothing for you to worry about. We have everything under control."

I gritted my teeth against the desire to question him. His gaze sought Amo who immediately stopped his workout and came over to us. Dad had wanted him to be present for whatever went down with the Bratva but Mom had talked him out of it. She couldn't stop protecting him.

"Hey Dad," Amo said. "Did you have fun smashing Bratva heads in?"

"Amo," Dad's voice swung with warning.

"Marci isn't blind. She knows what's going on." I sometimes thought that I understood the brutality of Dad's job better than Amo did. He still considered it great fun and didn't really see the danger. Mom was probably right to keep him away from the big fights. He'd only get himself killed.

"I need to talk to you. Come down on the boat with me," Dad told Amo.

Amo nodded. "Let me grab a sandwich. I'm starving." He jogged back to the house, probably to pester Lora to make him a grilled cheese sandwich.

Dad's face was tight with anger. He obviously wanted to talk right away.

"He thinks the conflicts with Tartarus and the Bratva are great fun, like another level in one of his computer games. He needs to grow up," Dad said. His eyes snapped to me, as if he'd forgotten I was there.

I shrugged. "He's fifteen. He'll eventually grow up and realize the responsibility."

"I wish he was as responsible and sensible as you are."

"Being a girl helps with that," I said with a smile. But it also meant my responsibility and sensibility would never be of use to me. I could never be a part of the business.

Dad nodded, his face becoming protective. "Don't worry about any of this, princess. You have enough on your plate with college and your engagement and wedding party planning..." He trailed off as if he was at a loss what else I did in my free time. Dad and I didn't have many common interests, not because I wasn't interested in Famiglia business, but because he didn't want me involved. He tried to show interest in the things he thought I liked instead, and I pretended to like them.

"The engagement party is already planned. And there's still plenty of time until the wedding." Our engagement party was scheduled in two weeks, even though we had been engaged for almost two years, but the wedding was still another two years away. A meticulously planned future lay ahead of me.

"I know you love it if things are perfect." He touched my cheek. "Will Giovanni come over?"

"No," I said. "He's too busy."

Dad's brows pulled tight. "I can call Francesco and tell him to give Giovanni a couple of days off if you want—"

"No."

Dad's eyes tightened with suspicion. "Did he—"

"He didn't do anything, Dad," I said firmly. "I just want a bit of me time to study and think about the color scheme for the party," I lied and smiled broadly as if I couldn't think of a better way to spend the afternoon than to mull over the difference between cream and eggshell. I hadn't even begun to plan anything for the wedding and didn't feel compelled in the slightest to do so right now. After a few days of relaxation after the birthday party planning, I'd probably feel more enthusiastic.

Amo came out of the house with a plate stacked with three sandwiches while already stuffing his face with a fourth. If I ate like that, I could kiss my thigh gap goodbye. Dad kissed the top of my head again before he and Amo headed down to the jetty to discuss Famiglia business. I sighed and picked up my book, immersing myself in the pages. Dad wanted to protect me from our world, and I had to accept it.

Maddox

"Do you know what this is about?" Gunnar asked as he pulled up beside my Harley. I swung off and ran a hand through my tangled hair. It was the shortest I'd ever worn it, only long on top so I could brush it back, but the helmet still made a mess out of it.

"Earl didn't say anything to me."

Gunnar got off his bike, an older model with plenty of chrome. My bike was an all-black Fat Boy, even the spokes were matte black. The only dash of color was the small Tartarus MC script stitched into the leather seat in blood red and the hellhound beside it.

Gunnar looked around. "Where's the kid?"

"Probably lost in pussy somewhere," I said with a grin as we headed toward the clubhouse. It was the fourth home base we'd had in the last two years. Vitiello and his men kept sniffing them out, so we had to abandon them frequently. There wouldn't be another massacre.

We settled around the oak table where Earl was already waiting, lounging in his fucking massage chair. We had to lug the heavy thing from one clubhouse to the next. Earl had an expression as if he'd won the fucking Nobel Prize. More and more brothers settled around the table until every member with a vote had gathered, except for one. Earl shook his head, got up and removed the vacant chair from the table, and moved it into a corner of the room. Then he settled back into his own chair, ready to begin the meeting.

The door flung open and Gray staggered in, his fly open and his cut put on the wrong way. His long blond hair was in complete disarray. I stifled a smile. This boy had a lot of growing up to do.

Earl's face darkened, accentuating the many scars even more. Even though he shared Gray's and my hair color, his had turned gray over the years. "You're late."

Gray seemed to grow smaller as he stumbled toward his usual spot at the table, freezing when he realized his chair was gone. He looked around, finally spotting it in the corner. He went to pick up the chair.

"You can sit in the corner until you learn to be on time, boy," Earl barked.

Gray gave him a disbelieving look but Earl sure as fuck wasn't joking judging by the pissed-off gleam in his eyes.

"Sit down or leave," he ordered. "And put your fucking cut on right, you idiot, or fuck off from this meeting."

Gray glanced down at himself, his eyes widening. He awkwardly pulled his cut off and turned it inside out then put it back on before he sat down in the corner.

"Done? I don't have all day. We have matters to discuss."

Gray nodded then sunk deeper into his chair.

I gave him a wink and relaxed against the upholstered headrest of my chair. Earl had a carpenter make the heavy mahogany chairs with the red padding to give our meeting table a royal look. Even his massage chair was upholstered with the red satin. Of course, after Earl himself had managed to get the first burn mark from his cigarette into the expensive satin, things had only gone downhill.

Gray still hunched in his chair like a drowned dog. He always took Earl's reprimands to heart. Maybe it was his age, but I hadn't been this eager for Earl's approval when I was seventeen. Yet, Earl had always given it to me more freely than to his son. But even I had hardly ever received a warm word. I'd learned at an early age to find warm words with women and not my club brothers, much less my uncle.

"So what's going on, Prez?" Cody asked.

Earl's disapproval was replaced by a sly smile. "I've come up with the perfect plan to kick Vitiello's ass."

"Hear, hear," I said. "What did your pretty head come up with?"

"We're going to kidnap Marcella Vitiello."

"His daughter?" Gray quipped. His open shock reflected my own feelings—only I had learned to keep them to myself. I'd later talk to Earl in private about my concerns.

Earl sent him a harsh look. "Who else? Or do you know anyone else with that fucking name? You'd think God didn't grace you with more than two brain cells the way you sometimes act."

Gray's neck turned red, a clear sign of his embarrassment.

"You think Luca Vitiello gives a rat's ass if we kidnap his spawn? She's not his heir. Maybe we should kidnap that giant boy of his," Cody said. He was Earl's sergeant at arms, and royally pissed because I was the second in command and not him.

"He'd eat the hair right off our fucking heads," I muttered, which earned me laughter from everyone around, except for Cody, and Gray who was still nursing his hurt pride.

"I want you to vet her, Maddox. You're going to lead the operation," Earl said.

I nodded. This was personal. I would have insisted on being part of the job even if my uncle hadn't asked me to do it. The spoiled Vitiello princess would be mine.

Earl shoved a newspaper article over to me. The headline announced the engagement of Marcella Vitiello with some slick asshole. My eyes were drawn to the image below.

"Fuck," I muttered. "That's her?"

Several men let out low whistles. Earl leered. "The whore who'll cost Vitiello his fortune and life."

"They must have used some kind of filter. Nobody's this goddamn gorgeous," Gunnar said. "I think my dick would fall off in awe if it ever got near that pussy."

"Don't worry, it won't," I said with a wink. "Your Old Lady would probably chop it off before you got close."

Gunnar touched his heart. He'd been the treasurer of our club for a decade now and often acted more like a father figure than Earl.

"The photo is manipulated, no doubt," another brother said.

I could only agree. Vitiello had probably paid extra so the photographers retouched his daughter's image until she looked like an apparition. Long black hair, pale skin, sky-blue eyes, and full red lips. The asshole beside her in his button-down shirt and carefully combed dark hair looked like her tax consultant and not the one who made her cream.

"Like Snow White," I whispered.

"What?" Earl asked.

I shook my head, dragging my eyes away from the photo. "Nothing." Sounding like a fucking imbecile wouldn't do me any favors. "I assume she's heavily guarded?"

"Of course. Vitiello keeps his wife and daughter in a golden cage. It's your job to find the loophole, Mad. If anyone can do it, then it's you."

I nodded distractedly as I scanned the photos on the table once more. Risky maneuvers were my specialty, but I had grown more cautious over the years. I wasn't a teen anymore. At twenty-five, I realized that getting killed before I got my revenge wouldn't do the trick.

My eyes drifted back to the photo as if pulled by an invisible string. Too fucking gorgeous to be true.

Vitiello had been the center of my attention, never his family, and definitely not his children. For some reason, it annoyed the fuck out of me that he'd managed to father such a stunning daughter. I really hoped the photos were heavily retouched and Marcella fucking Vitiello was butt ugly in real life.

I wore civil when I followed Marcella the first time. Her bodyguards would only get suspicious if a guy on a bike showed up repeatedly. Vitiello had certainly given out the headshots of every known member of our club to his soldiers so they could kill us on sight. Luckily, I'd laid low in the last few years and lost the boyish features and shoulder-length hair of my teenage years. Those wild years that had almost cost me my life and gotten me the nickname Mad. Right after returning to New York, I'd run one attack after the other on Famiglia establishments until a bullet grazed my head and almost ended my life. I'd die once Vitiello got what he deserved, not a day sooner.

Today, I even wore a goddamn long-sleeved turtleneck to cover up my tattoos and scars. I looked like a fucking mother-in-law's delight. But even looking like that, I made sure to keep my distance. Marcella's body-guards were as cautious as could be expected from soldiers who'd have to answer to Luca Vitiello if something happened to his precious off-spring. Worse than my choice of clothes was the Toyota Prius that Earl had organized for me to pursue our target. I missed my bike, the vibra-tions between my thighs, the sound, the wind. Riding in this car, I felt like an idiot. But my camouflage gave me the chance to trail Marcella's car closely, and when they finally came to a stop in front of a fancy bou-tique, I parked a few cars away. I got out of my Prius just when one of the bodyguards held open the back door for Marcella. The first thing I saw of her was a long, lean leg in red high heels. Even the goddamn sole was red.

When she straightened, I had to suppress a curse. This girl didn't need a filter. She wore a red summer dress that accentuated her narrow waist and round butt and made her legs look miles-long, even though she was a petite woman. I forced myself to keep checking the shop displays because I'd frozen in my tracks upon spotting the Vitiello princess. Her gait spoke of unwavering confidence. She never once swayed despite her ridiculously high heels. She walked the streets as if she owned them— her head held high, her expression cold and painfully beautiful. There were girls that were pretty, there were girls that were beautiful, and there were girls that had men and women alike stop in their tracks to admire them slack-jawed. Marcella was the latter.

When she disappeared in the boutique, I shook my head as if I was trying to wake from her spell. I needed to focus. Marcella's looks were completely irrelevant to our mission. The only thing that mattered was Vitiello's insane protectiveness. If we had her in our hands, we owned him, and then the bastard would pay.

I breathed a sigh of relief when I peeled out of the fucking turtleneck after returning to the clubhouse that night. Only in boxers, I went down to the bar area and grabbed myself a beer. Mary-Lu came out of Gray's room when I opened my door. She wore hot pants and a tank without a bra.

Her face lit up when she spotted me. "You look like you need company."

I took a swig from my beer. I needed a female body to distract me from Marcella Vitiello. "And I suppose you want to be that company?"

She sauntered over to me and raked her nails down my bare chest, tugging at my nipple piercing as she did so. She leaned up as if to kiss me.

"Did you just give Gray a blowy with that mouth?" I asked with a smirk.

She flushed. "He passed out drunk before he—"

"I don't want to know if my brother shot his load down your throat, Lu," I muttered then I opened my door wide. "No kissing, but I'm in the mood for a blowy and I promise not to pass out before shooting my cum down that pretty throat of yours."

She giggled when I clapped her ass and closed the door after us. Lu was one of our pass-around girls but she had every ambition to become an old lady. Not mine, that was for sure, though.

I woke in the middle of the night from a dream—or maybe nightmare, depending on the viewpoint. The last remnants of it still whirled around in my head. Blue eyes peering down at me, red lips parted for a cry of ecstasy and a pussy over my mouth.

My eyes opened wide. Fuck. I could almost taste it. Dreaming of eating out Marcella Vitiello was the fucking last thing I should do. A warm body stirred beside mine, and for a fucking heartbeat I wondered if I'd somehow managed to forget kidnapping Marcella and took her into my bed.

"Mad?" came Lu's drowsy voice, and my heartbeat slowed again.

"Go back to sleep," I said gruffly. My cock pulsed with excess blood. The last time I woke with a raging hard-on like that I had been a teenager.

Lu curled toward me, her hand brushing my dick. "Want me to suck you off?"

Yes, shit, but I'd only imagine it was Marcella.

That would take things down a very dangerous road.

"No, go back to sleep."

Her breathing evened out within minutes and I kept staring at the ceiling, ignoring my throbbing dick.

I should have known Luca Vitiello's spawn would make my life hell even before she was in our hands. Her father had haunted my nightmares for years. It was only fitting that now his daughter took over.

Chapter
Three

Marcella

I CHECKED MY REFLECTION ONE LAST TIME. EVERYTHING WAS perfect. At exactly four in the afternoon, the doorbell rang. Giovanni was never late. He wasn't even early. He was always on point. In the beginning, I'd found his desire to please me, and especially my dad, adorable. Now I had to stifle my annoyance as he stepped into the foyer after our maid Lora had let him in.

He wore a perfectly ironed dress shirt and pants, and his hair was in place despite the storm raging outside. I headed down the staircase to greet him. When I stood on my tiptoes to kiss his lips, he quickly dodged me and kissed my palm, slanting a cautious look at Lora who pointedly looked anywhere but at us.

I gave him a look, no longer trying to mask my annoyance. "Giovanni, my father isn't home and even if he were, he knows we're a couple. We're engaged for heaven's sake."

I could see that my words weren't making the slightest impact on him. His fear of my father was too great. This wasn't news and not even particularly shocking. Giovanni gave me one of his pleading smiles, which always looked a little on the verge of being painful. He took my hand.

"Let's go up to my room," I said, linking our hands.

Giovanni hesitated. "Shouldn't I greet your mother first?"

That was his miserable attempt to gauge if my mother was home. "She's not home either," I quipped, losing my patience.

He finally followed me upstairs but I could still feel his worry lingering, and it eventually came through when we reached the first-floor landing. "What about your brother? He's the master of the house when your father isn't home."

"My brother's in his room, probably playing Fortnight or whatever else he's into at the moment. He doesn't care if you say hi to him."

"But maybe we should alert him of my presence."

I was starting to lose my patience. Narrowing my eyes, I said, "He knows you're here, and he doesn't care. I'm the oldest Vitiello present."

"But you're—"

…a woman.

He didn't have to say it. Only a woman, and thus, completely irrelevant. I stifled a new wave of frustration.

"It's not like you're a stranger, Giovanni. You are my frigging fiancé."

Giovanni hated it when I cursed—he thought it was unladylike and not fitting for a Capo's daughter—which was exactly why I used it to annoy him. He obviously had no problem annoying me with his fear of being alone with me.

We finally settled on my bed after yet another argument if we should leave the door of my room ajar. I could tell Giovanni wasn't into our kiss. His tongue was like a lifeless snail in my mouth. Kissing him had never really set my blood on fire but this topped it off. He seemed miles away. I got up with a seductive smile and pulled my dress over my head, presenting the new La Perla bra and panty set I'd bought only last week in the hopes that someone other than myself would see it. They were black lace, revealing the hint of my nipples.

Giovanni's eyes widened as they raked over me and hope burst through me. Maybe we were actually getting somewhere. I crept back into bed but I could already see trepidation take over Giovanni's expression as if I was going to force myself on him. I kissed him and tried to pull him down on me but he pushed up on his arms, levitating over me, a pained expression on his face. I felt heat rise into my cheeks at his rejection. I wasn't even sure why I still felt this way when his pulling back had become a painful routine.

Giovanni shook his head. "I can't Marcella. Your father would kill me if he found out."

"But my father isn't here," I growled.

And yet he was. My father was always in the room when I was alone with Giovanni, not physically. He didn't have to be because he was in Giovanni's head. Everyone was terrified of my father, even my fiancé. My father's shadow followed wherever I went. I loved my family more than anything, but in moments like this, I wished I wasn't Marcella Vitiello. Even though my father allowed me to date, by merely existing he enforced the old traditions I technically wasn't bound to anymore. I was still expected to remain a virgin until my wedding night, but whatever else Giovanni and I did was our problem. Of course, it would be, if Giovanni had the balls to touch me.

I shoved Giovanni away and he gave in, leaning back and sinking against the headboard. He looked as if he would have jumped right off the bed if he wasn't scared of offending me. Scared to offend me, scared of my father. Always scared.

"What's your problem? We've been dating for over two years and you still haven't gotten anywhere near my panties."

I couldn't believe I was having this argument. I couldn't believe I was practically begging my fiancé to get it on. Whenever my friends talked about how they manipulated their boyfriends with sex, I felt a pang because Giovanni would probably cry in relief if I stopped pestering him with having sex. I felt undesired. I didn't even dare talk to my friends about this, and instead pretended I was the one who wanted to wait until marriage like the good, virtuous Capo daughter everyone wanted me to be.

"Marci—" Giovanni began in a tone that suggested I was a little girl in need of reprimanding. "You know how things are."

Oh, I knew. This wasn't about society. This was about his fear of Dad.

I was done with this, done being desired from afar. "I can't do this anymore. Three people is one too many in a relationship."

I grabbed my dress and dragged it angrily over my head, not caring when I heard it rip. It had cost a fortune but I could buy a new one. I could have anything money could buy and even things beyond that, if my father pulled the right strings. Everyone treated me like a princess. The spoiled princess of New York. I knew the nickname carried in nasty whispers through our circles. Good for nothing but shoe shopping and being pretty. I excelled at both of course, but I was also best in class and had goals in life that would never matter.

"I never—" Giovanni said, shocked, as he scrambled after me.

"Cheat, no, you didn't."

Part of me wished he had. Then I could drop him and pay him back, get revenge that could keep me busy but as it was, his confused expression made me feel guilty. "My father has always been and will always be a part of this relationship. He'll cast his shadow over our marriage too. I'm sick of it. Do you want to marry him or me?"

Giovanni stared at me as if I'd grown a second head. It drove me crazy. This wasn't his fault. It was mine for never being happy with what I had, for wanting a love that burned so bright, it would burst right through Dad's shadow. Maybe that love didn't exist, but I wasn't ready to swallow that bitter pill of acceptance yet.

"Listen, Marci, calm down. You know I worship the ground you walk on. I adore you, honor you. I'll be the best husband I can be for you."

He worshipped me like an unattainable princess. Every kiss, every touch was drenched with care, with respect, with fear… fear of what my father would do if Giovanni displeased me or him. I hated it.

In the beginning, his gentleness and restraint had been endearing. He'd known he was my first kiss and it had taken him three months to kiss me. I had to force the kiss on him. Every other step in our physical relationship had been initiated by me as well, and there hadn't been many to count. Sometimes I felt as if I was forcing myself on him. *I*, who had guys almost break their neck to check me out.

If I went somewhere nobody knew me, then I could have a new guy every night. But I didn't want to run. I didn't want to hide who I was, who my father was. I wanted someone who wanted me badly enough to risk my father's wrath. Giovanni wasn't that person. I'd realized it a long time ago but had clung to this relationship, had even said yes to his marriage proposal, when even back then I'd known he wasn't going to give me what I wanted. Two years, three months, and four days. Another day wouldn't be added to our relationship. Ten days after our engagement, everything was over. I could already see the uproar this news would cause.

"It's over, Giovanni. I'm sorry. I just can't do this anymore."

I turned and hurried away but Giovanni followed me. "Marci, you don't mean it! Your father will be furious."

I whirled on him. "My father? What about you? What about me?" I shoved him away and stormed off.

Giovanni's steps rang out behind me and he caught up with me on the staircase. His fingers closed around my wrist. "Marcella." His voice was low, frantic. "You can't do this. We're supposed to marry once you graduate."

In two years, I'll have my marketing degree. The mere idea to continue our relationship in the same way for that long made my stomach churn. I couldn't do it anymore.

Giovanni shook his head. "Marci, come on. We can even marry sooner if you want, then we can do whatever you want."

Whatever I wanted? A new wave of undesirable feeling washed over me. "I'm sorry that it is such a burden for you to get physical with me."

"It's not, of course not. I desire you. You are a beautiful woman and I can't wait to make love to you."

He kissed my hand but I didn't feel anything, and the idea of making love to Giovanni actually seemed less appealing than it ever had before. Giovanni's eyes begged me to reconsider, but I clung to my resolve even as I felt guilty. It would only get worse if I ended it later, and I would end it eventually. I shook my head.

Giovanni's grip on my wrist tightened. It wasn't painful yet, but close. He leaned closer. "You know of our traditions. The Famiglia is still conservative. If you don't marry me after dating me for two years, you'll lose your honor."

"We didn't do anything except for kissing and the few boob squeezes and one crotch brush I forced onto you."

"But people will think we did."

I couldn't believe his audacity. "Is that a threat?" I hissed, ready to smack him.

He quickly shook his head. "No, of course not! I'm just concerned about your reputation, that's all."

How considerate of him. "Amo's slept with half of New York. If the conservatives want to tear into someone for their sexual practices, they should choose him."

"He's a man, you're going to be ruined."

"Bite me." I paused. "Oh, I almost forgot that you can't. You'd probably shit your pants from fear of my father. So go away." I tried to jerk free of his grip, but he didn't let go.

We hadn't done half the things I wanted to, because Giovanni hadn't wanted to risk it, and now he dared to blackmail me with everything we didn't do but might have done? Asshole.

Something shifted down in the living room and Amo got up from the sofa where he'd apparently been busy with his phone and slowly came our way.

I narrowed my eyes at Giovanni. "Let me go right this second, or I swear you're going to regret it."

His eyes darted to the doorway where my brother was towering with a murderous look. Giovanni released me as if he'd been burned. "I have to go," he said quickly. "I'll call you tomorrow when you've had time to calm down."

My eyes widened in fury. "Don't you dare. We're done."

Amo came closer. "You're leaving *now*."

Giovanni turned and stalked toward the front door. Amo followed him and threw the door shut. Then he stalked toward me. I stood on the last step and he was still taller than me. His eyes burned with protectiveness. "What happened? Do you want me to go after him and kill him?"

When other brothers said those words to their sisters in a fit of protectiveness it was a figure of speech. Amo was deadly serious. If I said the words, he'd go after my ex-fiancé and end his life. Giovanni had pissed me off but he could find his happily ever after with someone else as far as I was concerned.

"Did he force you to do anything you didn't want to do?"

Of course, he'd think that was the case. No one would believe I had to beg a man to touch me. "No," I pressed out, feeling a treacherous heaviness in my throat and eyes. "Giovanni is Dad's perfect lap dog, the restrained gentleman."

Amo gave me a look that made it clear he worried for my sanity.

"If a girl was lying half-naked in front of you, would you tell her no?"

Amo's lips tightened in discomfort. "Probably not. But I really don't want to imagine you naked or having sex. If Dad knew, he'd kill Giovanni just because."

"Why? Giovanni was a well-trained lapdog and didn't dishonor me." I gritted my teeth against the hot feeling in my eyeballs. I wasn't going to cry because of Giovanni.

For a while, I'd been sure I loved him but now I realized I'd wanted to love him—had loved the idea of loving him. My relief over having put an end to this was too great for real love. Yet, sadness also settled deep inside of me. Sadness over wasted time or a future that was lost, I wasn't sure. I had thought I could force love, could recreate what Mom and Dad had by sheer force of will, but I'd failed.

"I need to think," I said and turned on my heel to head to my room. Amo was a great brother but talking relationships with him was moot.

The moment I stepped into my room, my eyes settled on the frame on my bedside table. It held a photo of Giovanni and me at our engagement party. Giovanni was beaming but my face seemed… off. I'd never noticed it before but I didn't look like a woman in love with her fiancé. I looked like a woman doing her duty.

I walked over to my bedside and turned the frame over. Staring at this photo wouldn't help me clear my head.

I felt a little lost as I stood in my room. Every moment that I hadn't spent with my family, working out, or on college had been dedicated to Giovanni. Now that was over. It wasn't easy finding someone to trust, to love, to be with, if you were me. I'd known Giovanni for a long time and he'd been part of my life since childhood. As the son of one of Dad's captains, we always attended the same social events.

I didn't want to think about it. Grabbing my iPad, I cozied up in the nook in my wide window and clicked on my favorite shopping sites. But even that didn't do the trick, so I grabbed my purse and headed down to the bodyguard offices in the adjacent building to tell them I wanted to go shopping.

Two hours later, I returned home with a dozen bags. I dropped them unceremoniously on the floor. Now that the shopping rush was over, a familiar emptiness spread in my chest. Shoving the sensation down, I grabbed the bags closest to me and opened them. I put on the Max Mara dress then pulled the shoebox out of the other bag.

Steps rang out and Amo appeared. He didn't say anything for several moments as he stood with his arms crossed in the doorway, muscles bulging.

I raised my eyebrows.

"When other girls get dumped, they cry their eyes out. You spend a fortune on clothes."

My chest tightened. I had *almost* cried but I'd jab myself in the eye with my stilettos before I'd let that happen. "I didn't get dumped," I said, slipping my new black leather Louboutins on. "Girls like me don't get dumped."

Giovanni would have never dumped me. The problem was I wasn't entirely sure if the reason for that was his fear of my father or his adoration of me. I tried to recall our good moments but looking back, none of them held the emotional depth I'd longed for.

"I can still kill him, you know. It wouldn't be any trouble."

Amo was trying to be like Dad, but he wasn't pulling it off. Not yet.

I straightened, then turned around to show off my new dress to Amo. "What do you think?"

He gave a shrug but his eyes remained worried. "Looks good."

"Good?" I asked. "I want to look hot."

Amo cocked an eyebrow. "You know fucking well how you look, and I won't call my sister hot."

"I want to go out dancing."

Amo shook his head. "Mom's going to kill me if I fuck up another math test." Amo had failed math last year, and only Dad's reputation had saved him. Now Mom forced him to do math tests even in the summer.

Rolling my eyes, I walked up to him and tilted my head back. "Really? You choose math over partying?"

Amo sighed. "Are any of your friends going to be there?"

"Half of them hate you because you dumped them. And the other half has the hots for you, so I'm keeping you the hell away from them." Not to mention that none of them knew of my breakup yet and for now, I had no intention of changing that.

"Then I'm out."

I made a pleading face. "Please, Amo. You know I'm only allowed to party when you are with me. I need a distraction."

Amo closed his eyes, growling. "Fuck. I really don't know how Giovanni could say no to you when you made that face."

I flashed him a smile, knowing I had won. He, like Dad, had trouble saying no to me. "He was too busy worrying about all the ways Dad was going to kill him."

Amo chuckled as he took out his phone, probably to ask the bodyguards for approval. "Yeah." The smile dropped. "You sure you're okay?"

I shoved his chest. He didn't budge. "I'm *fine.*" I tossed my hair back. "Now let's show New York's male population what they're never going to get."

"You're so fucking vain."

"Says Mr. Vanity."

"When are you going to tell Mom and Dad?"

I paused. That was a conversation I wasn't looking forward to. Not because I worried they'd force me to reconsider my decision. But I didn't want to explain my reasons to them, and they'd certainly ask for an explanation. Our circles would also certainly ask questions and if I didn't give satisfactory answers, they'd start spreading rumors—they'd probably do it anyway. People were looking for a scandal, especially where I was concerned. I had more enemies than supporters.

"Tomorrow morning when they're back."

Mom and Dad had their weekly date night, which they spent in a hotel. Valerio was with Aunt Gianna and Uncle Matteo in the meantime, probably getting up to no good with our cousin Isabella, and Amo and I had the house to ourselves—and the bodyguards.

"Did we get the go-ahead from the bodyguards?"

Amo nodded, looking up from his phone. "We can go to one of the Famiglia clubs."

That's what I'd expected. Amo and I had only once set foot inside a Bratva club and Dad had completely lost his shit.

"Then let's get ready. I want a distraction."

The club was frequented by many people from our circles, so Amo and I were under scrutiny the second we entered. But we both were used to it, so we ignored the constant attention. Or at least pretended to do so. From an early age, every one of our steps had been monitored and so we'd learned to keep up appearances in public. No meltdowns or smudged makeup. Too often paparazzi trailed us. I didn't want that kind of photo of me in a newspaper. It would make my family look bad.

Amo and I made our way toward one of the private balconies overlooking the dance floor. Because Dad owned the place, nobody cared if we were old enough to drink, and we weren't bound to the minimum beverage requirement of a thousand dollars for the evening, but most of the time, Amo and I easily topped that with our friends. Now that we were alone, this wouldn't happen. Drinking a Magnum bottle of Dom Perignon alone or with your little brother after a breakup was too sad. I checked my phone again. I'd asked Maribel and Constance, my two closest friends from college, if they wanted to join us, but they'd already made other plans because this was supposed to be my date night with Giovanni. I ignored their questions why I was suddenly free to spend the night with them and turned off my phone.

I just wanted to forget what had happened and who I was for a few moments, but seeing all of the judgmental gazes on me, at least the latter wouldn't happen.

Keeping my head high, I showed my perfect spoiled princess face, giving them what they expected. They hated me because they thought I had everything when the things I wanted most were always out of my reach. Money could buy so many things, but never happiness or love. Heck, I couldn't even choose the job I wanted.

Dad would never allow me to be a part of the business, to do what I was born to do and follow the path that ran in my blood. I tossed my hair over my shoulder and ordered a bottle of champagne.

My life was filled with all the riches money could buy and other girls hated me for it. I wondered if they'd still hate me if they knew of the invisible shackles around my wrists. Sometimes I just wanted to break free of them, but for me to do that, I'd have to leave the life I knew behind, and worse: my family.

Chapter
Four

Maddox

I SPENT FOREVER GROOMING INTO A SLICK VERSION OF MYSELF that would fulfill the entry requirements of the dance club. Earl was weary of me following Marcella inside one of Vitiello's clubs, concerned about the danger, or probably just about our plan being detected. But hiding right under the enemy's nose was one of the best places to be. Luca would never expect a member of the Tartarus MC to set foot inside one of his establishments. The asshole was too sure of himself. To guarantee my success, I'd chosen Mary-Lu to accompany me. She could clean up pretty well and pretend she belonged in a fancy Manhattan dance club. Guys with a female companion usually had it easier to access dance clubs.

"Take my hand," I said as we joined the line, and Mary-Lu did at once, looking as if I'd given her the greatest gift of all. It certainly didn't hurt that I'd given her a few hundred bucks to go clothes shopping so she'd look like a Manhattan chick.

When we reached one of the huge baboons Vitiello had picked as bouncers, he gave me the once over then checked out Mary-Lu and motioned for us to go inside. Mary-Lu clung tightly to my hand as we made our way into the club. This wasn't my usual crowd, nor the music I enjoyed. The monotone beat and the crowd spasming in rhythm with it made me want to hit a sledgehammer to my temple. I quickly scanned the club but it didn't take me long to spot my target. She and her brother throned high above the mundane crowd on their VIP balcony, over-looking their subjects like the king and queen of New York that they thought they were.

"Let's dance," Mary-Lu shouted.

I gave her a look. We were here on business, not for fun.

"We need to blend in," she reminded me, as if she gave a fuck about our mission, not that she knew exactly why we were here. Earl didn't trust the club girls to keep their mouths shut. But she had a point. We needed to blend in.

As usual, the Vitiellos had an entourage of bodyguards surround-ing them. Blending in wasn't their style.

The bodyguard on the staircase leading up to the balcony gave me a quick once over, but his face didn't show any recognition. With the stiff dress shirt and slicked-back hair, I looked too much like one of those Wall Street brokers that frequented Vitiello's clubs to blow cocaine up their noses.

I danced with Mary-Lu but my gaze kept darting up to the VIP balcony. Unfortunately, the angle wasn't the best, so I could barely make out Marcella Vitiello. The main reason why I knew she was up there were the many curious stares from the people on the dance floor.

"Let's go to the bar," I shouted, growing tired of dancing.

"I'm going to the restroom," Mary-Lu said, and I nodded

absent-mindedly because Marcella was heading toward the staircase leading down to the main floor.

Several people craned their heads to watch the spoiled princess of New York as she glided down the stairs in a boner-inducing dress. My eyes were glued to her as she headed for the dance floor through the parting crowd. She wore heels that had my head spinning. High and pointy, but she danced in them as if they were sneakers. Every move, every toss of her hair, even every bat of her lashes was in perfect sync with the music, as if she'd spent months perfecting a choreography. Marcella Vitiello was pure perfection. She knew it, and everyone around her better acknowledge it.

And I despised her for it. She lived a spoiled life, bare of hardships. She'd never suffered the way I had. Her father had put her on a throne, made her a princess without any achievements of her own. Hard work, pain, sacrifice meant nothing to the princess of New York.

Her fall would be steep. Fuck. I'd make her fall flat on her arrogant nose.

I let my gaze wander around the crowded club. Apart from her brother, a kid whose resemblance to his father made me want to slash his throat. She had three bodyguards with her. For once, her lapdog of a fiancé wasn't at her side. Trouble in paradise?

I smiled against my beer bottle and took another swig. I should leave. Even in disguise, the risk of being recognized by one of the Famiglia soldiers was too high. It would ruin everything, but tearing myself away was hard.

I stayed where I was for a couple more minutes and watched her dance. That girl didn't need bodyguards or her giant of a brother to keep everyone at a distance. Her gaze with those soul-suckingly cold blue eyes built higher walls than the Chinese emperors.

Another toss of those black tresses and suddenly those blue orbs locked on mine, for less than a second, but my pulse sped up. Fuck it. The only time I'd felt this arrested by a gaze had been her father's but in a very different way. The tables would soon turn. I smiled. Her brows puckered and I tore my gaze away. After leaving the bottle and cash on the bar, I found Mary-Lu and exited the club with her.

"What's gotten into you, Mad? You look as if the devil's after you," Mary-Lu said as she stumbled after me in her heels, displaying none of the grace that Marcella showed off with ease.

I got into the fucking Prius Earl had forced on me again and waited for Mary-Lu to get in as well before I hit the gas. "Let's go back to the clubhouse. I've had enough."

She gave me a curious look but I focused on the street and occasionally the rearview mirror as we hastened away. Marcella Vitiello had eyes that could freeze the blood in anyone's veins while the rest of her body had the opposite effect.

That night was the second time I dreamed of her, and from that day on, she'd haunt my nights.

Marcella

Usually dancing always worked wonders on my mood. It was my personal happy place, the medicine of my choice when I felt blue, but today it didn't have the intended effect.

I preferred things to go my way, to follow the plans I'd laid out meticulously for my future. So far all of my plans had worked out. I'd finished high school best in class, and had made it to the university of my choice. When I started something, I always finished it and when I finished it then I did it as one of the best. Breaking up with Giovanni, even if it was the right choice, felt like a failure, like admitting defeat on my part. I'd given up.

"Why are you pulling such a face? I thought we were here to have fun," Amo shouted over the sound of the music.

My eyes sought the club for something to catch my attention and distract me from my wandering thoughts. And then I spotted the guy who seemed completely out of place in this fancy Manhattan club, despite the standard outfit of dress shirt and dark slacks. Something in his eyes told me he despised everything about being here, as if he had to pretend he was someone else. I knew that feeling, but no one would ever suspect anything. I had perfected my mask over the years. Maybe he would too, eventually, or just stop doing what he hated.

He leaned against the bar, a bottle of beer in one hand. My gut instinct told me he didn't care for anyone's approval, which made his choice of outfit even stranger. He probably wouldn't give a damn if my father got mad. I wished I could be like that, not giving a damn about what people thought of me, but that was a luxury I couldn't afford, pretty much the only one. The guy met my gaze and his smile around the bottle rim became almost smug. My skin began to tingle in a treacherous way, a sign of impending danger, but my bodyguards looked unperturbed and so I ignored my body's reaction to the guy, but I couldn't stop looking into his eyes. Something in them raised goose bumps all over my body. Many people disliked me, but his feelings toward me seemed darker and deeper.

He turned abruptly and disappeared into the dancing crowd like a ghost. Sometimes I wished I could do the same, just vanish into the shadows, into anonymity for a little while. I glanced at my bodyguards once more, but they hadn't even paid attention to the guy. And Amo? He was dancing with two girls at least five years older than him who looked ready to tear his clothes off.

I rolled my eyes at him as I kept dancing on my own, the usual ban mile around me. Men didn't approach me for fear of my father and girls kept their distance so they could badmouth me. Amo waved at the two girls and danced his way over to me.

"You don't have to keep me company like I'm some loser," I muttered but I was glad for his presence, which said a lot about my day and my life in general. Having to rely on your younger brother to dance with you was sad in every regard.

Amo shrugged. "You are the only person I can be myself with, loser or not."

I rolled my eyes again, but my throat clogged with emotions. "Shut up and dance!"

It was almost two in the morning when Amo and I dragged our tired asses back home. Despite the three champagne cocktails I'd had throughout the evening, I felt disappointedly sober once I settled in my bed. All the thoughts of Giovanni and my now frustratingly unplanned future returned full force.

I remembered the guy who'd disappeared into the shadows and how in that moment I'd wished to do the same, but I wasn't someone who ran off. Even if this life often sucked, I was too grateful to my parents for what they'd done for me.

Despite my insistence to Amo that I wasn't nervous about talking to Mom and Dad, my stomach tightened as I made my way downstairs in the morning. I could already hear Mom and Dad talking, and the occasional clinking of cutlery.

When I stepped into the kitchen, they both looked up. Mom smiled brightly, looking as if she and Dad were fresh off their honeymoon. "How was date night?" I asked unnecessarily.

"Wonderful as always," Mom said, giving Dad one of those secretive smiles.

His face always filled with so much tenderness that I realized why it could have never worked out with Giovanni. I was striving for what Mom and Dad had, but while Giovanni worshipped the ground I walked on because of who I was, *of who my father was*, he never looked at me as if he'd walk through fire for me. Dad wouldn't have let anyone tell him how to love Mom. He definitely wouldn't have been scared of her father.

"Marcella?" Dad asked, worry tingeing his voice and his dark brows pulling together.

Steps sounded behind me and Amo trudged in, in sweatpants and nothing else, looking like death warmed over and squinting against the sunshine. The five o'clock shadow on his cheeks and chin still threw me off even though his facial hair had been growing for a while.

In case Mom and Dad hadn't known about our dance party yet, they would now. Amo gave the barest hint of a nod as he plopped down on a chair with a groan.

Dad's expression became stern. "What did I tell you about getting drunk?"

"I expect you to study for your math tests even if you have a headache," Mom added.

"It was my fault," I said because Amo didn't look as if he was in a state to defend himself and it wasn't fair that he'd get into trouble because of me.

Dad leaned back in his chair with an expectant look.

"I broke up with Giovanni," I pressed out.

Mom's eyes widened and she jumped up at once and hurried over to me. "Oh, Marci, I'm so sorry. What happened?" She touched my cheek. I was about an inch taller than Mom but she still managed to make me feel surrounded by her comfort.

Dad, however, looked as if he was about ready to hunt Giovanni down. "What happened?" His words, even if they were the same as Mom's, held a very different meaning. I could see that he was already imagining all the horrible things Giovanni might have done to upset me, and how to make him pay tenfold for his transgression. "What did he do?"

"Nothing," I said firmly. That was the problem. I couldn't tell Dad the exact reasons why I had broken up with Giovanni, especially because they were the reasons why Dad probably would have chosen him. They were most definitely the reasons why Dad had allowed me to date Giovanni in the first place. Dad could read people and he'd probably smelled from a mile away that Giovanni was too cowardly to ever touch me.

Dad looked at Amo as if he hoped my brother would prove my words wrong, but Amo only shrugged as if he didn't have the slightest clue and would rather die than suffer another moment of his hangover.

Mom's eyes softened further. "Maybe you and Giovanni can fix it?"

"No," I said immediately. If I returned to Giovanni, that would only happen out of habit and because I hated the prospect of an uncertain future, but those weren't good enough reasons to continue a relationship. "I just realized I don't love him. I don't want to settle for less than what you have."

Mom smiled softly. "Sometimes love takes time. Your father and I weren't in love when we married."

"I know. You didn't even choose to marry but it didn't take you years to love each other. Giovanni and I have been together for more than two years, but I don't love him, and I never have."

Dad finally rose from the chair as well. "There must have been an event that made you realize this."

"There wasn't, Dad. Honestly. I've realized it a while ago but I didn't want to give up too quickly, especially knowing that it might reflect badly on you and Mom if I break off the relationship and worse, our engagement. The Famiglia is still stuck in the Middle Ages in some regards."

Mom nodded but Dad still eyed me as if he expected me to give him a more satisfying answer to his question. "I'm going to have a word with Giovanni."

My eyes widened in alarm, and Mom warned, "Luca, that's Marcella's decision."

"It is her decision but I should still talk to Giovanni and see what he has to say."

"In his defense, you mean," I added angrily. I loved my dad and his protectiveness, but sometimes it went too far.

"It's my job to make sure you don't get harmed."

I lost it. "But you are the reason why it didn't work out in the first place! So if you want to find an answer to your question then you have to look in the mirror."

"Watch your tone," Dad said firmly, then he frowned. "Now explain. I supported your relationship with Giovanni. Didn't I?" he asked, turning to Mom.

"After your initial resentments, you were in favor of the relationship, yes," Mom said neutrally.

Amo stifled a grin, but I was far from being amused.

"You were in favor of Giovanni because of how easily you could control him. He was always eager for your approval. You could be sure he'd never do anything you didn't want."

"I don't see a problem."

"Of course, you don't. But what I want should matter in a relationship and not your wishes!"

"I am who I am, Marcella. My reputation carries even beyond our circles. Few men have the bravery to disregard my wishes. That's something you'll have to accept. I'm giving you more freedoms than most girls have, far more freedoms than your mother ever had, but you'll always be bound by certain rules."

"I guess then I'll just have to find someone who has the balls to stand up to you," I gritted out.

"Language," Mom said.

I shook my head and stalked off.

"Breakfast isn't finished," Dad reminded me, but I ignored him.

I headed straight for my room and flung myself on my bed, letting out a frustrated cry. Who would have the guts to go against Dad's wishes? Giovanni and all the other Famiglia soldiers even tried to anticipate Dad's *unvoiced* wishes. A man like that would never make me happy. But the normal guys I met in college were even worse. They barely glanced my way because they worried Dad would chase them Al Capone style. They didn't know any real facts about the Famiglia but even their imagination was bad enough to keep them at arms' length. If they really knew what Dad was capable of, they'd run away crying. No, I could never respect a man like that.

I stared up at the ceiling blankly. Maybe someone from another mob family. But I had absolutely no intention to move to the West Coast, nor to become a part of the Camorra. They were too crazy for my taste. And someone from the Outfit? I might as well just put a bullet in Dad's heart.

I guess I'd have to stay single indefinitely.

A soft knock sounded, and Mom came in. "Can I talk to you?"

I nodded and sat up. I didn't want to mope around on the bed like a five-year-old. Mom perched on the mattress beside me and gave me an understanding smile. She was always understanding. I supposed she'd learned that behavior in her marriage with Dad.

"Are you okay?"

"Yes," I said. I wasn't sad about losing Giovanni, not really. "I'm just sad I didn't end things sooner."

Mom tilted her head. "Is there anything you want to tell me that you couldn't say in front of your dad?"

I laughed. "Giovanni didn't do anything so I don't have to protect him. Dad would probably give him accolades for being such a perfect gentleman."

Mom bit her lip, obviously fighting amusement.

"Go ahead, laugh. I feel like a laughingstock anyway," I muttered. "Is it so wrong to want it all? Love, passion, and someone that Dad likes... or at least tolerates?"

"Maybe things would improve after your wedding."

I shook my head. "Giovanni will always try to please Dad with everything he does."

"I suppose that's true."

"You were so lucky that you got Dad. He is the one everyone fears. He'd never try to please anyone. He takes what he wants."

"I didn't see it that way at first. I was terrified of your father. Love and passion required some work on both parts."

"No matter how hard I try I can't imagine you being scared of Dad. You are like yin and yang, you complement each other."

"Someday, you'll find that special someone."

"Where?"

"Where you least expect it."

Chapter
Five

Maddox

GUNNAR AND I WAITED IN THE VAN, SMOKE FILLING THE inside. Since we'd left the clubhouse, I had smoked pretty much non-stop. Today was the day. I had to admit I was nervous like a virgin before her cherry got popped. We'd been trailing Marcella for weeks now, waiting for the perfect moment to abduct her. Unfortunately, the safety measures Vitiello had put in place for her were almost impenetrable. Earl was losing patience, but a risky maneuver would only alert Vitiello and not get us anywhere. Maybe this was our only chance. I wouldn't mess up.

"Maybe she left through another door," Gunnar said. His shoulder-length gray hair had fallen almost completely out of his ponytail because of his constant fretting. I'd never seen him so nervous.

"Nah," I said. "The cars are still here. Let me check the area."

I hopped out of the van and squashed my cigarette under my boot before I strolled along the pavement. I felt naked without my cut, but wearing anything that linked me to Tartarus would have been stupid and pretty much suicide. Even in civilian clothes, the risk of being spotted by one of Marcella's bodyguards was still high, but I could feel it in my blood that today was the day.

Eventually, I spotted the spoiled princess. She talked to an older man in loafers and a mustard-yellow suit coat, probably a professor. I hadn't even finished high school so I didn't have much experience with these things but he looked like someone who spent too much time with his nose in books.

Her bodyguards kept a respectful distance but were still too close for us to grab her. We had enough ammo and guns to conquer the entire college, but we wanted to keep things as low-key as possible. We didn't want the police on our backs. Having Vitiello and the Famiglia lighting fire under our asses was more than enough. Not to mention that Vitiello paid half the cops, so they'd probably hand us right over to him and then we'd be pulp.

I trailed Marcella at a safe distance on campus. I'd even grabbed a couple of books in the library to look my part. She studied business and marketing or pretended to do so. I bet her daddy bought her degree for her. Not that she needed a college education, she'd marry that sappy fiancé and become a trophy wife like all the mob women.

I hadn't seen Marcella and her boy toy together in over a week, which was unusual, but today he trailed her again like a lost puppy. He didn't know much about women if he couldn't see how annoyed she was by his simpering begging. But his whining eventually worked and she followed him to his car for a conversation. Of course, the posh boy had a fancy Mercedes Cabriolet. The Famiglia just swam in money.

She ordered her bodyguards away and they stayed back at the stairs to the main building.

I straightened and grabbed my phone to send Gunnar a text. Keeping an eye on Marcella and her boy toy, I jogged over to the old van and got into the passenger seat where I dropped the books on the floorboard. Slowly, Gunnar steered the car toward the parking lot where Marcella and her fiancé seemed caught in an argument in front of his sleek car.

Nothing was better to drive bodyguards away than an embarrassing fight between love birds. Her bodyguards pretended not to pay attention to the fight, obviously embarrassed by the scene. Well-trained dogs, all of them. I slid my silver knuckleduster on in case Marcella's fiancé put up more of a fight than he looked.

"Closer," I said to Gunnar who steered the car toward Marcella.

She looked furious. Cheeks flushed, looking absolutely striking against her porcelain skin.

"Fucking Snow White," I muttered. The Marcella from my dreams had a remarkable similarity to the angry Marcella of the present, only that her flushed cheeks had a very different reason then.

Gunnar gave me a curious look but I ignored him. Marcella shoved her fiancé's shoulder and turned on her heel, so her hair hit him smack in the face. After a gob-smacked expression, he grabbed her arm and her bodyguards were all eyes now. We only had one chance. Soon they'd be swarming around the princess again and we'd have no chance to get near her. I shoved the door open before Gunnar had come to a stop and jumped out of the car. I stormed toward Marcella with complete tunnel vision. Her eyes hit me and her face transformed from confusion to realization then shock. Those plump lips parted for a cry. Her bodyguards began running, pulling their guns.

Gunnar jumped out of the car, raised his pump gun and fired. The sound transformed the peaceful campus into a hellhole. Screams sounded and people scattered, running for their lives.

Their panic was to our advantage. They stumbled into Marcella's bodyguards who tried to reach us, slowing them down. I reached Marcella and her fiancé. He grabbed his gun, but I was faster and slammed my fist with the knuckleduster into his face. Blood shot out of his nose and mouth and he toppled to the ground. I didn't have time to off him, not with all hell breaking loose. It was only a matter of minutes before dozens of Famiglia soldiers would enter the scene to protect their princess. I knew what would happen if they got their hands on me. They'd deliver me to Vitiello and what he'd done to my father would look like kid's play in comparison to what he'd do to me for attacking his precious offspring. Not going to happen.

Nothing mattered as I finally grabbed Marcella's arm and jerked her toward me. Her wide, shocked blue eyes hit me like a sledgehammer. Her eyes locked on mine, not afraid, only surprised. The blue of her irises were accentuated by a darker outer ring. The momentum had thrust her against my chest. A cloud of her exotic perfume, something subtly sweet but also spicy, hit me. She was even shorter than I'd thought. Even with high heels, she only reached my nose. Before she could react, I pressed the chloroform-drenched tissue over her mouth. Her eyelids drooped and she sagged against me. I hoisted her over my shoulder and ran toward the van. Gunnar was still firing at the bodyguards who didn't have a choice but to seek cover, even if their fear of Vitiello's wrath made them reckless. I put Marcella down on the loading area of the van before I closed the door and slid into the passenger seat. After a signal from me, Gunnar jumped in and hit the gas.

"I got one of them."

He held out the pump gun and I took it in case I'd have to deal with pursuers. Soon the campus disappeared in the distance and Gunnar steered the car into a parking garage where we switched cars for the first time. The new van with the laundry logo belonged to a family member of one of the old ladies. I doubted Earl had told them what we'd use it for. He didn't care if Vitiello got their hands on them, as long as our plan worked out. Unimportant collateral damage.

Marcella didn't stir when I carried her from one car to the other.

After thirty more minutes, when I was fairly sure that we weren't being followed, I set the pump gun down onto the floorboard. Snow White was slowly coming to, groaning and moaning in a way that reminded me of last night's dream. I twisted around in the seat to watch her. The dose I'd hit her with hadn't been very potent. Her black lashes fluttered against her pale skin. I'd been almost one-hundred percent sure that her photos had been photoshopped heavily, but now from close up, I realized Marcella Vitiello was every bit as immaculately gorgeous as her Instagram and press photos had suggested. I had to resist the urge to move even closer, to touch her and find out if her skin felt as smooth as it looked. The short moment I'd grabbed her had been over in a flash and I hadn't had time to pay attention.

Her eyelids shot up and she looked at me, piercing and unafraid. I froze, stunned by the intensity of her gaze, by the way it grabbed hold of me and wouldn't let go. Luckily, the moment was over quickly. Her eyes rolled back and closed, and I stifled a sigh of relief to be freed of her penetrating stare. Fuck.

We changed cars two more times before we reached our new club-house out in the woods northeast of Morristown. My heart rate began to slow when we drove through the wire-netting fence gates. I'd half expected Vitiello and his soldiers to launch an attack on us. By now, Marcella was wiggling, still out of it, but growing increasingly more alert. This time I didn't make the mistake of looking at her again.

Earl waited on the porch of the old farmhouse, arms crossed. He'd received my message about our successful abduction. I jumped out of the van with a thumbs up in Earl's direction and opened the door of the loading area. Marcella sat up, supporting herself with one arm. She tossed her head back to glare at me when I towered over her.

"Time to move into your temporary home, Miss Vitiello."

I bent down to pick her up but she scurried backward. "Don't touch me with your dirty hands."

She aimed a kick at my crotch, but I grabbed her ankle before she could do real damage and jerked her in my direction. She didn't have any fight experience, so I had no trouble hoisting her out of the transporter. My attempt to set her down on the ground so she could walk by herself was thwarted when she aimed another kick at my shin.

"Fuck it, bitch."

Her indignant blue eyes hit me. Nobody had probably ever called her bitch before, and it wasn't usually a term I threw around, but she really pissed me off.

"Walk or I'll carry you over my shoulder so my brothers can see your perky ass."

She stiffened which gave me the chance to actually put her down on her feet and grab her arm to drag her along. Marcella struggled against my hold but I only tightened my fingers around her upper arm, snarling.

"Stop it."

She flinched before her mouth set in a thin, stubborn line, but at least she finally followed me without a fight.

Earl came down the three steps of the porch and met us halfway.

"Nobody followed you?" Earl asked, scanning Marcella from head to toe.

She shuddered. I wasn't sure if it was because of Earl or because she finally knew who we were. Unlike Gunnar and me, Earl wore his cut with the big Tartarus MC script on the back and smaller on the front.

"Nobody, don't worry. We were careful," I said. I moved toward the house but Earl raised his hand to stop me.

"The kennels," Earl ordered with a sharp nod in the direction of the line of cages down the slope from the house.

I hesitated, my brows pulling together.

Earl's eyes sharpened in warning. "Show the whore her rightful place."

Marcella tensed, but when I started dragging her toward the kennels, fight returned to her body. Eventually, I had enough and hoisted her up on my shoulder as I'd promised. She was a lightweight but what she lacked in weight, she made up with litheness and bite. She tried to scratch my neck and arms, every inch of skin that wasn't covered by clothes.

"You're going to regret this! My father will kill you."

Bearing the sting of her nails stoically, I muttered, "I'm sure he'd love to dismember me, but I won't give him a chance."

Barking welcomed us as we reached the kennels. They were one of the new additions to the property. Earl never went anywhere without a few of his fight dogs.

"Oh God," Marcella whispered. Maybe she thought I hadn't heard her. It certainly hadn't been meant for my ears, but for the first time, I sensed her fear and felt it in the tremor of her body.

It was strange, but I didn't feel any satisfaction at her distress.

I carried her into the only vacant kennel despite her struggling. Rottweilers filled the other cages, beasts that my uncle had turned into vicious fighting machines that only obeyed him, and sometimes me. Their barks and snarls rose in volume at the sight of a stranger.

I dropped her unceremoniously on her feet then turned and threw the cage door shut. The dogs sandwiching her kennel jumped against the bars, snarling and spit flying, as their vicious eyes fixated on Marcella, eager to tear into her. Earl earned good money with dog fights but rumor had it that he'd disposed of traitors that way in the past too, but that had been before my time.

Marcella flinched and backed against the wall of the dog kennel, clutching one of her expensive-looking black high heels. Earl watched everything with a satisfied smile before he strolled over to me. For some reason, seeing her in a cage gave me the same uncomfortable sensation I'd experienced whenever I'd seen a tiger in the zoo. She didn't belong in there, but this wasn't about my unreasonable feelings but about revenge. Her discomfort would be short-lived and nothing in comparison to the hell I'd lived after her father had butchered mine.

"Down!" he hissed and the dogs in all the kennels laid down obediently. He stopped beside me but only had eyes for the girl inside the cage.

"Marcella Vitiello, finally we meet."

"Am I supposed to know who you are?" she said haughtily.

I had a feeling she knew very well who we were. Her reaction to seeing the cut had been too strong. She couldn't be that oblivious. Though I was sure Vitiello did his best to turn her life into a fucking fairy tale. Yet even her shopping-fixated princess brain had to know the stories about our club and the Famiglia.

"Maybe you don't," Earl said with a shrug. He turned, showing her the logo of the hellhound with our script. "I'm the president of the Tartarus MC, and we have to settle a score with your father. Unfortunately for you, we intend to settle it with your help."

Marcella crossed her arms. "I won't help you settle anything. Your plan is doomed. My father will butcher all of you like he should have done a long time ago."

Not blind to what had happened obviously. Suddenly seeing her in the cage didn't bother me quite as much anymore. Maybe it would do her good to sleep with the dogs for a while.

"Let's see how long you can keep up that arrogance. Enjoy our hospitality," he said with a throaty chuckle. With a nod at me, he turned and headed back to the building.

Marcella didn't move. She still brandished that one shoe in her hand. Her feet were bare, so she must have lost one shoe along the way.

"You won't need fancy shoes around here, trust me," I said, leaning against the bars.

She glanced at her high heel then back at me. "I don't trust you, or any of the other hillbillies."

"Hillbillies?" I smirked and calmly took a cigarette from the package in my jeans. "Not a very clever thing to insult the people responsible for your safety." I lit up the cigarette, never taking my eyes off the girl.

Even her feet were immaculate. Her toes were painted red, probably by some fancy beauty salon in Manhattan. Girls like her didn't do their own nails, or hair, or anything else. They were used to having people do everything for them. Spoiled to the very core.

I finally tore my eyes away from her feet, not wanting to look like some pervert who was into sucking toes. Marcella was watching me like I had been watching her. Her face was a mask of control, but her eyes couldn't hide her fear. It didn't give me the amount of satisfaction I'd hoped for. Her father was who I wanted in my hands.

"I don't even know your name," Marcella said as if formal introductions could be expected.

"Maddox—Mad Dog—White."

I watched her reaction to my name, especially my nickname, closely. If she recognized the name, she didn't show it, but my middle name definitely caught her attention.

"Mad Dog," she said, shaking her head with a bitter smile. She flicked her manicured fingers in the direction of the dogs. "So they are yours?"

I scoffed. "You think they call me Mad Dog because I'm mad about dogs?"

"How would I know about biker etiquette, if there even exists any kind of etiquette among your kind."

I gritted my teeth. "Mad Dog because I know no fear, like a mad dog."

"Then you've never met my father."

I laughed quietly, shaking my head as I shoved the toe of my black boots into the dirt. If only she knew. She tilted her head in curiosity but I had no intention of telling her more right now.

"Why am I here?" she asked almost haughtily.

I had to admit she surprised me. I'd have thought she'd be begging and crying by now, but so far she kept up the cold mask she was notorious for. Maybe Marcella had more of her father in her than my uncle and I thought. "Like my uncle said, because of your father and the score we want to settle."

She shook her head. "Whatever you want from him, you won't get it."

"We want his life, and I'm sure we'll get it considering we have his precious daughter."

Marcella glanced over to the kennel on her left where Satan, Earl's favorite dog, sat behind the bars and watched her like her next treat. I'd never understood why he'd called a female dog Satan but understanding Earl's reasoning was wasted time anyway.

She swallowed and dragged her eyes back to me. "My father is the cruelest man you'll ever have the misfortune of meeting. The only thing he cares about is the Famiglia."

I chuckled. "You really think I believe that? Your father is good at keeping up his cold-bastard face in public but you and your mother look at him with love. If he was an asshole to you behind closed doors, you wouldn't look at him like that."

I'd spent hours looking at photos of Luca with his family in the last few weeks. The internet was full of official portraits, few of which conveyed any honest emotion, but a few unwanted paparazzi photos had revealed Marcella's and Aria's feelings toward the man I hated more than anything. By some miracle, they seemed to adore him, and while he always kept his cold-bastard façade up in public, I had a feeling he was at the very least protective and possessive of his daughter and wife. He would act now that we had her.

Marcella shrugged, trying to appear blasé, but she dug her red-painted nails into her upper arms. "If you say so. Many victims love and admire their abusers."

I took a drag from my cigarette. "Some do. But it is always mixed with fear, fear of displeasing their abuser and being at the receiving end of their wrath."

"How would you know?" she said sharply. "Did you major in psychology?"

I gave her a tight smile. She didn't need to know more about my past than the story about my father's death. "Nah, unlike you, I wasn't given the privilege of going to college."

"It can't be about money. I bet your club makes plenty of money with drugs and guns. It's a lucrative business."

"I'm surprised you know more about money than the price tag on your fancy shoes."

"I never look at price tags," she said dryly, giving a delicate one-shoulder shrug.

I actually laughed. She had bite. I liked that. I'd expected something else. "So your daddy shares his business stories with you?"

Maybe Marcella could actually be useful as more than bargaining material. Earl was keen on expanding our business but the Famiglia had a tight grip on drugs and guns.

"No, he doesn't. That's something everyone with a bit of brain knows."

I couldn't tell if she was lying. She had a good poker face. And she was definitely too confident for her own good.

As the silence between us extended, she looked around her cell cautiously.

"In case you're looking for the toilet, it's over there." I pointed at the rusty bucket in the corner.

"I won't use a bucket," she said in disgust.

"Then you can just let it go on the floor like the dogs do."

She looked over to the cage on her left again where Satan was now lying in her kennel, keeping a close eye on Marcella.

The roar of several bikes told me the celebrations of a successful kidnapping would soon begin. With cheers and hoots, several of my club brothers made their way over to the kennels. They clapped my shoulders and checked out the captive with leery eyes and dirty comments. After a few minutes, in which Marcella seemed to have tried to disappear into the wall, they left for the clubhouse.

Marcella gripped her forearms even tighter, glimpsing at me. "So what now?"

I tossed my cigarette on the ground. "You stay here and get comfortable, and I'll go to my brothers."

Loud country music blasted through the open windows and a few guys were singing along out of tune. They must have found the moonshine already. The door of the clubhouse burst open and Gunnar stumbled out, his shirt half unbuttoned and a bottle of moonshine in his hands.

"Maddox, you're missing the party," he shouted.

"I'm coming!"

"I suppose you're celebrating my kidnapping?" Marcella asked, tugging a strand of hair behind her ear. Today was the first time I saw her hair not perfectly straightened.

"That, and your father's upcoming painful death once he hands himself over for you."

Marcella surprised me when she pushed away from the wall and came closer. I narrowed my eyes and straightened from the bars. She was a petite woman, a head shorter than me, but sometimes appearances were deceiving. The smile she sent me was ice cold. "Enjoy the party while it lasts, but don't make a mistake, the only death you're celebrating is your own."

Gray arrived on his bike at that moment.

"Finally, Gray, move your ass over here. Your old man has been looking for you all day," Gunnar shouted.

Gray gave me a nod as he got off his bike. I shook my head, wondering what he'd been up to again. His eyes settled on Marcella and he grimaced. His sentiments toward the kidnapping hadn't changed. Mine hadn't really either but sacrifices had to be made if we wanted our well-deserved revenge.

Gunnar slung an arm around his shoulders and steered him toward the clubhouse, even if Gray looked as if he'd rather spend the evening at the kennels with me.

Marcella's gaze darted from them to me. "Your brother?"

I tilted my head, realizing she was watching everything closely. I wasn't sure how she knew we were related. We both had blonde hair but Gray had our mom's gray eyes and his face was softer than mine. "Half-brother," I said.

She nodded, as if she was filing away the information for later use.

I lit another cigarette and tipped an imaginary hat before I strode over to the clubhouse. "Enjoy the fresh air."

She didn't say anything but I could almost feel her furious eyes on my neck.

Inside the clubhouse, the party was in full swing. Word about the success of the mission had spread quickly.

Everyone wanted to clap my shoulder and congratulate me on my success. I only shook my head with a grin. Earl came toward me and handed me a Budweiser. "Why aren't you celebrating?"

"It's too soon," I shouted into his ear. "We've won a battle but not the war."

"It's an important battle, son. Let our men celebrate and give them the feeling we're close to winning the fucking war."

I nodded, then took a swig from the beer before I allowed Cherry, one of the newer club girls, to rub herself against me in a very explicit dance. My mind was elsewhere. I couldn't stop thinking about the girl locked in the kennel outside. She had been a figment of my imagination for so long that having her this close was a shock to my system.

The moment I'd finished the beer, Gray shoved a bottle of moonshine into my hand. I took a small sip then put it down on the bar.

I preferred to stay sober with Marcella in our hands. I wouldn't underestimate Luca Vitiello. The man was a homicidal maniac with an army of loyal soldiers at his hands, and he was deadly protective of his family. Kidnapping his daughter could be the nail in all of our coffins if we didn't play this right. Earl should have postponed the celebrations, even if our brothers wouldn't have liked it. Alcohol and pussy could wait until Vitiello was dead.

Cherry pressed up to me. "You look bored. Let's go up to your room. I know how to entertain you."

I let her pull me up the stairs and into my small room. The only piece of furniture was a bed and an armchair that I used to throw my clothes over.

She shoved me on the bed and began to strip. I'd always been satisfied with the girls in the club, but now I couldn't stop comparing them to Marcella fucking Vitiello. And fuck me, Snow White played in a league of her own. Cherry dropped her bra but that wasn't why my cock erected a tent in my jeans. An image of cold blue eyes, black hair, and plump red lips lingered in my head.

I needed to stop fantasizing about Snow White, especially now that she was in reach.

Chapter
Six

Marcella

I WATCHED MADDOX DISAPPEAR INSIDE THE SHABBY FARM building, a confident swagger to his gait. His biker buddies probably hailed him like a king after he kidnapped me. I moved toward the cage, trying to ignore the disapproving snarling of the dog in the cage beside mine, and my quickening pulse in response. It must have rained not too long ago because the stench of wet fur and pee made my stomach churn violently. The humidity and lingering heat only made things worse. I tried not to think of all the things my bare feet came into contact with on the dirty ground. I climbed on the hut, wincing as splinters from the rough wood speared my palms, and pressed against the rough stone of the back wall. It was growing dark around me, only making my situation seem more desperate. Out of habit, I reached into my back pocket for my phone, but of course they'd disposed of it.

Dad had always warned me about the dangers of our life, but neither he nor I had ever thought it would really come to this. That I'd actually be kidnapped.

I shuddered. It still seemed like a nightmare.

I didn't know what time it was. I must have lost my watch like one of my shoes in my struggle, but hours must have passed since I'd been kidnapped. The idea that I had been passed out for hours perhaps sent an icy shiver down my back, wondering what these animals had done in the meantime.

By now, Dad would know. I wondered if he'd told Mom yet. He preferred to keep certain dark topics from her and me, but we weren't stupid and knew more than he thought. Still, I wished there was a way to keep this news from Mom. She'd break down if she found out. Mom had never been built for this world.

And Amo? He'd probably do something absolutely stupid, even more stupid than his usual actions. I smiled, but soon tears filled my eyes. I blinked fast to push them back. I wouldn't cry. Instead, I stared stubbornly ahead into the forest that surrounded the area, listening for sounds of a nearby road or human life. But apart from the occasional bird saying farewell to the sinking sun and the rustling of trees, I didn't catch anything—except for the ruckus from the clubhouse.

Night fell and the bird song died away. The howls from the biker party increased in volume and were joined by the sound of breaking glass on occasion. Exhaustion, more emotional than psychological but just as potent, took hold of me. Yet, I wouldn't fall asleep until my body couldn't take anymore. Not with these animals—dogs and bikers alike—so close.

Pebbles crunched. I tensed and sat up as a man in his twenties stumbled in my direction. He was drunk and couldn't even walk straight but had his gaze fixed on me. He collided with the bars then clung to them, his forehead pressing into the gap as if he wanted to squeeze through the metal. My eyes darted to the door, which was locked, but what if he had the keys?

He gave me a wide grin. "There she is." He sounded as if he was trying to be a snake, dragging the s grotesquely. "Pretty princess." He undressed me with greedy, hooded eyes.

My hands shook even worse and so I clung to my knees. His eyes darted to the cage door. I prayed he didn't have the keys. Maybe he was drunk enough so I could overwhelm him and get away, but maybe he wasn't, and he was definitely stronger than me. He stumbled toward the door, and rattled it, lightly at first, then harder. I breathed a sigh of relief when his angry shaking at the door didn't do anything.

"Pity. Maybe later," he said with a stupid cackle. Then he began to unbuckle his belt. It took him two tries to get the fly down, and I jerked my head away in disgust. Was he going to jack off right in front of me?

But soon the sound of liquid hitting the the side of the hut inside the cage echoed through the silence. A few warm drops hit my hands and I let out a disgusted scream, pressing even closer to the wall. "You animal!"

Steps rang out. "Denver, you asshole!" Maddox roared and shoved the other man's chest so hard he just toppled over and laughed drunkenly, then fell silent.

Maddox was in his baggy jeans, but without a shirt, and his boot laces dragged over the ground. In the soft glow from the porch, I could see that he had several tattoos on his chest, one of them, over his sternum, a skull spitting fire. The shadows accentuated the ridges of his muscled stomach right down to the V of his hips.

"Fuck," Maddox growled and kicked an unmoving Denver whose head lolled to the side. "The asshole passed out and pissed all over himself." He turned to me, eyes crinkling. "Are you all right?"

"What do you care? You locked me in a dog cage." My voice had become nasal as I fought tears. I held my hand away from me, wondering how I could get rid of the pee. My stomach lurched just thinking about it.

"I don't," he said coldly and turned to go. "Good night."

"He peed against the cage and I got some of it on my hands," I rushed to say, hating the desperate note to my voice. I was never desperate, at least not in front of strangers.

"Stupid asshole," Maddox growled in the direction of his biker buddy, who definitely didn't hear him before he said to me, "I'll get you a towel."

He turned and stalked up the pebbled way leading to the clubhouse.

I eyed the passed-out man on the ground but he didn't stir. A couple of minutes later, Maddox returned with a towel. He held it out to me through the bars. I hopped off the hut, making sure not to land in the pee, and grabbed the towel. It was cold and wet. I smelled it, not trusting anyone around here, but I only caught the barest hint of detergent.

"It's water and soap, or did you expect me to give you a towel with more piss?" Maddox said. He actually sounded offended. What right did he have to be offended? Was he the one in the kennel?

I wiped my hands, muttering. "How should I know? That guy wanted to pee on me, and you probably think that's what I deserve for being my father's daughter."

Dad evoked hatred in many people, and by merely sharing his blood, I reaped the same emotions. Dad's power had protected me from the force of people's viciousness, their fear always greater than their dislike. Now I was left unprotected.

"No. Just because you're a captive doesn't mean you should be treated like dirt. I want your father, not you."

I kept rubbing my hand with the towel, but the stink of pee from the kennel floor clogged my nose, so I still felt dirty. "So a dog cage is your version of not treating me like dirt?"

"That was a club decision."

I tilted my head curiously. "And where would you have kept me?"

"We have a basement."

"Sounds splendid." I held out the towel.

He shook his head, watching me in a way that felt too personal. "Keep it."

I nodded then made a beeline around the pee puddle and climbed back on the hut.

"I'll have someone clean this up in the morning, or maybe afternoon, depending on when everyone's sober." He had the barest accent, one that didn't belong here and one I couldn't place but was definitely southern.

"You realize my father would have it easy if he attacked you now."

"He would, but your old man doesn't have the slightest clue where you are. We only recently moved into this clubhouse."

"Where are we?" I asked casually.

Maddox watched me closely and slowly a smile formed on his lips, dimpling his right cheek. "For some reason I think it might be a mistake to tell you too much."

"Maddox!" a high-pitched female voice called out.

Maddox sighed, looking up to a window where a naked woman waved.

"Your girlfriend is waiting for you to keep her entertained," I muttered.

"Not my girlfriend, but I should go," he said. He grabbed the guy on the ground and dragged him away.

Once he was out of sight and earshot, I released a shuddering breath. Tears pressed against my eyeballs. I wasn't strong enough to hold them back.

Sitting in the dark, listening to the grunts and howls and barks of the dogs around me, silent tears trailed down my cheeks. It wasn't cold but I couldn't stop shaking. I'd always known Dad's business was dangerous but it had only been a distant danger despite the bodyguards following my every step. They were dead now. Either the bikers had killed them, or Dad had done so the moment he found out they'd allowed me to be kidnapped. I didn't blame them. Giovanni had annoyed me so much until I'd ordered them away to have a private conversation with him and get him off my back. Dad wouldn't see it that way. He'd blame my bodyguards in his rage and I wasn't there to tell him otherwise and take the blame.

I wiped the tears away eventually and stared off into the darkness blankly, listening to the occasional yowling of the bikers as they got more drunk. The huge dog in the left kennel began pacing, ears perking. It scratched at the ground then curled up. Despite my fear of the dogs, I felt sorry for them for spending their life locked in a small cage.

How long would I spend here? Maybe Dad and Matteo were already on their way to save me. I prayed that was the case. I didn't want to find out what those bikers had in mind for me. Maddox might have saved me from being peed on, and pretended I was going to be treated decently, but so far everything pointed in another direction.

My beauty had been a weapon all my life, something to intimidate others without guns and violence, but now it was a liability. I'd been in my early teens when I'd realized the look in many men's eyes, and I'd soon learned to twist it to my advantage, but now…

After I'd allowed myself one good cry, I promised myself to be strong in order to get out of this alive. Dad would do everything to save me but I needed to make sure he and Matteo didn't get themselves killed while they did. I had to figure out a way to make it easier for him, or maybe even escape. These bikers weren't the brightest candles on the cake. I had to find a way to trick them so I could run away.

My eyelids soon became heavy but I forced them open until they burned fiercely. The dogs snored in the kennels beside mine, probably dreaming of having me as their next meal.

A figure moved out of the house long after the party had settled down.

I recognized Maddox as he leaned against the porch, backlit by window lights. He was the tallest of all bikers. Occasionally the tip of his cigarette glowed up. Even without seeing his eyes, I could tell he was watching me. It was a tingling sensation. One I'd felt in the club where I'd first seen him.

Maddox White.

I knew who he was. Dad never shared the darker parts of his life with me or Mom, as if we couldn't handle them because we were female. Mom didn't want to know, and I had never really made an effort to find out more, because it seemed futile. It would have only piqued my interest further and made me resent the fact that I could never be part of the business even more. Yet, I'd heard the story of the bikers in New Jersey that my father had eradicated single-handedly. I made sure to keep my eyes and ears open at all times, and this massacre was still a popular topic among Made Men on social events. Since most men tried to be exceedingly entertaining around me to impress me, stories like that always reached my ears.

I took a deep breath and pressed against the rough wall. My fingers hurt from clutching my high heel. Maddox was the son of one of the bikers who'd been killed. He must really hate Dad, so I trusted his friendliness even less. So far, I hadn't tried to think about their revenge plan. It would have only made me more nervous but having a clear overview of what might happen next could mean the difference between escaping here alive or in a coffin.

My pulse quickened at the realization of how close to death I was. All my life a possible threat to my safety had dangled over my head like a Damocles sword, but it had always been abstract, never something palpable I could grasp. Now Dad's worries had manifested into reality and my annoyance for his insistence to keep me heavily guarded at all times seemed childish and naïve. Maybe it would have been good to prepare me in a similar way like he had Amo, really show me the dangers of our world. Now I was confronted with them with little preparation.

These men wanted my father, but to get him, they would certainly not shy back from hurting me. I'd never suffered a scar in my life. I prayed for the strength to remain dignified even if faced with torture. I wanted to do my family proud. These bikers wanted to sully the name Vitiello, but I'd do my best to thwart them. I had to trust that I had more of my father in me than he ever wanted for me.

I didn't have any weapons, but one. Amo always said my looks were lethal. I had to hope I could prove him right.

Chapter
Seven

Maddox

DESPITE THE BONE-DEEP TIREDNESS TUGGING AT MY brain, I couldn't fall asleep, even long after my club brothers had succumbed to their alcohol-induced slumber. Eventually I gave up trying and spent the night on the porch, watching Marcella's hunched shadow on the hut, sensing that she, too, kept her eyes on me. The occasional owl hoot or a raccoon fight broke the peaceful silence. Only a small part of the reason for my watch was to make sure none of my uncle's men lay a hand on our captive, especially after Denver acted like a fucking animal and pissed in Marcella's cage. The other reason was I wanted to find out more about Marcella Vitiello, and through her, about her father. The name Vitiello had haunted my life for so long, it seemed stupid to let the opportunity pass to find out more about the family.

When the first hazy sun rays peeked over the treetops, I flipped my cigarette into the ashtray and pushed away from the porch and headed toward the kennels. Deep down, I knew I should stay the fuck away from Snow White. For one, I called her Snow White and second, I couldn't stop thinking about her.

She sat atop the dog hut with her legs pulled against her chest and her chin resting on her folded arms atop her knees. Her eyes were glassy and red. She must have cried. It had been too dark for me to see. The thought of her tears made me uncomfortable. Marcella wasn't the person I wanted to lock in a cage and put through hell. She was only the bait for a much bigger prey.

Her high heel rested on the hut beside her. The bucket was pushed into the corner as far from her as possible. But even if she had a will of steel, her body's needs must have won out through the night. The hut's wood was darker where Denver's piss had hit it.

When she spotted me, she straightened and sat crossed-legged, her back ramrod-straight. Her blouse was wrinkled and her pants covered in dirt, but she still managed to look like this was exactly how it was meant to be. Shit. That girl still managed to look blasé and like a goddamn society girl in a fucking kennel.

The dogs whined and jumped up at the cages, eager for food. But that was Gray's job, not mine. I suspected he was nursing a hangover from our party last night. I'd send one of the prospects over to clean everything later.

I stopped in front of the cages, regarding the girl inside for a few minutes without a word. Unfortunately, Marcella simply stared back at me, hiding her discomfort, if she felt any. "Your eyes are red. Did you cry?"

"My eyes are red because I fought sleep all night. I won't close my eyes with so many disgusting animals around." She paused for emphasis. "Not to mention the dogs."

I smiled. "Your insults pearl right off me." She slid off the hut with elegant ballet dancer feet, making sure to stay away from the piss spots, and grabbed her shoe. I had to stifle my amusement over her insistence to keep that shoe close.

"I won't go looking for the second shoe, no matter how expensive those heels were. And nobody cares how you look. You won't need fancy shoes any time soon." Not to mention that the girl looked like a sex bomb even in her ripped clothes. She'd probably still look like a fucking model in a potato sack.

Marcella smirked and came toward me, her hips swaying from side to side in the most mesmerizing way, before she stopped close to the bars. Last night when I'd caught Denver pissing against the hut, I'd seen behind her arrogant mask for a moment but now her expression was steel again.

"You care from the way you keep checking me out. I've been thinking about you all night…"

I raised an eyebrow. "I won't release you for a quick fuck, no matter how fuckable you are. But nice try."

Her lips thinned. "I'd rather sleep in a kennel with those dogs than fuck you. But I can tell you've given it plenty of thought."

Her eyes held so much arrogance I had to resist the urge to shove open the door and jerk her against me to shut her up.

"Early in the morning, I realized where I'd seen you before. In the club a few weeks ago. You watched me like all men do, as if you would sell your left kidney for a night with me."

I grabbed a bar, chuckling. "Damn, you are conceited as fuck. I was watching you because I was looking for an opportunity to kidnap you."

Marcella grabbed the bar below my fingers, leaning forward, bringing our faces so much closer. The top buttons of her silk blouse had ripped off, giving me a view down her cleavage and the enticing swell of her breasts. I tore my gaze away but was met with her soul-crushing eyes. I'd never seen eyes as blue as hers, but with a darker ring around them, never seen skin so immaculate, almost pearlescent, especially against her black hair. It was as if she'd really materialized out of a fairy tale. A very dirty, adult fairy tale. Snow White indeed.

"But that's not why you couldn't take your eyes off me. I know the look you had on your face. You can deny it all you want, but I bet you fantasized about me after that day."

I wished she was wrong. But the girl was right. She was so gorgeous, that even after a night in a kennel without any access to a bathroom, she made the dolled-up girls in the clubhouse look like gutter rats. "Your beauty won't get you out of here, it won't save you."

Her smile widened as if she knew better, as if she was absolutely sure that she would be saved.

"Even your father won't find this place if that's what you hope for. He can't save you," I continued.

"My father's going to save me. He's going to kill everyone who stands in his way. Every man, every club girl, even your little brother. He'll kill them as brutally as he's capable of, and my father is the most capable man when it comes to brutality, Maddox. You'll watch them all bleed to death at your feet, their bowels strewn about the floor like confetti. Gray will die, and in the last moments of your life, you'll listen to his cries and feel guilty for bringing this upon him and yourself."

Her words caught me by surprise, especially the vehemence and fierceness in them. This girl didn't seem like she shied back from the dirty side of life, but I doubted she'd ever seen blood and death, certainly not like I had.

Her words also revealed how attentive she truly was. From seeing us interact for barely a moment, Marcella had already figured out that I felt very protective toward Gray and she was trying to play on my worry for him. She was good, and more dangerous than I'd given her credit for. I needed to be careful around her for more than one reason.

"You think you know everything, don't you? But you don't, Snow White," I growled. Marcella's eyebrows twitched upward. "I know how capable your father is. You only heard the stories, but I've seen him in action. I watched him dismember and skin my father and his men when I was only a little boy. I kneeled in their blood while your father kept hacking at their corpses like a goddamn maniac. I pissed my pants, terrified he'd find me and kill me too. I still hear the screams in my nightmares. And you want to tell me I don't know what your father's capable of?"

For the first time, my words broke through her cold beautiful mask. Her face softened with realization then understanding and worse, compassion.

Seeing the softer angles of her face hit me like a fist to the stomach.

Marcella

I'd heard the stories, countless versions of the events. If my father's men told the story, it glorified him and his actions as if he was superhuman. If outsiders whispered the stories in hushed voices in my presence, even their words still rang with respect and sick fascination. I'd been proud whenever I'd come across that story. Now for the first time in my life, I wasn't. For the first time, I saw the other side of the coin, a very bloody, painful truth.

Maddox's words had been vicious, but I'd seen the pain the memory brought in his blue eyes. I didn't want to imagine how horrible it must have been for a little boy to watch his father being killed, especially in such a brutal way.

I masked my feelings, not wanting to feel pity for the man who had kidnapped me. Whatever cruelty he'd suffered as a boy didn't justify his actions now. "Then you should be reasonable and release me before my father gets his hands on you," I said.

Maddox stepped back from the bars. "I've been waiting all my life for the chance to kill your father. Nothing will take this from me. Nothing."

There wasn't a flicker of doubt in Maddox's eyes. He would go through with his plan and the whole club seemed to back him. My father's death was their only goal. They would stop at nothing. "So your biker friends are willing to die so you can get your revenge?"

"It's not just my revenge. Every single one of us hungers for revenge. Your father killed an entire chapter. My uncle lost his brother. None of us are going to rest before the score is settled, and we are all willing to die for it."

"You will," I said with a shrug, sounding certain even when I wasn't. Dad was powerful but he might act without thinking where I was concerned. He didn't have any weakness except for his love for his family. He wouldn't listen to reason if my life was on the line. And, Mom, the person who could usually reason with him when he was going berserk was probably in no state to think clearly.

"Revenge is a waste of time and energy," I lied.

Maddox smiled cockily. I had to admit I was surprised by his straight, white teeth, and pleasant smell. For some reason, I'd always imagined bikers to be a little raggy, with unwashed hair, matted from their stinking helmet, and yellow-tinged teeth. Even his hair looked silky smooth as it fell into his eyes. He pushed it back, a habit I'd noticed before.

"Do you use bleach to keep your teeth so white? With all the smoking you're doing, that seems like the only way for you to have nice teeth."

Maddox shook his head with a disbelieving look, a chuckle bursting forth. "Fuck, only you can think about someone's teeth while being in captivity by your father's mortal enemy."

He leaned against the bars, and I tried to see him as a man I might have met in a club, not my enemy and captor. He would have been off-limits then, with his tattoos and his non-Famiglia heritage, and so I wouldn't have given him the second glance I gave him now, but he wasn't hard on the eye with his sharp-angled face, blue eyes, and tall, muscled frame. The dark jeans, white tee, and black leather cut really worked in his favor, even when I'd never been a girl who liked the casual look.

Playing the only card I had, using my best weapon, wouldn't be impossible with him. If it were any other of the bikers, even my life on the line, couldn't have made me flirt with them. But with Maddox…

He had been checking me out from the first moment he saw me, and not just in a captor-captive way. A man's desire was a thing I was familiar with, at least from a distance. And Maddox desired me. Not as much as revenge. Not yet.

"There isn't much else I can do," I said, my voice less hostile, softer and almost playful.

"You could cry and beg for mercy."

"Would it change anything?" I asked dryly.

"No."

"I don't like to waste my time," I said. "Life's too short not to do the things we enjoy…"

He smiled, the dimple, which wasn't really one, but a scar, appearing in his cheek. "Then why are you wasting your time flirting with me, spoiled princess? Maybe you think I'm an animal, but my cock's not running the show. Sorry to disappoint you."

He tipped an imaginary hat and stepped back from the bars, the smile dropping and his eyes becoming more vigilant. "Keep your feet still, and don't flirt with my club brothers, they might take more than you bargain for. But if you keep your head down, then you'll soon return home without a hair out of place. Your inheritance will guarantee you a life full of shopping trips after you've dried your tears over your daddy's death."

I stifled my fury. "Do you think my father's death will dry your tears over having lost your father?"

He narrowed his eyes. "I didn't just lose my father, he was ripped from me in the most barbaric way possible."

"And you think by being barbaric, you'll feel better."

"This isn't about feeling better, it's about revenge."

"But if you kill my father, you don't hurt him. My father doesn't fear death. If you want revenge, you need to hurt him like he hurt you."

"And how could I hurt him?"

I smiled bitterly. If Maddox really wanted revenge, he should hurt me. My father would suffer in the worst way if I paid for his sin of the past.

Maddox tilted his head. "I suppose hurting you would do the trick."

I didn't say anything. I wasn't really sure what I was doing here. I wanted to be freed as soon as possible, but knowing Dad, he'd hand himself over in exchange for me without hesitation.

"You aren't the person we want. I have absolutely zero interest in hurting you. Your father will pay, not you." The words sounded final.

"If you kill my father and let me live with the guilt of having been the reason for his death, I pay for his sins."

"But if I hurt you to make your father suffer, you pay for his sins too, only in a more painful way."

"I guess I'll pay either way," I said softly. "But you're wrong, physical pain wouldn't be more painful."

"Unless you've experienced both, you can't be sure."

"I guess I'll find out soon."

"You won't experience physical pain while you're here, but I can't spare you the grief of being the reason for your old man's death," he murmured. He hooked his thumbs in the pockets of his jeans. "Maybe it's a consolation to know that he deserves whatever we have planned for him."

My stomach lurched as my mind imagined the gruesome details. "Maddox," I said quietly. "Men like you and him always deserve death. At some point, the mutual killing has to stop. If you kill my father, my brother and uncles will seek revenge."

Matteo loved my dad, and Romero respected Luca and was almost like a brother to him. They wouldn't rest until every biker had found a painful end.

"I live for revenge."

"Seems like a pointless life if it's only filled with a desire for revenge."

"Enough for me."

"Will your club brothers and uncle mourn you as deeply as my family will mourn my father? Will anyone miss you as profoundly because they loved you with all their heart?"

He gave me a harsh smile. "I'm afraid I don't have time for more chitchat. Have a good day."

By not answering, he gave me the answer I'd expected. "That's what I thought."

He tilted his head in farewell and turned without another word. I had definitely hit a weak spot. Movement on the porch drew my eyes in.

Another biker, much older than Maddox, with shoulder-long black-gray hair watched me. Goose bumps rose on my skin at the look in his eyes.

Maddox passed him by on his way into the clubhouse, saying something to him that had the man look away from me briefly.

But my reprieve was short-lived. Soon his greedy gaze returned to me, and now Maddox was gone. I could only hope my words hadn't driven him away. I had a feeling he was my best bet to get through this unscathed.

Chapter
Eight

Maddox

CODY KEPT OBSERVING THE KENNELS LIKE A WOLF ON THE hunt. He had his eyes set on Snow White, sensing easy pussy. He'd never had much of an understanding of the meaning of consent.

I stopped by his side on the porch. "Don't you have better things to do than to salivate over the Vitiello girl?"

He scoffed. "I don't spend half my morning gossiping with the cunt."

"I'm trying to gather information from our captive while she's in our hands," I lied. It had been the original plan but whenever I was near her, any carefully laid out plans evaporated.

"What kind of info? How much cock she can take into that filthy mouth of hers?"

"Just stay away from her. We both know your dick has a life of its own."

I strode into the house and was immediately hit with the smell of a wild party. After hours outside in the fresh air, the stench almost made me pass out. Gray had thrown up in an ice bucket and someone else had pissed into a beer bottle. That mixed with the odor of a dozen sweaty bodies was a potent mixture.

I found Earl already up and in his chair at our meeting table, smoking a cigar. He could hold his liquor pretty well after decades of training. A half-naked girl lay on top of the table, fast asleep.

"You left the party early," he said, not bothering to take the smoke out of his mouth.

"I've had enough parties to last me a lifetime, and I still don't think we have reason to celebrate just yet."

"When I was your age, I didn't say no to a party or pussy."

"So nothing changed," I said with a grin.

He chuckled then coughed and finally took out the cigar. "What did the bitch say? Did she cry and beg you to release her?"

I shook my head. "She's too proud. Got more of her father in her than I thought."

Earl's expression darkened. "We'll see how long she keeps that Vitiello arrogance."

Something in Earl's tone made me uneasy. If he disliked someone, truly disliked someone, that person better made sure to stay away from him.

"When are you going to ask Vitiello to exchange himself for his daughter? I want to get this over with and finally get my hands on Vitiello himself."

Earl didn't react, only squinted down at the cigar in his hands.

"That's still the plan, right?" After my initial reluctance regarding the kidnapping, Earl had insisted we'd keep Marcella as briefly as possible. Now he seemed to be having his thinking hat on again, and that was never a good thing.

"It is, but it would be too easy, and that's the last thing I want to give Vitiello, an easy way out of this. He needs to suffer emotionally before we really tear him apart."

I was the last person who wanted to spare Luca Vitiello pain in any form. He needed to suffer as much as possible for ruining my childhood.

"We've gone through plenty of shit but we need to stay on track or we risk getting our asses kicked again. I'm sure the asshole already suffered plenty after he found out we got our hands on his daughter."

"One night. That's what you call plenty of suffering? You pissed your goddamn pants every night for the first three months you lived with me. That's suffering, Mad. Let Vitiello piss his pants from fear for his precious daughter's life. Once he's come crawling, we can still exchange her for him and torture him to death."

Earl's voice made it clear that the discussion was over for him, and he being as stubborn as a mule, I knew it was futile to keep talking.

A man's scream rang out, followed by cursing and Marcella's cry of pain.

"What now?" Earl muttered, annoyed, pushing out of his chair, but I was already on my way out of the room.

I stormed out of the house, my eyes darting to the kennels where the noise was coming from. The dogs were barking up a storm, jumping against the cages, but my eyes were drawn to Marcella's cage. Cody was inside, grabbing Marcella by the arm and shaking her.

He slapped Marcella across the face so hard she fell to the ground with a yelp. I charged down the pathway and into the cage and grabbed his arm, stopping him from hitting her again.

"What the fuck is going on here?" I growled.

Marcella sat on the ground, touching her cheek, which was bright red. From the way she pressed her lips together, I could tell she was fighting tears.

"Answer me," I hissed, giving Cody a shake.

He shook off my grip and clutched the side of his head where he

By Sin I *Rise*

was bleeding profusely from a cut in his hairline. He made a move as if to attack her again but I shoved him against the bars.

"What happened here?"

Why the fuck wasn't anyone answering me?

"The whore attacked me with her fucking shoe," Cody seethed.

I followed his pointer finger toward the high heel on the dirty floor, and almost started laughing.

"That's a Louboutin, not some shoe," Marcella said haughtily, still holding her cheek, but no longer appearing close to tears.

I had no clue what that meant. I owned exactly two pairs of shoes.

I sent her a death glare. "You better shut up."

Cody was a vindictive asshole. Provoking him would not only make her life a whole lot more difficult but also mine if I wanted to make sure she got out of this unscathed. Earl stood on the porch, watching over the events. I wasn't sure what his angle was, so he probably wouldn't keep Marcella safe. It was ironic that it fell upon me to protect my worst enemy's offspring.

"What were you doing in her cage?"

"I was supposed to feed her. The cunt doesn't deserve food, if you ask me."

"Nobody asks you, Cody. Next time you better pay attention before she pokes your eye out," I told him. "Or better yet, let me or Gray handle the meals."

I preferred Cody far away from her. Eventually he wouldn't be able to keep his ugly dick in his pants. I really didn't want to add that kind of shit to my list of sins.

"Whatever," Cody muttered, rubbing his head as he left the cage. The last look he sent Marcella told me I'd have more sleepless nights. He stalked away, muttering insults.

Earl shook his head at Cody. His disapproval would only increase Cody's desire to pay Marcella back for humiliating him.

I turned to Marcella. Her blouse had lost another button and was covered in grime just like her feet but the look in her eyes was as proud as the first time I'd seen her. I held out my hand to her and to my surprise she took it without hesitation. I pulled her to her feet. She stumbled against me and I wasn't entirely sure if it was an accident. Instead of pushing her away at once, I enjoyed the feel of her breasts pressed against my chest for a moment as I looked down at her face. Grabbing her shoulders, I moved her back. "Does it hurt?" I asked, motioning at her red cheek.

She shrugged. "Your biker buddy has it worse. I think I knocked his last brain cells out of his head."

"Maybe you should get down from your high horse before someone knocks you down. Everyone around here is eager to break the spoiled princess. Keep that in mind before you act out again."

"My father will save me soon. I bet he's already on his way with an army of loyal followers at his heels. And you'll find I'm difficult to break," she said simply.

Her absolute certainty that her father would save her rubbed me the wrong way. Her absolute trust in her father enraged me. I wanted her to doubt him, to hate him. I wanted her to show a crack in her cold New York princess façade. This side of her was too much like her father.

I smirked. "Maybe because nobody's tried to break you yet, Snow White." I stepped closer again until I towered over her and inhaled her scent. "You grew up in a castle behind protective walls built by your fucking father."

Fuck, part of me wanted to break her, but the other, the other wanted to find out more about her, wanted to win her over to my side. Breaking women wasn't my thing anyway. Cody and a few other guys, on the other hand might find it enjoyable.

Marcella only watched me but there was a flicker of unease in her eyes. She knew what I said was true. She'd had a very sheltered life. The only problems she'd encountered so far were if her shoes didn't match her dress. I came from a very different world, one filled with blood and pain.

"Do you want to break me, Maddox?" Marcella asked, and the way she said my name, her tongue caressing every syllable, raised goose bumps on my skin. Fuck. Never before had a woman given me goose bumps.

Her blue eyes seemed to bury in my soul, digging and searching. "I'm pretty busy." I backed away and picked up the shoe. "I'm afraid I'll have to confiscate this until your release. Though, I'm sure you've got an impressive collection at home and won't miss a pair."

"When will I be released?"

I walked out of the cage and closed the door. "When your daddy is ready to hand himself over." She didn't need to know the truth. Maybe she'd finally learn to despise her father if she thought he hesitated to offer himself for her.

"Will you give me clothes to change or an opportunity to wash myself?"

I shook my head. I wasn't sure if she was trying to piss me off on purpose. "I'll send someone down with a bucket of water later. But I don't think any of the girls want their clothes ruined in the kennels."

"You'd probably prefer me to sit here naked," she muttered.

"No," I said, and I wasn't even lying, because I had a feeling seeing Marcella naked would mess with my brain in a way that I really didn't need.

I got off my bike. Since Marcella's arrival three days ago, I always parked my bike farther down the hill so I had to walk past the kennels and could catch a glimpse of her. What I saw made me pause.

Her blouse was ripped. One of those fancy see-through sleeves hanging by a thread. This morning before my run that definitely hadn't been the case yet. Fuck. Why did Earl have to insist I check our gun and drug storage?

I made a beeline toward her, my pulse already speeding up. "What happened?"

Marcella poked around in her bowl of scrambled eggs. I got why she didn't eat them. They looked like they had already been eaten.

"Someone needs to take a cooking course," she said, as if she didn't know what I was referring to. She had a talent to drive me up the wall. I unlocked the door and a subtle tension entered Marcella's body. I'd noticed it before and as usual it rubbed me the wrong way.

I motioned at her ripped sleeve. "What happened?"

She finally looked up from the bowl. Her cheek was still slightly swollen from when Cody had slapped her and the sight still upped my rage.

"Cody wasn't happy with my refusal to acknowledge his presence so he made himself unmistakably known."

I gritted my teeth against the onslaught of fury I felt toward the idiot. He always needed someone to pick on, preferably someone female. "What exactly did he do?"

Marcella narrowed her eyes in that assessing way that she had. "Why do you care?"

"You are our leverage against your father. I won't allow anyone to mess up my plans by damaging the leverage."

"Newsflash: the leverage has been damaged before." She motioned at her cheek. "And I doubt ripping my sleeve will be the last thing Cody does. He seems to like it too much." She tried to sound flippant and cool, as if nothing that could happen concerned her in the slightest, but there was the slightest tremble in her voice that betrayed her cool to be a charade.

"Cody won't touch a fucking hair on your head again. I'll make sure of it."

"Your last warning didn't have the intended effect. And your uncle doesn't seem to care if he damages the goods."

That was true. Earl's concern over Marcella's physical intactness was limited to her being alive long enough to torture Vitiello with her safety and blackmail him into handing himself over.

My phone rang. I picked it up. It was Leroy, one of the prospects detached to our old clubhouse to keep watch. His breathing was harsh.

By Sin I *Rise*

"Mad, they burned down everything." His words tumbled over each other, ripe with fear.

"Slow down, who burned down what?" I had an inkling what might have happened though.

Marcella put down her plate and pushed to her feet. I realized it might not be the best idea to let her find out too much. Even if she didn't have any implants that we could detect, I had a feeling she was clever enough to use any morsel of information against us.

Listening to Leroy's rambles, I left the kennel and locked it again, to Marcella's obvious displeasure. As I'd feared, Vitiello had burned down our previous clubhouse—which had also been in a secret location and not easy to detect. "You safe?" I asked the prospect.

"I don't know. A few of them followed me but I must have shaken them off. I don't see them anymore."

"You know protocol. Don't come here until you're absolutely sure nobody's following you. Until then, stay with one of the pass-arounds." Going to an old lady would be too risky and until we could be sure our safe houses actually were safe, he needed to stay away from those as well.

"Will do," he said. He still sounded haunted.

Ignoring Marcella's curious expression, I hung up and jogged up to the clubhouse to give Earl the bad news. I found him in his office with a club girl, one of the pass-arounds, on his lap. In the past, the sight had always made me furious on Mom's behalf but she always said she didn't care as long as she was his old lady. Bikers couldn't be faithful, especially the prez. I thought she was being too easy on Earl, but her gratefulness after he'd taken her into his house—and bed, after Dad's brutal death reached further than my reasoning.

"Club business," I said.

Earl unceremoniously pushed the girl off his lap and I didn't look anywhere near his groin area. I'd seen his dick on too many occasions like this already.

"What's so important?"

"Bad news about our old clubhouse."

81

Earl leaned forward on his chair as if he was preparing to lunge.

"Vitiello found it and burned it down. He must have hoped to find his daughter there and probably wanted to send us a message with its destruction."

Earl jumped to his feet. "Motherfucker! I'll give him a fucking message if he wants one!"

He looked livid. His head didn't just get red, it got purple and a vein in his forehead swelled grotesquely. That was never a good thing.

"He's trying to intimidate us. If we ignore his message, this will only enrage him more."

"Ignore it? The fuck I'll do that. He needs to realize who's pulling the strings, and it's sure as fuck not him."

"What's your plan?" I asked carefully as he paced the room, cracking his tattooed knuckles.

Instead of an answer, he stalked out of his office like a man on a mission. "Gather at the kennels!" he barked at the guys lounging in the common room.

Most of the club brothers were on runs, but Cody, Gunnar, Gray, and a prospect were around. They all got up and sent me questioning looks as if I knew what kind of madness Earl had in his mind.

"Take your phone with you, Gray!" Earl ordered.

I followed Earl as he rushed outside.

"Why do you need a phone? You can use mine as well."

"Calling Vitiello is a big risk, Prez. He can track us," Cody butted in.

I almost rolled my eyes. As if Earl didn't know that. Everyone who's been doing illegal shit for more than a day knows how easily phone calls could be tracked.

"Do I look like an idiot?" Earl snarled. "It's to record a video for the motherfucker, Vitiello."

My pulse sped up, wondering what kind of video Earl had in mind.

Marcella's expression turned worried when she spotted us heading her way. "Hey princess, time to show your daddy not to mess with us."

Marcella's eyes darted to me, then to Earl.

"Get naked," Earl ordered.

My head swiveled around. "Why?" I asked, my voice alarmed.

"Someone's eager to see pussy," Cody snickered, mistaking my worry for excitement. He was such a fucking moron. Earl, on the other hand, seemed to know exactly how I felt about the situation.

"Can you upload the video on the internet without any link to this location?" Earl asked Gray.

Gray looked put on the spot. "I guess so."

Earl slapped him over the head. "I guess so won't do if you don't want Vitiello to skin your balls."

"I can do it," Gray said quietly.

"You want to post a video of Marcella naked online?" It wasn't as bad as what I'd feared when Earl had asked her to get naked, and it would definitely coax a strong reaction from Vitiello.

Earl nodded but he looked at Marcella. "Get naked!"

She shook her head, her head held high. "I certainly won't undress in front of any of you."

"Oh, you won't? Then we'll have to do it for you," Earl said with a nasty grin.

Cody was already salivating at the prospect of getting his hands on Marcella. "I can do it," he said, sounding like he'd never seen a pussy before.

"No, I want to do it," I growled, sending Cody a scowl. Then I glanced at Earl and allowed my expression to become leering. "I want Vitiello to know that I'm the one who undressed his precious princess."

Marcella sent me a disgusted look.

Earl gave me a benevolent smile. "Go ahead." He nodded at Gray. "Get your phone ready."

I unlocked the door and stepped inside the cage, straightening my cut so it would look good in the recording.

"The rest of us will howl and hit the bars in the background," Earl instructed, as if Cody needed an incentive to do so.

Gray positioned himself in a corner of the kennel so he could film Marcella but also the others as they swarmed around the kennel.

The dogs began to bark and jump against the bars, fired up by the heated atmosphere.

Marcella took a step back when I approached her but then she caught herself, straightened her shoulders and lifted her head to send me the most condescending look I'd ever seen, as if I was a cockroach not worthy to be squashed under her expensive shoe. Anger rushed through my veins. In moments like this, she reminded me too much of her father. Why was I even trying to protect her?

I stopped right in front of her, torn between fury and concern. This was quickly getting out of hand.

"Get her out of those clothes," Earl shouted.

"I'll count to five then I'll start to record," Gray said.

I reached for Marcella's blouse and noticed the slight tremor in her body. My anger quickly evaporated but I couldn't reason with Earl and I sure as fuck wouldn't allow Cody to put his hands on her. I began to unbutton the remaining buttons of her blouse. My fingers brushed across Marcella's skin and goose bumps erupted all over her body, but all I could think about was that I'd never touched skin softer than hers.

She jerked back when I reached her midriff. "I'll do it myself."

"Hurry the fuck up, will you?" I snarled, knowing this would reach Vitiello.

I took a step back and watched as Marcella unbuttoned the last button then pushed her blouse over her shoulders. After that, she shimmied out of her black pants. The fabric floated to the dirty ground, leaving her in black lace panties and a black strapless bra. I didn't even try not to check her out. It would have been physically impossible. The draw was simply too strong.

"The rest too," Earl growled.

Marcella's fingers trembled when she unhooked her bra and she swallowed visibly when it dropped to the ground. Her pink nipples puckered. I dragged my eyes away from her round breasts and met her gaze, trying not to act like a fucking pervert but it cost me every ounce of self-control I never knew I had.

In the background, Earl and the others began to howl and hit the bars. The dog's barking soon became shrill and excited. Marcella hooked her fingers in the waistband of her panties, her hateful eyes hitting me before she shoved the flimsy fabric down. For a heartbeat, my gaze darted down, like a reflex I couldn't control, but there wasn't enough time to soak up the full enormity of her beauty. I only caught a glimpse of a triangle of black and slim thighs before I caught myself. I fought the urge to step in front of her to shield her from the hungry eyes of the others. I didn't want to share the sight with anyone, even though I didn't have any right to see it myself. Fuck. I never cared if any of the girls I slept with were passed around my club brothers, so why did I care about Marcella?

"Turn around," Earl ordered. Marcella's wrath now hit him. She was trembling and fear swam in the depth of her blue eyes but you couldn't tell from her cold expression.

With a grace few people would have managed in a dirty kennel, surrounded by leering men and raging dogs, Marcella turned around slowly. I realized I'd stopped breathing when the last item of her clothing had hit the ground and quickly sucked in a deep breath. I needed to get a fucking grip. I focused on Cody, trying to gauge his reaction. He was practically salivating, eager to mount her. Luckily, Earl's expression was mostly calculating, even if he too watched her with a sort of slack-jawed hunger—which any man would upon seeing Marcella's body.

Eventually, Earl motioned Gray to turn off the recording. Marcella stood still, her arms hanging loosely by her side. Looking the way she did, she had no reason to be shy about her body, but that wasn't why she seemed completely unfazed by her nakedness. She was too proud to show any weakness. I wondered what was really going on in her mind.

"Let's hope for you that your daddy gets the message," Earl said before he turned and headed back to the clubhouse, probably to dip his dick in club girl pussy.

Gray, the prospect, and Gunnar soon followed him. Only Cody remained, still checking out Marcella.

"Why don't you fuck off?" I muttered.

"Why? So you can dip your cock in that virgin pussy? I didn't hear you call dibs."

I glanced at Marcella. Virgin? She had been dating that Italian douchebag for over two years. I knew the Italian mob was traditional but even they must have stepped into the twenty-first century by now. Marcella's face was still hateful and eerily proud.

"Nobody's going to call dibs," I growled.

"We'll see," Cody said and finally turned around and left. The moment he was gone and out of earshot, I turned to Marcella. "You can get dressed."

She smiled harshly, but I didn't miss the glistening of her eyes. "Are you sure that's what you want? Don't you want to call dibs on my virgin pussy?" She spat out the last two words in disgust. It was obvious that she wasn't used to talking dirty.

I almost asked if she was indeed a virgin. Then I decided it was better if I didn't know. It was completely irrelevant to our plan, and yet my thoughts circled around this tidbit of information since Cody had brought it up like flies around shit. "Just get dressed," I said sharply, annoyed at myself.

Marcella covered her breasts as she bent down to retrieve her clothes then tiptoed toward the hut where she draped them as if they weren't ripped and dusty.

"I didn't know this would happen," I said, even though I wasn't sure why I was telling her this. I didn't have to justify myself or the club's actions to her.

"You enjoyed it," she muttered as she pulled her panties back on. I'd seen her wash them in the bucket of water from my window last night.

There was no denying it. Marcella was prettier than in my imagination. Fuck, pretty was an insult for her. "Are there men who wouldn't?"

"At least one," she said as she dressed herself fully. I wondered whom she was referring to.

"Your fiancé?"

"Ex-fiancé." She fixed me with a look. "So what's next? Are you going to post a video of every biker having a go at me?"

My pulse sped up. "No," I growled. The mere idea of letting that happen set my blood aflame. "We aren't animals."

She gave me a doubtful look. I couldn't even blame her after the show Earl had just put on.

Marcella

The fierceness in Maddox's voice caught me by surprise. "Why do you care? Or do you want me for yourself?" I asked.

I resisted the urge to rub my arms. That wouldn't get rid of the dirty feeling on my skin where they had leered at me. Focusing on Maddox had helped a little. His gaze, other than that of his biker friends, hadn't made me feel dirty. I wasn't sure what it was about him that calmed and exhilarated me all at once. It was an absolutely irrational feeling.

Still, my stomach dropped when I thought of the recording that would soon find its way into the internet, onto millions of computer screens, even Dad's and Amo's. I hoped they wouldn't watch. I also wished none of the girls who despised me would see me like that, but that was wishful thinking. They would all jump at the chance to see me humiliated. At the mercy of these bastards. I wouldn't allow them to make me feel degraded.

Maddox stalked out of the cage and locked it, as if he couldn't stand another moment in my proximity. He lit a cigarette and glowered up at the clubhouse but didn't answer my question. I wasn't blind. I had seen the way he looked at me, no matter how hard he tried not to look.

He took a deep pull from the cigarette and exhaled. "I'm a better choice than Cody," he muttered.

My stomach coiled at the implication. The mere idea of Cody touching me made me want to throw up. Maddox, on the other hand... I wasn't repulsed by his body, and I didn't dislike him as much as could be expected. Not to mention that he was probably the only chance to get out of here. None of the other bikers had shown the slightest interest in my well being.

"You aren't any kind of choice. Nobody asked me what I want."

Maddox nodded. "I've got to go."

Fear overwhelmed me and I lunged forward, grabbing on to the bars. "What if Cody comes down here to get what he wants? I doubt your uncle would care."

Maddox tensed, but I couldn't read his expression when he turned to me. A few blond strands fell over his baby blue eyes and the gash that looked like a peculiar dimple deepened further as he scowled. "Cody can't do anything without my uncle's permission."

Was that supposed to calm me? Cody was like a starving man who'd spotted his next meal when he looked at me.

Maddox's gaze held mine and what I saw in his was pure hunger. I shivered and pressed even closer to the bars.

"You can't let him have me," I whispered. I could be yours, I let my eyes say. He wanted me, had wanted me from the very first moment. I needed him on my side if I wanted to survive this. I couldn't rely only on Dad and Matteo to save me.

A war was raging in Maddox's eyes. Maybe he realized why I was flirting with him. He flicked away his cigarette, stomped on it before he moved very close to me, only the bars between us. The dogs let out yaps of excitement. He brought his face so close our lips were almost brushing.

"I'm not stupid," he growled. "Don't think you can manipulate me. I'm not like that sappy ex-fiancé."

His furious eyes darted down to my mouth, *wanting*, despite everything. He suspected me and yet he couldn't stop wanting—wanting what he shouldn't. I didn't look away. I exhaled, then drew in his scent, a mix of leather, smoke and sandalwood. Nothing I'd ever appreciated but Maddox made it work. My body wondered, longed for something I'd been denied for so long.

"Who says I'm manipulating you?" Then I amended. "But even if I were trying to do it, you don't have to let me succeed. You could just use me like you think I'm using you."

"I don't have to use you. You are at our mercy, Marcella, maybe you forget. I could do with you whatever I want without any consequences whatsoever."

"You could, but that's not who you are. You want me, but you want me willing."

Maddox's knuckles turned white as his grip around the bars tightened.

"You don't know me."

"No, I don't. But I know one thing for a fact," I whispered and then brushed my lips so very lightly over his, trying to ignore how my body heated from the light contact. "You can't stop thinking about me, and after today you'll dream about my body and how it would be to touch me every waking moment and even when you sleep."

He jerked back from my lips as if they'd electrocuted him. I too had felt the zap rushing through my body at the brief kiss. "Don't play with things you can't control, Snow White. You don't know what you're getting yourself into." He turned around and left. He was probably right. Maddox was a different type of man than I was used to. He was crude and didn't have an ounce of respect for my father. He'd love to piss him off. But that was part of why I was drawn to him, despite the horrible situation. Not that my desires held any meaning. I needed to get out of here, no matter how.

Maddox kept his distance the rest of the day, and luckily no one else came by either.

My stomach rumbled again. After the recording, I'd been sure I'd never be able to eat again, I felt so sick. The last few days I'd longed for my cell phone, now I was glad it was gone. My Instagram and Messenger were probably bursting with messages because of the nude recording. I shoved the thought away and glanced to the left.

Satan paced the kennel beside mine again. She probably was hungry too. I hadn't seen anyone bringing the dogs food. I hopped off the hut, the only place in the shadow, and moved cautiously closer to the dog.

She threw me a quick look, then paced back and forth in front of the cage door again. Her water bowl was empty too. I peered toward the house. In the afternoon heat, the dog needed something to drink, even I knew that. I considered calling Maddox. Maybe he was in his room and would hear me but I couldn't bring myself to do it.

The door of the house opened and I called, "Hey, the dogs need water and food!" Then I realized it was Cody. I snapped my mouth shut but he already headed my way with a wide grin.

I stepped back from the bars, wanting as much distance between us as possible.

"What do you want, princess?"

I swallowed my revulsion and pride. "The dogs weren't fed today and Satan doesn't have any water."

"The dogs are more vicious when they are hungry. There's a dog fight tonight, so they need to be sharp."

I grimaced. "I doubt they can fight if they die of thirst."

Cody leaned against the bars, letting his eyes travel along my body in a very disgusting way. "What do I get in return for giving them water?"

I scoffed. "Not what you want."

His face hardened. He picked up the hose they used to fill the bowls but instead of pointing it there, he brandished the end at me. My eyes widened a second before cold water hit my chest. I stumbled back but there was nowhere I could seek cover, unless I crawled into the dog hut, which I'd never do. The dogs barked excitedly. I turned around so the water hit my back. Eventually Cody turned the water off. I was completely drenched. Looking over my shoulder, I saw Cody grinning maliciously.

"There's your water. You sure you don't want to give me a little something so I fill the dogs' bowls?"

I scowled, and he tossed the hose away before he walked off. My kennel was completely wet but the water slid down the slight slope toward the cage doors and didn't reach the other cages. Satan got on her belly and tried to squeeze her muzzle under the gap between the bars and the ground to lick water up but she didn't succeed. I picked up my bowl, which was filled with water, but the thing didn't fit through the bars. Satan watched me closely. I didn't have any experience with dogs, so I couldn't tell if she was friendly or waiting for a chance to eat me.

My pity for the beast won out even as my pulse quickened. I scooped up water in my hands and carefully moved them through the bars. After a moment of hesitation, Satan approached me. I tensed when she opened her muzzle but only her tongue darted out and she began to drink eagerly. I repeated the process several times until she seemed satisfied.

"What are you doing?" Maddox asked, startling me so much, I bruised my wrists when I jerked them back through the bars. Satan let out a sharp bark at the quick movement.

"Giving her water."

Maddox scanned my drenched clothes. "And why are you wet?"

"Cody hosed me down instead of giving the dogs water when I asked him to fill their bowls."

Maddox's expression flickered with fury. "Asshole," he muttered, then he frowned. "Why do you even care if the dogs have water or not?"

"They're locked inside a cage without a fault of their own, just like me."

Maddox shook his head with a strange smile as he picked up the hose and filled all the bowls with water. By now, it was getting dark.

"Is it true that the dogs have to starve so they fight more viciously tonight?"

"Yeah," Maddox said. "Earl's orders."

"It's wrong. Dog fights are disgusting. I feel pity for them."

"I don't like the fights either, but the prez makes the decisions and we all follow them even if we hate them."

I was surprised by his honesty and I could see in his face that he hadn't meant to reveal as much. "Were you against kidnapping me?"

Maddox shook his head with a strange smile. "Do you need a blanket or towel?"

"No, it's warm enough."

He tipped an imaginary hat before he headed back to the clubhouse where he perched on the banister and lit up a cigarette. I had a feeling he'd watch me as long as he could forgo sleep.

Soon Denver, who hadn't dared come near me again, and Gunnar picked up several dogs, among them Satan, and led them away. Deep in the woods, lights were set up but I couldn't make out any details. Yet, when the first snarls and later yelps and whines echoed through the area, I closed my eyes and held my hands over my ears.

Chapter
Nine

Maddox

T HE DOG FIGHTS WERE ABSOLUTELY UNNECESSARY, especially because tonight we didn't even have any visitors who could bet on the outcome. This was solely for Earl's and the club's entertainment. When I was a kid, Earl had forced me to watch the dogs tear each other apart but by now I was old enough to stay away. Gray wasn't as lucky. Earl still thought he needed to harden the boy by making him watch this sadistic spectacle.

I tried to ignore the sound of the fighting and watched Marcella instead. She was sunken into herself, cupping her ears with her palms. She'd surprised me today. I wouldn't have thought she cared for anything but herself. Seeing her help Satan by risking her fingers had done something to me I couldn't quite explain.

It was close to midnight when Cody and Gray led the surviving dogs back to the kennels while Earl shot the ones that were too badly injured. Marcella sat up when Satan limped into the kennel and rolled up on the ground. Cody said something to her that made her face twist with disgust.

I straightened, ready to rush down there and ram my boot into Cody's ass. He was pissing me off more every day and unlike Denver, he seemed content to ignore my warnings. His interest in Marcella was getting out of hand. Finally, he walked off in the direction where Earl always shot the dogs, probably to watch eagerly. Marcella said something to Gray and he shrugged.

I narrowed my eyes, wondering what they were talking about. She said more and Gray nodded then he headed to the shed with the dog food and grabbed a handful. I tensed when he handed it to Marcella through the bars, but she simply took it without trying anything. Gray headed back up to the clubhouse, looking pale.

"What did she want?"

"Dog food for Satan."

"And?"

"That's it. She asked me if I was okay because I looked sick," he said, rubbing the back of his head in embarrassment.

"Tell Earl you don't want to watch."

"I did, but he doesn't care. Today was really bad." He shook his head as if he didn't want to think, much less talk about it.

"I need to drink myself into a stupor," he muttered and disappeared inside.

I resisted the urge to go to the kennels for a few minutes but then the draw was too strong. Marcella looked up when a twig broke under my boot. She kneeled beside the bars and tossed food at Satan who ate it but was obviously too exhausted to stand and go closer.

"It's barbaric," she seethed. "She's bleeding. There's a tear in her ear and muzzle."

"If those are her only injuries, the other dog's probably dead," I said.

Satan was Earl's favorite for a reason. She was big for a female, and since she had a litter, which Earl took from her right after birth, she was a vicious fighter within the ring.

"She shouldn't be forced to fight against other dogs."

I watched her, not saying anything. The moonlight made her skin glow and her hair shone like petroleum, but what really made her gorgeous in that moment was the caring expression she had for the dog. She slanted me a look, tossed the remaining food toward Satan, and cleaned her palms on her pants before she got up. She approached me with a look that made my fucking stomach flip. She grabbed the bars and peered up at me. "People who enjoy dog fights usually enjoy torturing humans too. I don't trust Cody and Earl. Do you?"

I laughed. "They are not my enemies."

"Cody sure is."

I shrugged. "I can handle Cody." I didn't trust Cody, and I trusted Earl to some extent.

"He's not going to stop coming to the kennels. He's drawn to me. He can't stand being rejected. Eventually, he'll take what he wants, Maddox."

I knew she was right, but I couldn't let her make us out to be allies. We weren't. She was the captive and the daughter of my worst enemy.

She leaned even closer, her voice low. "Do you really want to come down here one day and find out he forced himself on me? Do you want that on your conscience?" I gritted my teeth. "Could you really live with yourself if Cody took what you deny yourself?"

I jerked back, my pulse racing. Her words seemed to sink into me and fester.

"Don't—" I warned but didn't even know how to finish the sentence. I whirled around and stalked back to the clubhouse.

Fuck, fuck, fuck.

Marcella Vitiello was trying to lead me around by the balls to save herself, and I had half a mind to let her try. I risked another glance over my shoulder back at the kennels as I headed toward the clubhouse. She was still pressed up to the bars, watching me. Her hair was a mess and her clothes had seen better days but she looked as if it was exactly meant to be like that, as if she were staging some fancy post-apocalyptic Vogue photo shoot. I gritted my teeth and tore my eyes away. It became harder to ignore her, to forget her. My dreams were completely out of my control by now and after what I'd seen today, things would certainly not improve. But my cock was the least of my problems. Cody's horniness was the real fucking problem. Seeing her naked would give him a ton of new fantasies he was going to follow up on at some point. I couldn't let that happen. The reasons for my need to protect Marcella were fucking irrelevant. All that mattered was to get her out of danger. Her father would pay for his sins—not his daughter. Maybe she was spoiled and had led a good life thanks to his rotten character, but that didn't warrant a punishment, and I was certainly the last person who should judge a person's blood money.

Pacing the porch, I smoked two cigarettes before a plan formed in my mind. It was risky on so many levels but the only other thing I could come up with was letting Marcella go and hell would freeze over before that happened. She was our ticket to Vitiello's demise.

I put out my cigarette in the overflowing ashtray and went up to my room, determined to talk to Earl in the morning. After dog fights, he wasn't in a state to discuss anything with him. I perched on the windowsill. Marcella's words repeated in my head. What if he takes what you deny yourself?

Fuck. I would spend the night watching over the kennels again.

After a quick power nap in the morning, I went in search of Earl, but didn't get a chance to talk to him because he sent me out to collect money from one of our dealers. Luckily Cody wasn't around, so I didn't have to be worried for Marcella. I'd just have to hurry the fuck up.

When I came home late in the afternoon, Cody's bike was already parked in front of the house. I dismounted my Harley quickly and jogged up the path until I spotted the kennels. Marcella sat next to the bars and was talking to Satan from the looks of it. The dog was stretched out beside her, only the bars between them.

Reassured, I went inside. Following the sounds of bullets hitting cans, I headed through the backdoor and found my uncle in his favorite rocking chair, shooting at cans on tree stumps. His cut with the stitched words **President of the Tartarus MC** hung over the backrest. As usual, my chest swelled seeing it. One day I would wear that cut, would lead our club. For a long time, I hadn't considered it an option, had been certain Gray would follow in his father's footsteps, but three years ago Earl had told me that I and not Gray would be the future prez of Tartarus. I had been more than a little surprised, and Gray had been devastated, but Earl was a stubborn asshole and wouldn't change his mind once he'd come to a decision.

Earl glanced over his shoulder then he kept shooting at the cans. "Don't stand behind my fucking back, it's giving me a fucking itch."

I sank down in the rocking chair beside his but firmly planted my feet on the ground to stop it from moving. I hated the monotone back and forth. I preferred to make progress. The feeling of bridging hundreds of miles on my bike, that was the kind of motion I liked. Well, there was one back and forth motion I didn't mind...

"Spill. You're fucking with my aim."

"Have you made more plans with the girl you haven't told me about?" I asked.

Earl's face pinched angrily. "If I have, you'll find out when I see fit, boy."

I nodded grudgingly. "I thought this was our plan, our chance to get revenge on my dad's murderer. I thought we were in this together, but now you're doing your own thing."

Earl sighed and leaned back in his chair, the gun balancing on his thigh. "You'll get your revenge, don't you worry. We need to use the Vitiello brat as long as we have her, really drive her father to the brink, see that Italian asshole crumple bit by bit."

I braced my elbows on my knees. "You got it," I said then smiled twistedly. "That's why I want her in my bed."

Cody, who had stepped outside without me noticing, let out a disbelieving laugh. "Right."

But I ignored him and just continued, "Nobody has more reason to get revenge than me."

Earl regarded me curiously and lit his cigarette. "Why the change of heart? Didn't you say she's just bargain, and we shouldn't hurt her. Now you want to drag her into your bed?"

I had absolutely no business protecting her. Her father had killed my father brutally before my eyes, but I couldn't allow Cody to get his hands on her. "Not dragging anyone," I said with a grin. "Girl's been flirting with me like crazy, probably trying to get on my good side. I suppose she's used to getting what she wants by using her tits and cunt."

"I bet she is. She's got great tits and a pretty cunt as far as I could see so she's got plenty to work with."

I lit my own cigarette, allowing my grin to become dirty. "If she wants to influence me with her pretty cunt, who am I to deny her? Especially when it'll piss Vitiello off."

Cody's face became more and more frustrated. "Be careful not to fall into her trap. I bet she's led more than one man around by his dick."

Earl still watched me. His poker face was one I'd learned to be wary of.

"Don't worry. My hatred for what her father's done will help me. I sure as fuck won't be led around by my dick, but if she wants a good biker creamin', who am I to say no?"

I chuckled to myself, grabbing my crotch.

Earl let out his raspy laugh. "Horny as fuck. For all I care, you can fill her holes as long as that's not messing with our plan. You're the one who deserves some Vitiello cunt, like you said. I won't forbid it. But watch your back. I'm sure the pretty face is a mask and the cunt will stab you in the back the moment you don't pay attention."

Cody crossed his arms over his scrawny chest. Maybe he should restrict his physical movements to bench press instead of fucking every available pussy in the club. "I think it would be only fair if each of us got a go at her. We're all in this. I don't think it's fair if only Mad gets his dick wet."

"Mad had to watch his father and his club brothers being ripped apart by Luca Vitiello and risked his fucking hide trailing and kidnapping Marcella. How's that unfair?"

Cody turned to Earl. I listened to him trying his damnedest to get his dirty hands on Marcella, and while Earl shook his head, I wondered how much longer he'd deny Cody's request. Keeping the mood good in the club was one of the main tasks of a prez. So far none of the other club brothers had openly asked for a go at Marcella but if Cody started spewing his bullshit that might very well change. He was like a fucking bulldog when he wanted something.

But if anyone got cozy with her then it was going to be me.

"She's not a pass-around. I won't hand her around like a trophy. That's only going to lead to more arguments among you perverts. I won't have fights because someone had ten minutes more with the whore. As long as it's only Mad getting his bonus after all the shit Vitiello has put him through, everything will be good."

Cody looked as if he'd swallowed a bitter pill but he didn't dare bug Earl more. His face made it clear the topic was settled for him and he wanted his fucking peace to shoot cans.

I sent Cody a smirk and nodded my thanks at Earl before I stalked away to tell Snow White the good news.

My heart was beating like a jungle drum. I was fucking ecstatic, but at the same time I knew this could mess things up. I already had trouble getting my mind out of the gutter. Sleeping in the same room with Snow White definitely wouldn't help. Cody's warning had hit home. For one, I didn't know much about Marcella. She might very

99

well stab me in the eye while I slept. I'd have to get rid of every potential weapon in my room, which would take a while.

"Good news, you're moving today," I told her. She scrambled to her feet, eyes growing wide with hope.

"You're helping me," she whispered, her gaze flitting to the clubhouse as if this was a secret. In moments like this, her protected upbringing showed. Everything had always gone to plan in her life. Her daddy had made sure of it. That someone might not fall to his knees before her mightiness and follow her command was impossible to grasp.

"I hope you're not thinking I'm taking you back to Daddy or letting you go. Not all of my blood has left my brain yet."

She frowned, becoming vigilant. "Where are you taking me?" I unlocked the cage and entered, growing annoyed by her reaction, especially when she backed up a step. Did she think I'd grab her and throw her over my shoulder? I'd risked my fucking head for her and she acted as if I was some kind of perv.

"Up to my room. That's where you're going to spend the rest of your stay here until your daddy decides to hand himself over for you."

Her mouth went slack. "Have you lost your mind? I'm not going to share a bedroom with you."

"If you stay in my room, I can protect you from Cody. Out here, you're at his mercy, especially at night. I won't stay up all night and watch you through my window. Sorry, princess, not going to happen."

"You want me to think you're some kind of knight in shining armor?" she hissed. Those blue eyes shone with distrust, and she had every reason not to trust me.

"I don't care what you think Marcella, but if I tell you to stay by my side for your own fucking protection, you should really do it."

Her eyes narrowed farther. "I don't believe you're doing this out of the goodness of your heart."

"You can either stay here and wait for Cody to get his eager hands on you or you can come with me to my room."

"For you to get your eager hands on me."

I let out a sarcastic laugh. "Don't overestimate yourself." Then I tilted my head. "And if I recall our last conversations correctly, you made a move on me, and not the other way around."

The look she gave me made it clear she knew very well of the effect she had on me, and fuck, she was right.

I shrugged and turned on my heel to leave the cage. I wouldn't beg her to sleep in my room. If she wanted to stay with the dogs. That was her decision. They'd be the least of her problems anyway. Cody was already salivating at the idea of getting his tiny cock into her pussy.

Of course, her refusal only meant I would spend all day and night watching the kennels from my window to make sure nobody touched Snow White.

"Wait," she shouted when I was about to close the cage. I masked my relief and cocked an eyebrow at her.

"I don't have all day for you to make up your mind. Maybe everyone's catered to your every whim so far but I won't."

I could tell how she fought with herself to keep a comeback in. "I'll go with you," she said grudgingly.

"Then come on. Hurry."

She tiptoed out of the cage, but Satan jumped against the bars eagerly, making her jump. She turned to the dog. "I'll make sure my father frees you once he destroys this place."

I scoffed. "Your father will make a rug from her fur."

"You don't know anything about my father."

Shaking my head in annoyance, I motioned for her to go ahead. She finally picked up some speed as I led her to my room. The club brothers gathered in the common area hollered and whistled as they saw us. I sent them a grin, which increased the look of wariness on Marcella's face.

The moment we entered my room, both she and I became tense, only for very different reasons.

101

As the vice president of the Tartarus motorcycle club, getting pussy had never been an issue. Sexy women eager to please walked in and out of our clubhouse every day. But spending the night in a room with Marcella, was a fucking temptation unlike any I'd ever encountered. I'd taken her into my room to protect her, but now that she was here, I wondered if this would seriously mess things up for me. I wanted her, had wanted her from the very first second I'd seen her if I was being honest with myself.

"I need a shower," she said, tearing me from my thoughts. She scanned my room. She was used to better of course. I'd lived in every imaginable hut and I didn't give a fuck if she thought this was beneath her. She was lucky that she was out of the kennel.

"Be my guest. There's a shower behind that door. Of course, nothing as fancy as a marble bath with rain shower."

She pursed her lips, her eyes settling on me. "Maybe you think I'm spoiled…"

"I think?"

"Maybe I'm spoiled, but I don't think you have any right to judge me. I don't go around kidnapping people."

"No, you only profit from your father's crimes, and kidnapping people is the smallest of his sins."

Whenever I attacked her father, her walls came up as she went into protective mode. Could nothing make her doubt him? "My father would never kidnap a woman or someone's child. He's got honor, unlike you and your idiotic biker club."

"You think too highly of your father. If you knew everything he's done, I'm sure you'd change your mind."

"Nothing you can say would ever change my mind, Maddox, so don't waste your breath on convincing me."

There wasn't a flicker of doubt in her expression and it infuriated me. I wanted to destroy her image of her father. I wanted her hatred for him to match my own. I wanted her on my side. That would truly break Luca Vitiello.

Marcella

I desperately needed a shower but I could hardly wear my dirty clothes a day longer. They stank of wet dog and sweat and were stained with whatever had clung to the dog hut.

"You should get ready for bed. I have an early day tomorrow and can't afford to discuss bullshit with you all night," Maddox said. He kept a few steps distance between us, for which I was glad. I wasn't sure about his motives.

"I need a change of clothes. Mine are ruined."

He motioned at the heap of wrinkly clothes on the armchair in the corner. "Pick a shirt and boxers for sleep. I won't go shopping for you."

After another glance at the queen-sized bed, I went over to the armchair. In the two years of our relationship, Giovanni had never spent the night. It was ironic that the first man I'd spend the night with in a room was the very man who'd kidnapped me and wanted my father dead. A biker. A man who definitely didn't share any of our values. I had flirted with him but sleeping in his room had never been part of the plan. I looked around his room curiously. There wasn't much to it. A bed, a chair, and a desk. The latter two only served as objects to throw clothes on.

I carefully picked up a piece of clothing, acutely aware of Maddox's eyes following my every move. From the messy pile, it was hard to tell if the clothes were dirty or clean.

Maddox let out a low laugh as he perched on the windowsill and blew smoke outside. "Everything's clean. But as you can see, I don't have a wardrobe, so the chair has to do."

"Ironing and folding too complicated for you?" I asked after I'd picked up a simple black T-shirt and black boxers. It felt strange touching Maddox's underwear. The idea of wearing them felt even stranger. My relationship with Giovanni had always been too formal for me to get the chance to run around in his clothes, not to mention that he would have never allowed me anywhere near his underwear.

"Be my guest if you want to stay in your dirty clothes."

I grabbed the T-shirt and his boxers and disappeared into the bathroom. The room was clean but small. Maddox was right. I'd never been in a bathroom as simple as this. Even my friends came from money and had bigger and more luxurious bathrooms than most people. I washed my underwear in the sink with soap but my pants and blouse were ruined. After a quick shower, I dressed in Maddox's clothes. His shirt reached my thighs and his boxers hung low on my hips, almost slipping off. It felt strange being this vulnerable around a man like him.

When I left the bathroom, Maddox was gone. I walked toward the window, unsure what to do. Lying down in Maddox's bed felt like a bad idea. I was dead tired but my suspicion kept me wide awake. After a while the door opened and Maddox came in with a plate stacked with sandwiches. He paused briefly, his eyes tracing from my bare feet over my naked legs all the way up to my face. He didn't give away anything. Usually men always went slack-jawed but *usually* I dressed up.

"I have some sandwiches for you."

"You made them?"

He shook his head with an amused expression as if the mere suggestion was absurd. "I had Cherry make them. She's a decent cook."

"The girl you got cozy with a few days ago?"

He nodded, as if it was no big deal. "Didn't she mind that she had to make dinner for another woman who'd spend the night in your room?"

"We aren't dating, only fucking. She's a pass-around. She doesn't care. I'm not the only guy she's got an eye on. If someone else asks her to be his old lady, she'd dump me in the dust in the blink of an eye. All these girls want is a cut that declares them a biker's property."

My lips curled. "A pass-around, really? How sexist can you be?"

"Don't act so high and mighty. In your circles women are used as bargain. I mean, who still uses arranged marriages?"

"They worked for centuries," I said haughtily. "And I'm not promised."

"Anymore. Weren't you and that sappy guy supposed to marry in two years?"

"We didn't have a date yet. But for your information, I chose him, not my parents."

"You chose someone your father allowed near you so you would choose him."

I had never seen it that way, but it was true that only certain boys had been allowed near me once I hit puberty. All of them well-behaved and respectful, not to mention terrified of my father. "You know nothing of our life. But it's certainly better than this lawless hillbilly life you lead."

"I'm free to do as I please. You are bound by your old-fashioned rules."

Even if he had a point, I couldn't just let it drop. I motioned at the hellhound tattoo on his upper arm, the sign of his club. "You can't just leave the club either. That's not freedom."

"I live for that club. I'd never leave it. It's my fucking life."

"And my family is my life, so I'm not less free than you."

"I don't think you really understand what freedom means."

I'd often longed for freedom, but not away from my family and the world I grew up in.

Maddox held out the plate again, then set it down on the night-stand. "You can eat in bed if you want, I don't mind."

"What about crumbs?" I asked, more to gain time and get rid of my sudden nervousness.

"These sheets have seen worse," Maddox said with a chuckle, making his way over to the armchair.

My lips curled. "I think I'll sleep on the floor."

Maddox gave me a pissed-off look. "I changed them this morning, so don't get your panties in a bunch. But if you prefer the floor, be my guest. I don't give a fuck."

He removed his cut and draped it over the backrest. It was the first time I saw him without it since the kidnapping. The way he looked at it, the piece of leather seemed to be important to him.

He slanted me a warning look. "Don't touch my cut while I take a shower."

"Don't worry."

He turned in the doorway to the bathroom. "And don't try anything or I'll dump your perky ass in the kennel again." He closed the door.

"Asshole," I muttered, but I was almost thankful. If he really did this to protect me, then it was a nice gesture. However, I couldn't believe it was only because of that.

I'd inherited my father's distrustful nature and it was rearing its head now. When water began running, I headed for the door and pushed the handle down but it was locked. Male voices and boisterous laughter sounded downstairs, so the locked door was probably for the best anyway.

Glancing at the stack of sandwiches and hearing my stomach's angry rumble, I finally took one with cheese and ham. I usually didn't eat carbs or dairy. One made you fat and the other gave you pimples, but I really couldn't bring myself to care. I stuffed one-third of the sandwich into my mouth and bit off, chewing eagerly. After living in a stinking cage for days and being at the mercy of those bikers, most of my previous worries seemed awfully irrelevant. Briefly my mind touched on the video, wondering who had seen it, but I shoved the thought aside. It wasn't useful at the moment. The past was the past. I needed to figure out a way to improve my future.

Sooner than expected, Maddox came out of the bathroom and I almost had a heart attack. He wore nothing but boxers, revealing a muscular upper body covered in tattoos. Now the pull-up bar hanging from the ceiling by the window made sense. That body required work. I had to force my eyes away from him. His body screamed bad boy. I'd grown up around bad men, but Maddox carried his very own forbidden, bad boy aura.

Maddox looked at me as if I were an intruder in his space, as if I'd asked to be here, as if any of this had been my choice. He walked over to the small table and grabbed the cigarette package that lay there. "Did you touch my cut?"

I rolled my eyes. "It's a piece of leather."

He raised his eyebrows.

"No, I didn't touch it."

He nodded, obviously satisfied. He picked up the packet of cigarettes from the windowsill.

"You're smoking in your bedroom?"

He put the cigarette into his mouth, lit it and took a deep drag before he finally deemed me with a reply. "Got a problem with that?"

I shrugged. "It's unhygienic and disgusting. Not to mention dangerous, considering how many people fall asleep with a burning cigarette and set themselves aflame. It's your health. But I'd prefer if you'd choose something that kills you quicker than nicotine."

Maddox's expression twisted with anger and he stalked toward me. I forced myself to stay put and not back away from his fury. "I'm the only thing that stands between you and a bunch of horny bikers who want to get a taste of mafia pussy."

Why did this enrage him so much? He'd been particularly tense since we arrived in his bedroom. I stiffened. "Why do you even care? Why don't you let them have a go at me if you hate my family so much?"

"I hate your father. You only annoy the fuck out of me because you don't even realize how privileged you are."

Due to his outburst, he'd come very close to me so the scent of his brisk, minty shower gel flooded my nose. His hair was still wet and messily hung down his forehead. My eyes were drawn to the tattoos all over his upper body and arms. Images of hellhounds, knives, skulls and bikes.

"Stop playing the victim here," I said eventually.

Maddox glared at me but something in his eyes made me feel hot. "I was a victim a long time ago, I'm not now."

My eyes flickered from the piercing in his tongue to the bar in his nipple.

"I have more," he said and took another drag.

"Where?" I asked.

His gaze moved down to his boxers. "Two more."

My mouth fell open, trying to imagine where exactly he had them.

My cheeks became hot. "You're toying with me." I narrowed my eyes. "You just want to make me nervous."

"Why would two piercings in my dick make you nervous?" he asked, but his voice had a new, deeper timbre.

I shrugged. "They don't."

He smirked, seeing right through me. Everything about Maddox made me nervous. "Go to bed, princess."

He always succeeded in making the word sound like the worst insult imaginable.

Not wanting to appear scared, I sat on the very edge of the bed, my toes on the floor. The bed linen smelled fresh and not like smoke or sweat. Maybe he normally only smoked with the window open and just didn't to annoy me.

Maddox gave me a half amused, half annoyed look. "The sheets are clean like I said, don't worry."

"I'm not worried about that."

He nodded, narrowing his eyes in thought. "Then what are you worried about?"

"Isn't it obvious? I'm not too thrilled about sleeping beside my kidnapper without protection."

He pointed at his chest. "I'm your protection, and you sure as fuck don't need protection from me. Your pussy is safe."

I gritted my teeth, then finally laid back on the bed. It was much harder than I was used to from home but felt like a soft cloud after the hut.

Maddox finished his smoke but even then he stayed in front of the window, looking out. The letters Tartarus MC were written across his back and shoulders, and below it a skull was spitting fire, the same image as on his sternum. "Why the skulls?"

He glanced down at his chest. "My father had the same tattoo. I don't remember much about his appearance. Whenever I try to recall how he looked, I see the bloody pulp your father turned him into. That tattoo is all I got."

I swallowed. "I'm sorry for what my father did."

He nodded, watching me intensely. "Not your apology to hand out, and I doubt your old man will ever utter the words."

He probably wouldn't.

I looked away from his too personal stare and scanned his other tattoos. The words "no regrets" graced his left forearm.

"You only regret the things you didn't do," I murmured. It was a quote I'd read on a motivational post on Instagram once and it had resonated deeply with me.

Maddox sent me a confused look until I pointed at his tattoo. He smiled wryly. "What do you regret not doing?"

The list was long, but nothing I felt comfortable discussing with Maddox. I tore my eyes away from him and stared up at the ceiling. The fan was spinning around in slow, mesmerizing circles. "Nothing."

He laughed and my belly flipped. He appeared at the bedside, towering over me, still only dressed in his boxers. "I don't believe you. I'm sure there are plenty of things you're dying to do but can't because your ol' man is always watching your back."

I didn't say anything. Maddox sank down on the other side of the bed and I curled my hands into fists. "Don't try to smother me while I sleep. If you try anything, I'll hand you over to Cody myself."

I nodded, not trusting my voice. I felt too hot when Maddox stretched out beside me. His bed was entirely too small for two people who weren't dating. Our arms were practically touching. You could hardly count the half inch between us. I folded my hands on my belly to bring more space between our arms.

"For someone who's been flirting with me in the kennels, you're awfully quiet now," he joked, his face tilted toward me.

I turned my head in his direction. Despite our closeness, I wasn't half as scared as I should have been. If I wanted my plan to work, I should have been flirting with him now, but this was definitely out of my comfort zone. "I thought you wanted to sleep."

"I do," he said, but his eyes said something else. I swallowed when he finally looked away and extinguished the lights.

I listened to his breathing, clinging to consciousness, hoping he'd fall asleep before me. But I just knew he was wide awake. I wondered what kept him from sleep. It couldn't be worry for his life. Maybe he was imagining all the things he could do to me. My pulse sped up. Problem was it wasn't only from anxiety.

Chapter
Ten

Marcella

WHEN I WOKE THE NEXT MORNING, I JERKED UP IN BED, looking around. Maddox perched on the windowsill. His cheek dimpled upon meeting my eyes. "You survived, see?"

I cleared my throat and brushed down my hair, feeling vulnerable knowing Maddox had seen me sleep. It was a very personal thing, and one I'd never shared with anyone outside my family. The sun had only just risen, but Maddox looked as if he had been awake for a while.

"Why are you up?"

Maddox shrugged. "You took up too much space in bed."

I tilted my head in consideration. It almost appeared as if Maddox felt uncomfortable with me in a bed. At least, I wasn't the only one who wasn't at ease. I got up and stretched. Maddox followed the movement. Maybe he was scared of his own desire. I needed to use this. As I strode over to him, under his unwavering attention, my courage slipped away. Like he had said, he wasn't like Giovanni. Maddox wouldn't hold back from fear of my father. He'd probably send him a detailed recount if we ever had sex.

A hot wave passed through my body at the thought.

I wrapped my arms around my chest as I stopped beside him, and the cold morning air hit me. My nipples hardened and I was acutely aware that Maddox could see it through the thin fabric of the T-shirt.

"I'll be gone on runs most of the day but I'll leave enough food and water, and keep the door locked."

I nodded, following his gaze out over the horizon and marveling at how strange the situation was. In a blink, my life had been turned upside down and I had a feeling this was only the beginning.

I checked out Maddox's profile, the sharp angles, then lingered on the scar that looked like a dimple. "How did you get that scar?"

Maddox touched the spot and smiled wryly. "When I was nine, I tried to set Earl's dogs free on a fight night. A few of them managed to run off. He hit me with one of the spiked collars he uses on the dogs."

"That's horrible. But why did it heal so badly? The wound couldn't have been that deep."

"He said if I wanted to pick the dogs' side, I'd be treated like one and their wounds always have to heal without treatment. He locked me in the cage for a couple of days too, so I know how it feels."

My mouth fell open. "No wonder you're so messed up."

He laughed a deep, full belly-laugh. "That's one reason, yes, but your old man still wins the prize of messing me up."

I leaned against the wall, frowning. "But Earl was supposed to take care of you after your father died not scar you mentally and physically."

He sighed and shook his head. "I don't know why I even told you."

"Because you don't have anyone else, you trust enough to share it with."

I spent all day sitting on the windowsill. At first, I'd been surprised that Maddox didn't lock the window. But I soon figured out why escaping through the window, apart from the risk of jumping down from the second floor, wasn't an option. I spotted guards patrolling a wire-fence, and one of them had a Rottweiler on a leash. He'd probably send the beast after me if I tried to run. Remembering Satan's sharp teeth, I shuddered to think what they'd do to my flesh. Satan and I had made—at least temporary—peace but I wasn't blind to the danger the dogs posed.

I searched the horizon for signs that Dad was on his way. I wasn't even sure what I was looking for exactly. He'd certainly try to keep his attack secret for as long as possible to surprise the bikers. I knew he was searching for me but being unable to contact him or anyone else from the family felt as if a part of me was ripped away. Even when I'd been away from home, I'd always had my phone with me to contact them whenever I pleased. Now I felt more alone than I ever had in my life.

Maddox came home after nightfall, looking disheveled and pissed.

"What happened?" I asked, sitting up in bed.

"Your father."

He didn't elaborate, only disappeared in the bathroom. I couldn't help but smile.

Maddox came out ten minutes later and got into bed without another word, but he didn't turn down the lights.

"I told you my father would stop at nothing to save me," I said, not able to hold in my giddiness.

Maddox scoffed. "How did he brainwash you into being his biggest fan, despite all his faults? Whatever drug he gave you must be worth millions."

"He's my father, of course I believe in him. And the drug you're looking for is love." I cringed inwardly at how sappy that sounded, but it was true. Dad didn't only spoil me with presents and money, he spoiled me with love and affection as well.

"I'm going to throw up." Maddox twisted around, facing me fully.

113

"Come on, be honest for a moment. You must realize what kind of man your father is. Don't tell me you don't care."

"I know what kind of man he is. Everyone in my family is involved with the mafia. And your family members are outlaws so don't tell me there's much of a difference. You justify your actions with club loyalty and your cut, and the members of my family justify it with their oath and the loyalty to the tattoo on their chest."

Maddox shook his head. "You defend the Famiglia even if they look down at you. I'll be president of the club one day, but you'll always only be the wife of a mobster. Your word won't ever matter in the mafia. Still, you defend the cause. You don't seem like a woman who likes to sit back and do nothing."

"Who says I'm going to do nothing?"

"You can't rule over the Famiglia like your father."

"My brother will be Capo."

"Aren't you pissed that your brother will become the boss even though you are older?"

On occasion I'd imagined what I'd do if I became Capo, but I'd never really considered it a valid option. "Are women allowed in your club?"

"Of course, didn't you see them?"

I rolled my eyes. "Not for fun, or pass-arounds. I mean as members."

"No, it's against the rules."

"So if you had an older sister, she couldn't get involved with the club?"

He frowned. "Okay, both the club and the mob don't allow women. But you seem like a girl who's used to getting what she wants. It must be hard to be in second place, and not even that. Your word will never mean anything in the Famiglia. If you marry some pompous Italian mobster, he'll rise in rank in the Famiglia and you can raise his kids and give him blowies if he returns home from a hard day at work."

"Blowies?" I repeated with a disgusted twist of my lips while heat traveled up my throat in a very embarrassing way.

Maddox used his tongue to tent his cheek in a very obvious way.

"That's disgusting."

"A blowy or my interpretation of it?"

"Both," I muttered.

"Don't tell me you never gave that poor asshole a blowy in two years of relationship. No wonder he always looked so pinched. I would too if I didn't have a nice long blowy in years."

"Stop saying that word," I muttered. I'd never wanted to give Giovanni oral, and he would have never dreamed of asking me. He'd never even allowed me near his fly in our relationship. "This discussion is over."

"Do I make you feel uncomfortable?" Maddox asked, obviously enjoying himself.

He made me uncomfortable for various reasons, none of which I'd discuss with him, especially not while sharing a bed.

Flirt with him.

That had been the plan but following through was more difficult.

Maddox watched me and my palms became sweaty. My body had never reacted to someone's presence like that. I made others nervous, not the other way around.

"Why would anyone pierce his genitals?" I blurted, wanting to break through the silence.

Maddox's answering smile only made me feel hotter. "To receive more lust, and even more importantly, to give more lust."

My mind went into overdrive. Maddox and I stared into each other's eyes, then he shook his head with a chuckle and rolled over on his back. "Go to sleep before we both do something we might regret."

"I doubt you'd regret me," I said.

Maddox closed his eyes with a sardonic smile. "I wouldn't."

His confirmation stunned me. My eyes traced his chest, which wasn't covered by the sheets.

"And you, would you regret me?" he asked eventually.

"Definitely," I said. I didn't even want to consider the social media shitstorm I'd be submitted to if word got out that I'd slept with a biker, even if it was to save me. In our circles, women were condemned in the blink of an eye. And my family? Dad would lose it.

Maddox nodded, his eyes still closed. "Yeah. You'd definitely regret me."

Maddox

Marcella had spent the last three nights in my bed, and every night had been more torturous than the last. I felt her presence everywhere. When I lay awake beside her at night, and I hardly slept anymore, I was driven almost insane by her scent and by the images of her body replaying before my closed eyes.

I'd half hoped, half dreaded Marcella would make a move at me, even if only to save herself, but so far she'd held back. Despite her killer body, she wasn't used to making advances on men. I wasn't sure if it was due to her conservative upbringing or because she was used to men throwing themselves at her feet.

I had half a mind to do the same.

Some women dressed in expensive dresses and put on tons of makeup to look presentable, but Marcella in my clothes and no makeup was an apparition that put them all to shame.

"What are you thinking?" she asked out of the blue.

"Isn't that a question you ask your fiancé when he spends the night?"

She shrugged. "Giovanni never spent the night."

Douchy name for a douchebag, then my brain registered her words. "Why?"

"We hold on to our old values," Snow White said matter-of-factly. "And I live with my parents."

I couldn't stop staring at her blue eyes, glowing against the dark coal of her hair.

"Let me guess, your fiancé pissed his pants because of your ol' man."

She smirked. "Most people do."

"Not me."

"No," she agreed in a soft voice. "Not you, Maddox."

Fuck. I wished she'd stop saying my name in that gentle lilt. Yet, I'd never ask her because the moment the last syllable died on her lips, I longed to hear it again. She was like a drug I couldn't resist, and I hadn't even tried it yet. She'd be like crack, without a doubt. One taste and you'd be addicted, and ultimately, she'd ruin you.

"What's your favorite childhood memory of your father?"

I hadn't expected that question. No one had ever asked me something like that. I racked my brain, trying to come up with an answer. Most of my memories weren't happy. My old man hadn't been the best father, but he had been a father.

Images of my father fighting with my mom, or sitting on the couch with a beer, or not present at all flashed through my mind.

"He died before we could make many good memories," I said. But deep down I knew that happy memories would have been few and far between even if Vitiello hadn't killed him. But having a bad father was better than not having one at all.

"But you miss him?"

Most of all, I missed what could have been. I missed that we never got the chance to have a good relationship. I missed that my old man never got the chance to be a good dad. "Of course," I said, but the words sounded hollow.

Marcella tilted her head so her hair fanned out like pitch on the pillow. "What about your mom?"

"She became my uncle's old lady a few weeks after my old man got killed."

That should answer her question. My mom never really missed my dad. She might have missed the position as the old lady of a prez if my uncle hadn't immediately made her his.

I motioned at her. "Your turn."

I still couldn't get over the fact that Marcella Vitiello was lying in bed beside me, in my black T-shirt and my boxers, and talking to me as if it was the most normal thing in the world.

"You want me to tell you my favorite childhood memory? Are you sure you want to hear any stories about my dad?"

I sure as fuck didn't want to imagine Luca Vitiello as a good dad. I wished Marcella's memories of him were as bleak as mine of my dad, but I wasn't a pussy. I could take the truth. "Go ahead."

Marcella's gaze became distant, then a soft smile curled her lips, one I'd never seen on her usually so controlled and cautious face before. "When I was seven, I had a phase when I was convinced monsters were in my walk-in closet and under my bed. I could hardly sleep. So Dad made sure to check every possible hiding place in my room every evening, and even when he came home late in the night after a difficult workday, he still snuck in my room and made sure I was safe. Once he'd checked the room, I knew the monsters were gone and I always fell asleep within minutes. But seconds before I drifted off, Dad would always kiss my forehead."

I couldn't imagine Luca Vitiello as Marcella described him, as the loving, caring father. He had been the monster that still haunted seven-year-old me. When I thought about him, I always saw the ax and knife wielding madman who slaughtered the people who were like my family. He was the man who'd been our enemy even before I had been born. This wasn't a new feud, but it was one to last generations.

Marcella regarded me. "You don't believe me?"

"I believe that's how you see him, but it doesn't change my feelings toward him. Nothing can erase my hatred, nothing ever will."

"Never say never."

"You'll rather learn to despise your ol' man before I'll forgive him, that's a fact, Snow White."

I cringed. This was the second time I called her by that name outside of my head.

Her eyebrows puckered and she regarded me as if she was trying to see right into my brain.

"Snow White?"

I shrugged and rolled over on my back, staring up at the ceiling. She kept watching me expectantly.

"Come on, don't be surprised. I can't believe no one's ever called you Snow White before. Black hair, pearlescent skin, red lips."

One dark brow twitched up, and I realized I was only digging myself a deeper grave with every word out of my stupid mouth. The ghost of a smile passed her lips, and it was all I could do not to pull her on top of me and kiss her.

Women have a certain place in motorcycle clubs, and it isn't on equal footing with men. They were only supposed to speak when spoken to and had to please their man. I'd never just talked to a woman for more than the meaningless chitchat before and after sex, and if possible, I'd even avoided that. The only woman I'd ever shared a halfway decent conversation with was my mom, but in recent years, I'd closed off even around her.

I wasn't sure what it was about Marcella that made me want to talk, or at least listen. She was sophisticated and chose her words carefully. I'd never talked to a woman who was even half as educated and intelligent as her. And sometimes I just enjoyed getting a reaction out of her. "What happened with your fiancé? Did he dump you for not putting out?"

Her lips thinned. "Girls like me don't get dumped. I broke up with him."

"So fucking arrogant. You think you're a gift to men that no one would dump your perky ass?"

"Nobody would dump me because of my father," she muttered.

I perked up at the bitter note in her voice. "Too scared of the old man, I get it. But why do you sound like this pisses you off? Don't you enjoy the perks of being feared because of your scary daddy?"

"I'd rather be feared or rather respected for who I am."

Her words surprised me, but I couldn't hold back a snide comment.

"People generally don't respect or fear people for their extraordinary shopping skills."

She narrowed her eyes. "There's more to me than shopping. You don't know me."

"Then enlighten me, Snow White."

"My life's not a fairy tale, so stop calling me that."

My grin widened at her obvious anger. "Pity, I'm sure the big bad wolf would love to eat you."

A blush traveled up her throat and her cheeks, making her look even more like the fairy tale princess.

"I study marketing and I'm among the best."

I couldn't stop smirking.

She glowered. "I suppose you see yourself as the big bad wolf, Mad Dog?"

I would definitely love to eat her.

She shook her head and became very quiet. "It's been over a week. When's this going to be over?"

I hadn't asked Earl again. He'd punished Vitiello with silence, hoping the asshole would die from worry over his daughter. And I didn't mind having a few more days with Marcella.

My smile died. "Soon. When your old man is dead."

She closed her eyes. "What would it take for you to give up your plan?"

"Don't waste your time looking for a way to convince me. I won't lie, my dreams are filled with images of your naked body on top of mine, but even that won't change my mind, so don't try to manipulate me with sex."

"Nobody said anything about sex," she murmured. Then she tilted her head curiously. "So you'd prefer if I didn't try to seduce you?"

"I've been waiting every fucking night for you to finally try, but don't do it for any other reason than because you want to."

"As if you'd care why I'd make a move on you."

I smirked. "I wouldn't, as long as I ended up between your thighs.

But I want to spare you the disappointment if you don't get anything out of it except for dirty, amazing sex."

"If sex is all I wanted, I could have slept with more sexy guys than I can count. There are few men who wouldn't say yes to a night with me."

Without a doubt...

"Maybe you didn't choose one of them because all of those men cowered before your father. I'm the first guy that isn't scared of him, and that, admit it or not, turns you on."

She didn't deny it, only looked at me in a way that sent a rush of desire through me.

Chapter
Eleven

Marcella

IPERCHED ON THE WINDOWSILL, PEERING OUT. AS SO OFTEN I tried to find landmarks that would give me a clue where I was, but the forest around the clubhouse didn't offer any hints. After ten days in the hands of the bikers, I was starting to give up hope that Dad and Matteo would find me. A floorboard creaked in the hallway, causing me to tense. Whenever Maddox wasn't around, my nerves were frayed. No matter how insane it was, he protected me. I'd seen the looks the other men gave me, hungry and hateful. I couldn't expect mercy from them, and even though I'd like to say I didn't want their mercy, I was terrified of what they might do to me.

"Oh, Spoiled Princess, where are you hiding?" Cody called in a sing-song voice. It was his favorite hobby to lurk around in front of the door when Maddox was gone and torture me with comments of how he'd rape me. He made loud sniffing sounds. "I can smell that Italian pussy. Let a real man fill that dirty hole."

I made sure not to make a sound. Maybe then he'd go away. Instead he rattled the door handle. Even though I knew he was trying to scare me on purpose, I couldn't help but feel anxious. Only a door and the bikers' respect for Maddox kept me safe. Both weren't things I wanted to rely on.

The longer my captivity took, the higher the chances got that Earl White would eventually snap and hurt me to pressure Dad. I didn't want to wait for that to happen but escape without Maddox's help was futile.

He had made it clear that he wouldn't help me no matter what I did, but at this point, I wondered if I shouldn't test his theory. I'd heard him murmur my name in his dreams at night.

The roar of an engine turned my head toward the driveway and I couldn't help but smile when I spotted Maddox on his Harley coming to a stop in front of the porch. He removed his helmet and ran a hand through his unruly hair. I had to admit that the sight of Maddox mounting his beast of a motorcycle was strangely attractive. Even his biker outfit with the cut looked good on him. He swung off his bike then looked up to his window. Our eyes met and my belly twitched in a way I didn't even want to analyze. I turned away from the window as if I didn't care that he was back, but the overwhelming relief in my body spoke a very different language.

It was dark and Maddox's warmth was everywhere. Eventually I rolled over. I could hardly make out his silhouette. The curtains kept too much of the moonlight out. Maddox wanted me, and even if I'd never admit it, I felt attracted to him. Turned on even, as he'd said. I could follow my desire and hope it would save me, or I could deny myself what I wanted and rely on others to save me. Maybe I was a spoiled princess, but I didn't need a prince to wake me from eternal slumber.

Maddox

The dark seemed to cover us in a cocoon full of possibilities. I lay on my back beside Marcella. She smelled like trouble and temptation. She'd shifted and now her knee lightly touched my thigh, and the touch seemed to electrify my whole body. Her closeness wreaked havoc with me. She was warm and so goddamn close.

Being close to her every night was torture. Earl had mentioned that he'd contact Vitiello soon to make the exchange, and instead of looking forward to getting revenge, my only thought was that I'd lose Marcella before I even had her. I was such a dickhead.

"What are you thinking?" she asked.

"That I'll regret ever inviting you into my room," I said.

"Why?"

I had a feeling she knew of her effect on me. It was almost impossible for me not to check her out, not to fantasize about her day and night. "I think you know," I said gruffly.

She moved, bringing us closer, but still only her knee touched me. I wanted to roll over and pull her against me, kiss her, taste her, especially that pussy I had been fantasizing about.

"Do I?"

My patience snapped. I rolled over, bringing our faces impossibly close. Even her breath was sweet as she exhaled sharply. I didn't touch her, even though every part of me wanted to. "I can't stop thinking about your pussy and if it's dripping," I said crudely, hoping to make the spoiled princess shy back, but she only swallowed.

"Nothing's stopping you from finding out," she whispered.

I was sure I'd misheard her. I touched her hip and after briefly tensing, she softened under my touch. "What are you doing? Do you think you can seduce me into helping you? How often do I have to tell you that's not going to work?"

"And even if I were, wouldn't it be worth it to get a taste of the spoiled princess?"

Fuck. I couldn't resist. I stroked along her upper thigh then trailed my fingers inside the boxer shorts. Marcella's warm breath brushed over my lips as she exhaled when my fingers slid under her underwear. I stifled a groan at the feel of her silky warm flesh. Her pussy was so fucking soft. She held her breath as I brushed my index finger along her slit. My fingertip discovered the subtle hint of wetness between her pussy lips. "Fuck," I groaned.

Determined to tease more of it out of her, I traced my finger up and down her slit.

Her breathing was still slow and controlled but picked up when I began to scissor her pussy, stroking her between my index and my middle finger, and brushing my finger joints over her clit. She began to pant and soon my fingers were slick with her arousal. I couldn't resist. I dipped one finger into her and stifled a curse. She felt as if I'd died and gone straight to heaven. She was so tight, Cody's words came back to me. Maybe he was right. Fuck, I fingered her leisurely, wanting to savor every moment of this. She grabbed my shoulders and began to move her hips in rhythm with my fingers, chasing the heel of my palm with her clit. I slowed, and as I'd hoped she rubbed herself against my hand, driving my finger into herself over and over again. My cock was ready to explode.

"Don't stop," she whispered thickly.

"Fuck, you really think anything would stop me from fingering you until you cream? I'd even keep doing it, if my fingers fell off."

"Shut up," she groaned, then sucked in a sharp breath. I pumped faster, almost drunken on her moans and the feel of her tight walls around my finger. I added a second finger, my dick twitching at her sharp exhale. Her lips found mine for an uncoordinated kiss.

And then she exploded with a cry, her walls clenching around my fingers. Her orgasm was like an unstoppable avalanche, her juices running down my fingers and wrist. "Dripping," I rasped.

Marcella only moaned softly as I kept pumping in and out of her slowly, prolonging her orgasm. Eventually I stopped but kept my fingers inside of her, relishing in the occasional spasm that took hold of her walls. I pulled out my fingers and brought them to my lips, licking them clean, making sure that she could hear what I did.

"That's disgusting," she whispered.

"I have to disagree." I smirked as I inhaled her after orgasm scent. "I'm still not sure this isn't a dream."

Marcella turned on her back. "I'm sure you'd get off in your dream."

I laughed, even if my dick pulsated with raging need. "That's not going to earn you extra points."

She leaned over and brushed the softest kiss across my cheek. "Sleep well, Maddox. I can't wait to hear you murmur my name in your sleep again."

Fuck.

Of course, I dreamed of her and woke with a hard-on. Maybe the blood hadn't left my cock all night. My balls hurt like a bitch anyway. After a quick shower, I pranced around completely naked in my room, done playing hide and seek with Snow White.

She followed my movement with an indignant expression but her eyes held the same desire I felt. Soon my cock stood proudly again. Marcella's gaze took in the bar piercing at the base and the one at the tip. The latter had actually been the result of a lost bet but I'd quickly realized I enjoyed the feel of the cool metal and the ladies did too.

Marcella's fascination was definitely worth it. I stroked over the piercing at the base, bringing her attention there. "This one is positioned so it stimulates the clit," I said, my voice rougher than usual. "And this one," I continued, touching the piercing at the tip. "Stimulates the G-spot."

Marcella didn't say anything but after last night she couldn't pretend she wasn't turned on by me. I knew I'd find her wet again if I touched her pussy.

Marcella

Last night with Maddox had been a revelation. His simple touch had ignited my body. Maybe because I'd been starving for touch.

I'd worried that I'd feel regret after but regretting something you want to do again seemed hypocritical. I tried to console myself with the fact that I was in an extraordinary situation that couldn't be judged by standard rules. Yet deep down, I wondered if that was the only reason for my desire.

When I came out of the bathroom that night, Maddox lay stretched out on the bed, watching me with a hungry smile.

He was only in boxers, showing off his muscled, inked body.

I feigned disinterest.

"Earl said he's getting there with your ol' man. This might be one of our last nights together."

My heart sped up. "Really?"

"Can't wait to be rid of me?" he asked.

Surprisingly, I wanted more time with Maddox, no matter how infuriating he could be. Being locked in Maddox's bedroom, away from the disgusting bikers, I'd almost forgotten the danger I was in. This had seemed like a strange version of a sabbatical away from my usual life.

"Maybe you should use tonight to have your pussy eaten out before you return to your fiancé."

"Ex-fiancé," I said immediately.

Giovanni had never gone down on me, only touched me a couple of times through my jeans (because he'd been scared to have me naked in case my dad burst into the room), which wasn't an experience I'd enjoyed very much. Yet, considering that his tongue had felt as if a goldfish was floundering for its life on land in my mouth whenever we'd kissed, I hadn't been overly eager to have him go down on me. I hadn't come the few times he'd touched me, which had been a blow to his confidence, and which he'd blamed on me wanting to wait until my wedding night… at least subconsciously. That was utter bullshit of course.

Maddox lay on his back, grinning dirtily. "I could make you cream real good."

My lips curled. "Cream, really? Don't waste your breath, I'm not into oral."

"Giving."

"Receiving," I snapped back, even though I couldn't really know.

I hadn't ever gone down on a guy. Giovanni had been too terrified of my father and didn't dare to sully me like that before our wedding day.

Maddox's smile became even dirtier and heat washed through me. I was slightly slick between my legs only from looking at him. "Your fiancé's a real loser. He didn't eat you properly or you wouldn't be spouting this bullshit. If you were my girl, you'd be squirting like a fountain just thinking of my tongue in your cunt."

I didn't correct him in his assumption that Giovanni had gone down on me. It was irrelevant to what we had. I stepped closer to the bed, glaring down at him. "You have a foul mouth."

You only regret the things you didn't do.

"I have a magic tongue," he growled, flicking his tongue out so the piercing flashed in the light. I couldn't stop wondering how it would feel to have him pleasure me with the piercing. Just thinking about it, my thighs clenched in anticipation. If this was really one of our last nights, this was also my last chance to get him on my side… and enjoy myself a little while I did.

I wasn't sure why I did it, but I stepped on the bed and glared down at Maddox.

He dipped his head back so he could look beneath my shirt. I wasn't wearing panties. He whistled between his teeth. "Fuck, Snow White, let me eat that royal pussy."

I raised one eyebrow. "Only if it shuts you up."

He grinned devilishly. "Straddle my head. Come on. Spread those milky thighs for me."

I gave him my most condescending look and stepped up on the bed so I was towering over him with my feet on either side of his shoulders. I knew what kind of premium view I was giving him, and he enjoyed it. Yet, I couldn't deny that I too got increasingly aroused by the situation, by Maddox's dirty mouth, by the hungry gleam in his eyes. I'd doubted myself so often in the past, but with Maddox, his desire for me was blatantly clear. There was no room for doubt.

"Kneel so I can eat you out."

"Vitiellos don't kneel."

He grabbed my calves and tugged so hard, I lost my balance and fell forward, my knees sinking into the soft mattress beside his head.

"I could have smashed your face in with my knee!" I hissed. Maddox was my only chance out of this hellhole. Even if I wanted to kill him, which I wasn't entirely sure about at this point, I'd have to wait until I was free.

Maddox grabbed my ass and jerked me toward his face. His eyes captured mine and then his tongue slid out slowly, a dirty grin on his face. The tip of his tongue brushed over my pussy lips, parting them to caress the sensitive inside. I shivered at the almost overwhelming sensation, momentarily worried I'd come from the brief contact. "Fuck," he said in a low rumble, his lips vibrating against my pulsating flesh. He began licking me with slow movements, the piercing teasing my clit. I tore at his hair, jerking his mouth closer to my pussy and he took me up on the invitation, dipping his tongue into me. I rotated my hips, riding his mouth, his tongue deep inside of me, his piercing teasing what I assumed was my G-spot. I watched him as he took his time, sometimes even closing his eyes as if he was having a tasty meal that he needed to savor fully. The piercing flashed as his tongue flicked my clit leisurely. I gripped his hair, tugged almost viciously but Maddox only smirked and closed his lips around my clit. My teeth sunk into my lower lip to keep a moan in.

"You need to scream and moan. All women do when they're in my room. My club brothers will get suspicious if you're silent like a church mouse."

I glared.

Maddox only seemed to take it as a challenge to coax sounds from my lips as he sucked and licked, nibbled and flicked. Soon my breathing came in sharp bursts and my hips rocked almost desperately. By now I was riding his mouth without shame. Maddox's strong hands cupped my ass-cheeks, kneading and guiding my movements. He pulled back about an inch and I almost jerked him right back by his hair. So desperate for release I was close to losing any semblance of control.

"Come in my mouth, Snow White," Maddox growled. His blue eyes stayed locked on mine as his lips cupped my clit once more. Pleasure radiated from my core, through every inch of my body in unstoppable waves. I came so hard, every muscle seemed tightened to the max. I gasped, my hands flying to Maddox's muscled shoulders to steady myself. Closing my eyes, I succumbed to the sensations and screamed as if nothing around us existed. And it felt so good. I rocked my hips back and forth, driving his tongue deeper until the waves of pleasure began to ebb away. Eventually my lids peeled open and I peered down at Maddox.

Maddox lapped up my release eagerly, smirking, his face shiny with my juices. I watched him and kept grinding my pussy against his lips. Loving how dirty this was, how wrong. This—Maddox—could be my salvation, or it could be the fall from grace so many had been waiting for.

I still kneeled above him, my chest heaving.

His lips and chin were shiny. "See, I told you I'd get you to cream in my mouth."

"You realize that sounds disgusting, right?" But deep down, I was wickedly turned on. Maddox was forbidden and crude and daringly free of conventions. This was meant to be a means to an end, but I couldn't bring myself to feel guilty for enjoying it at the same time.

Maddox raised his head and stretched out his tongue. Tracing its tip along my folds then sucking one of them into his mouth. "Who doesn't like cream? Especially if it tastes this good."

I got up, the shirt falling to my knees once more, hiding my nudity. But my legs were sticky and my core still throbbing from my release.

Maddox sat up slowly. "Won't you return the favor?"

I cocked an eyebrow. "Why don't you ask one of the pass-arounds to do it for you?" Despite the harsh note of my words, the idea that Maddox could get it on with another woman didn't sit well with me. He pushed into a sitting position, his jeans tented. Remembering the piercings and his sinfully sexy body I felt compelled to get on my knees and do what he asked, but my pride kept me in place. He took a cigarette out of his packet and pushed to his feet, looking as if he didn't care. He shrugged and sauntered over to the door. "Suit yourself. I know just the right girl to suck my dick."

A hot ball of fury built in my chest. "If you do this—" I seethed, not sure what I was going to threaten him with. We weren't a couple so I couldn't break up with him. We were nothing except captive and captor, which made the situation all the more ridiculous. I didn't have anything I could blackmail him with.

"Then what?" Maddox asked, turning with a satisfied grin, as if my reaction had been his plan. Had he tricked me into an emotional outburst?

I couldn't believe him. I shook my head in disgust. "I don't care. Do what you must. For all I care you can let all the old ladies…" I wanted to say something crude to match him but the words stuck in my mouth. "…have their way with you." I finished lamely, and my face heated.

Maddox's smile broadened, becoming so smug I wanted to strangle him with the gold chain around his neck. "Have their way with me?" he echoed, all teeth and smugness. "Suck my dick is what they would do. Can't you say the words, Snow White?"

"Unlike the women you choose to do your bidding, I have some style."

"Oh, you got style and plenty of arrogance to match it. Don't you feel hypocritical bashing those girls when your pussy's still wet from my magic tongue."

He had a point but I couldn't admit it. "They chose this lifestyle. I got kidnapped. Nothing is my choice."

"Riding my mouth with your pussy like a fucking rodeo rider was your choice, princess. Your cream on my tongue's proof of that."

As often as his crudeness turned me on, just as often it annoyed me.

"That's what experts call Stockholm Syndrome," I muttered, hating my cheeks for heating further because I felt caught. Even if I was telling myself that this was part of the plan to get Maddox on my side, so he'd help me escape, I enjoyed our physical encounters too much to blame it on strategy. I felt wanton, sexy, and naughty in a way Giovanni had never allowed. I felt freed from shackles that had weighed me down more than I'd realized.

"Bullshit, Snow White. Don't insult my intelligence and definitely not your own goddamn backbone. You'd never let some shitty syndrome determine your actions. I doubt anyone or anything could ever force you to do anything you don't want." He paused. "And you want me. In your prim society life, you'd never be allowed to get nasty with someone like me, but now you got the chance and you took it greedily with your perfectly manicured fingernails."

He was right. I wanted him. I felt freed of the rules of the Famiglia for once. This was a lawless zone. Whatever happened while I was being held here, I would never be blamed for it.

This was cowardice, not wanting to risk living the life you desire.

His eyes trailed the length of me, making me feel hot all over again. "You don't even have to say it. I know you want nothing more than to get even nastier with me, to really unleash the sexy vamp you hide behind that Snow White face."

His grin became even dirtier. "Aren't you curious?"

"About your genitals?" I said sarcastically.

Maddox laughed, a deep bark I began to like way too much. "Not quite the words I would have chosen, but yes."

"No, thank you. Curiosity killed the cat."

His smile widened. God, a smile had never made me feel as if my insides were being lit on fire.

He reached into his jeans and freed his length. I couldn't look away even though I wanted to do it. But the piercing in his tip captured my attention and didn't let it go. He flicked his thumb over the shiny piece of metal repeatedly as he rubbed his tip.

I stepped closer. "You're really going to do this in front of me. Don't you have any shame?"

"No shame whatsoever, Snow White. But if you're so concerned about my dignity, give me a hand."

I shook my head. "You're impossible, and crude and absolutely shameless."

"Guilty as charged. But you are a coward, a hypocrite, and a liar."

I narrowed my eyes. "I'm not." But I was. Maddox cupped my neck and pulled me down until I had to support myself with one knee on the mattress. "You are," he murmured before he kissed me. He kept rubbing himself and when I finally freed myself from his kiss, my gaze darted down to watch his hand work his length.

My mouth watered seeing his abs flex with every move.

"Coward."

"Shut up. You can't taunt me in to touching you. If I touch you, then I do it because I want to."

"Of course," he said. The sarcastic note in his voice barely registered because I simply couldn't pay attention to anything but the rhythmic up and down movement of his hand. A droplet of milky liquid had gathered on his tip.

"You're impossible," I seethed, kissed him angrily and finally reached for his length. My fingers closed around his firm, but smooth cock. He blew out a breath before he said, "Finally brave."

I silenced him with another kiss and began to move my hand up and down, effectively shoving his hand away. My thumb explored the piercing in his tip, thrilled at the sharp intake of breath followed by a low moan. I trailed my fingertips lower, to the other piercing at the base, like a decoration for his balls, and was again rewarded by a hiss from Maddox.

"Get naked," he growled.

My eyebrows skyrocketed. I hadn't yet made up my mind if I wanted to go all the way with Maddox. In the last thirty minutes, the scale had definitely tipped in Maddox's favor. I just couldn't stop wondering if sex would be a revelation like oral had been. Why should I wait for another Made Man, a future husband, who'd banged countless girls before our wedding night? Why couldn't I enjoy myself a little?

And more than that, a little voice, one I used to call my instinct, told me that Maddox was the guy I should lose it to.

Maddox chuckled as if he could read at least part of my thoughts. "I want to cum all over your perfect body."

"I'm not sure if I want to get whatever sexual diseases you have."

"If I had any diseases, you would have gotten them through the pussy-tonguing you just had."

He had a point, and I hated feeling stupid.

"But don't worry, I usually use condoms and if I forgot, I got tested. I'm clean."

I stopped rubbing him and pulled my shirt over my head. Maddox's gaze caressed my curves. My nipples pebbled even though it wasn't cold in the room. I started rubbing him again. Maddox reached for my breast, capturing one hard nipple between his fingers and twirling it between them. His other hand stroked my ass before it snaked between my legs from behind. His thumb parted me, brushing up against my clit, which was already throbbing with eagerness again. One flick of his pad and I was alight with desire, ready to let loose.

"I thought it was your turn," I said in a hushed voice as his thumb worked me up again. I had to admit, getting Maddox off at the same time was a huge turn-on, driving me toward the edge so much faster than expected.

"Watching you cream will make me cum so much harder, Snow White."

For once, I didn't have a clever comment. I was too lost in the sensations, in the heat radiating off Maddox's skin, in the surprising hardness of his cock, and in the pulsating need between my legs. Soon my hips began to shift, chasing Maddox's thumb.

When my second orgasm took hold of me, he, too, came all over his abs. After a deep sigh, he grabbed my neck and pulled me down for a kiss. "I'll really loathe letting you go."

Chapter
Twelve

Marcella

SOMETHING WAS DIFFERENT TODAY. THE BIKERS WHO arrived after Maddox and Gray left for a run, seemed agitated as they buzzed around the porch. When Earl White peered up to the window, catching my gaze with a superior gleam in his eyes, my stomach plummeted. I doubted I'd be released today. He had more in store for me.

Earl nodded at Cody who grinned.

My eyes darted to the locked door. A few moments later, I heard steps thundering up. I hopped off the windowsill, then rushed toward the bathroom just when the lock sounded. "You can't run anywhere, cunt."

Cody grabbed me by the hair and jerked me backward. I cried out from the sharp pain that shot through my skull. I clutched his wrists, digging my nails in, but he kept dragging me out of the room and down the stairs. My knees bumped against several steps, making me cry out in pain again.

He didn't stop until we reached the common area downstairs. My already churning stomach turned when the stench of spilled alcohol and old smoke filled my nose. What was happening? Would they exchange me for my dad? The atmosphere was way too tense for that.

"Fuck, the stupid whore scratched me." Cody shoved me away from himself. I landed on my knees before Earl, gasping from the sharp twinge, but I quickly pushed to my feet. I'd never kneel before someone like him.

He sneered. "Still too proud to bow to your betters?" He shook his head. "Just like your old man."

"One day my father's going to make you regret the day you were born," I said, lifting my chin. A feeling of utter helplessness washed through me, but I didn't let it take control.

Earl smiled in a way that froze my blood. "I was so close to allowing your old man to exchange himself for you, but something about his voice was just lacking the necessary submissiveness I was expecting in a situation like this, you know?"

I swallowed, not liking the way the bikers were looking at me. I couldn't blame Dad. It wasn't in his blood to be submissive. Even if he'd tried to appear that way, it would have never been convincing.

"Today, I'm going to make him regret the day he went against Tartarus and teach him his new place."

He nodded at Cody who grabbed my neck and pressed me against the bar counter. Sharp pain shot through my hipbones from the impact. He shoved my head down so my right cheek pressed against the sticky wooden surface. The stench of cheap liquor was almost overwhelming. Earl came into view, holding a long knife. I tried to move back but Cody held me tightly, his body pressed against mine in the vilest way. The blade gleamed in the light of the lamps over the bar. Panic worked its way through my body like poison.

Earl held up the knife with a vicious smile, watching my reaction. I wished I managed to look brave and indifferent, but I was too terrified of what he might do. "You are too fucking pretty, whore. That perfect face makes me angry every time I see it."

Fear choked me as he moved even closer, holding the sharp tip of the knife right before my left eye.

"I wonder what you'd do without those lethal looks." He smiled in a bone-chilling way, revealing one golden tooth.

"Don't," I pressed out. I wanted to sound fierce and threatening but sounded terrified and almost begging, but I couldn't help it. What if he blinded me? There was still so much I wanted to see, so many things I hadn't appreciated enough because I'd thought I'd have time to look at them. My heart throbbed furiously, blood pumping through my veins like an avalanche.

"I'm sorry, sugar, but I need a little gift for your old man. He needs to know we're not playing. We'll destroy him."

He moved the knife even closer. Where was Maddox? God, where was he?

When the blade sliced into me, a high-pitched scream tore from the deepest part of my body until everything pitched into darkness.

Maddox

The moment I stepped into the clubhouse, I knew something was fucking wrong. Ruby, Earl's favorite girl and stupid enough to think he'd ever make her his old lady, had a satisfied smirk on her face as Earl wiped blood off his knife. Blood also covered the bar. My heart lurched. "What happened here?" I asked, trying to hide my worry.

Earl sheathed his knife calmly, looking bored as fuck. "Taught the Vitiello princess a lesson and her old man too."

Fuck. Earl must have used his spare key to get inside my room. I shoved past a grinning Cody and stormed upstairs, my pulse pounding. What the fuck had he done? I thought Vitiello was ready for the exchange? I unlocked the door and shoved into the room. Blood splatters covered the ground, leading into the small bathroom. Blood had never bothered me. After the carnage Vitiello had caused before my eyes as a little boy I was too hardened to be bothered by it. And yet, the sight of these few blood splatters made my heart race.

I followed them into the bathroom then came to a staggering stop in the doorway.

Marcella perched on the edge of the toilet, face ashen, shoulders and wife beater covered in blood. She pressed a towel over the left side of her face. "What happened?" I asked, fearing the worst. Earl had been like a father to me, but I knew what he was capable of. Over the years, his obsession with revenge had grown rapidly, even worse than my own.

She lowered the towel that her trembling hand had been clutching against the side of her head. Seeing her blue eyes intact, relief washed over me, but then I registered her ear, which was bleeding profusely. It took me a moment to see that Earl had cut her left earlobe off.

My vision turned red and I whirled around and thundered down the creaky stairs. I could barely breathe from fury. My ears were ringing, my temple throbbing. I stormed into the common area. Earl and Cody sat on barstools and downed bourbon as if to celebrate their success.

I charged toward Earl and grabbed his cut, jerking him off the stool. "We agreed not to torture her! You swore it." I'd never talked to my uncle like that, especially not in front of others.

Earl's eyes narrowed and he grabbed my wrist in a bone-crushing grip, trying to unlock my fingers but I didn't release him. He'd grown old, but not less vicious. "What have you done?" I seethed. For the first time in my life, I wanted to kill him.

"Don't forget who's pulling the fucking strings in the club, Maddox," he muttered, his expression full of warning. "And don't forget who took you in when the little whore's old man slaughtered your father."

Cody had stood from his barstool and was ready to interfere. He'd had an eye on the position as second in command for years, always saying I was too young for the position. Killing me would make his day.

I unfurled my fingers, took a deep breath and stepped back. "You shouldn't have done it. You went too far. I never agreed to this shit. I want to torture and kill Luca Vitiello, not Marcella."

Earl tilted his head, stepping closer and regarding me with a challenging smile. "Is she getting under your skin? Where are your loyalties?"

"With the club," I said.

Earl's lips tightened. In the past they'd always lain with him but after what he'd done today, I wouldn't follow him blindly ever again. "I am the club, don't forget that, Maddox. If you want revenge, you better stop getting into bed with Vitiello's spawn. She's making you lose focus. Maybe it wasn't wise of me to allow you to take her into your room. Maybe we should all share her."

Cody's face lit up like a fucking Christmas tree. I'd cut his dick off before I'd let him anywhere near Marcella.

"I'm not losing focus," I said in a much calmer voice. "But provoking Vitiello like that could lead to rash actions on his part. You know what he's capable of."

Earl smiled grimly. "This time, we are in control. He won't catch us by surprise like last time. With his daughter in our hands, he'll think twice before acting."

Up until this point, I would have agreed with my uncle's assessment. Luca wouldn't risk Marcella's wellbeing, but now that my uncle had started torturing her... my blood boiled, my chest constricting. Earl didn't take his eyes off me. "With your actions, you forced Vitiello's hand. He won't wait for you to cut off more pieces of his daughter, Uncle. I thought he was ready to exchange himself."

"He won't find us. We're well hidden. And if he attacks another of our brothers, we'll send him another piece of her until he learns his place." He climbed back on the barstool and emptied his bourbon. "He wanted to exchange himself but I didn't like his tone when we talked. He still thinks he's better than us. Until he learns his place, his daughter stays with us."

I'd secretly wished for more time with Marcella, but not like this.

"The longer this takes, the higher the risk for all of us," I said, fighting to keep my voice under control.

"I'm in control," Earl said, his voice laced with spite.

I gave a terse nod, seething. Cody gave me a superior look that made me want to smash his face against the wall. I could imagine how he'd gotten off on seeing Marcella being tortured. Just thinking about it made me want to put a bullet through his and even Earl's head. Fuck.

I stalked back to my room, my mind reeling for a solution to the predicament I was in. Marcella was no longer safe in this place. Now that my uncle had begun torturing her, he wouldn't stop. He enjoyed it too much. Fuck. I, too, wanted blood, but not Marcella's. I wanted her father's brutal end, not hers. I found Marcella still in the bathroom. She hadn't moved from her spot on the toilet seat and was watching blood drip from her ear, drop after drop, and landing at her bare feet. By now, most of her nail polish had peeled off, but what remained of it had the same color as her blood.

She ignored me and peered down at her feet. Then slowly she lifted her head but she still wasn't looking at me. I stared at her profile, trying to sort through my whirlwind of emotions.

Even in a tattered and bloody wife beater and my old boxer shorts, Snow White looked more regal than any queen on a throne of gold and diamonds ever could. She carried her invisible crown with unabashed pride. Fuck, this woman had been born to be a queen and she fucking owned that title.

I kneeled down beside her but she didn't look my way. Instead, she kept staring straight ahead, her eyes distant.

"Snow White," I murmured. She didn't react. "Marcella."

Her eyes dragged down to mine, as cold and impenetrable as ice. She couldn't hide the traces of her tears. "Let me take a look at your ear," I said in a beckoning voice.

"At what's left of it, you mean?" she said hoarsely, her eyes full of hatred and accusation, but beyond those obvious emotions, emotions she wanted me to see, I detected her pain and fear, and those emotions cut me deeply. Maybe I should have seen it coming. From the first moment I spotted her, she hadn't left my mind. What had been lust in the beginning had morphed into something more. I enjoyed talking to her, teasing her. Fuck, I even enjoyed watching her sleep. Whatever I felt and I wasn't ready or willing to analyze my emotions yet, was at odds with my pure hatred for her father.

"I didn't know. I wouldn't have allowed this to happen. It's not part of the plan."

Her lips pulled into a tight smile. "And what's the plan?"

"You were meant to be exchanged for your father, like I told you. It was supposed to happen this week."

"But what's the plan now?"

I wasn't sure telling her would make things better but I knew Marcella was too clever not to realize what was going on. "Earl wants to punish your father through your suffering."

She nodded as if it all made sense. She jerked her head away again, her shoulders stiffening. I shifted, trying to get a glimpse at her face. I could see the struggle in every perfect inch of it but finally the tears tumbled out. Restrained at first but then her walls came crashing down.

"Snow White, I'm sorry, fucking sorry," I murmured, touching her cheek.

Her eyes flashed. "This is not a fairy tale. And it's your fault this is happening."

She was right. It was irrelevant that Earl would still have gone through with the plan even without my help.

"Let me treat your wound," I said.

She glared. "It's your fault. Go away."

But I didn't leave, not with her crying openly in front of me, vulnerable like I had never seen a Vitiello before. I took out bandages and antiseptic before I started cleaning her wound. The cut was fairly clean and I was sure there were ways plastic surgeons could replace an earlobe, but that wasn't the point. Marcella sat quietly as I took care of her, and

By Sin I Rise

I wished she'd say something, even if it were words of spite. Anything was better than this sad, quiet version of her.

"Done," I said.

Finally, her gaze returned to me. The smile she gave me was bitter. "This is what you wanted, huh? Bringing a Vitiello to tears."

"The wrong Vitiello. Even if I've never seen a woman who can cry prettier than you, I never wanted your fucking tears."

For some reason, this caused a new wave of tears, which only seemed to make her angrier. I slid my arms under Marcella's knees and her back and lifted her into my arms. She didn't resist, instead, she sagged against me. What this did to me caught me by surprise. I felt a wave of protectiveness and affection that almost knocked me over.

I put her down on the bed and stroked her back. Certain that she didn't want me close, I stepped back, wanting to pace the woods to clear my head and figure out a plan.

Her arm shot out, grabbing my hand. "No, stay with me."

"Marcella, are you—"

"Stay."

I stretched out behind her and wrapped my arms around her. I'd never hugged her like that, simply to show affection and give consolation. I didn't remember the last time I'd hugged someone at all.

"It's only going to get worse," she whispered. "Your uncle wants to break my father, but my father can't be broken, so he'll break me."

I knew she was right. Maybe I should have seen it coming but I had been too desperate for revenge. "I'll protect you," I swore. This oath would be my downfall, I could feel it deep in my bones. Yet, I had no intention of taking it back.

When I left my bedroom to a sleeping Marcella an hour later, my mind was still reeling. I wasn't sure how to convince Earl to go ahead with the exchange, especially after our argument. He was probably still pissed at me. The common area was filled with guys. Word about my reaction to Marcella's torture must have gotten around judging by the curious and sometimes even questioning looks I got. I just nodded at them and stalked outside, not in the mood to justify myself.

I paced the forest when I spotted Gray. He hunched on a fallen tree, smoking, his hair falling down his face. Like me, he had been in the club since he was fifteen, even though prospects usually needed to be at least eighteen years old.

"Hey, why are you hiding out here?" I asked as I went over to him and sank down beside him. Looking up in surprise, he offered me a smoke, which I took.

He didn't say anything, only squinted at the glowing tip. I inhaled deeply but noticed a bit of blood from Marcella on my fingers. A new wave of anger mixed with despair over the hopeless situation crashed down on me. This was such a goddamn mess.

"I heard about what happened to the girl," Gray said eventually.

His expression made it clear that he felt sick to his stomach about it.

"It was a mistake," I said.

Surprise crossed his face. I rarely criticized Earl's decisions.

"I thought you wanted the kidnapping."

"Not at first, but then I figured it was the perfect way to get our hands on Vitiello."

"And now you don't think it is?"

"I still think we should let him exchange himself for Marcella. But Earl wants Vitiello to crawl and beg, and even then, he probably wouldn't be satisfied."

"The guy will go crazy when he sees his daughter's earlobe," Gray murmured. "Earl had me sent it off to him."

I shook my head. "Fuck. This is a fucking mess."

"How is the girl? She's in your room?"

"Yeah, she's sleeping now. Of course, she was freaked out. Who wouldn't be after what happened?"

Gray sighed. "I hope this is over soon."

"The kidnapping?"

"The kidnapping, the revenge. All my life, I only heard Earl and you talk about revenge on Vitiello. I just want us to move on and really focus on making Tartarus stronger."

A life without revenge as a focus seemed impossible. It had become such an integral part of the club. Revenge was the reason why Earl's authority had never been questioned. Fights within the club just weren't an option while in war with the Famiglia. Maybe that was why Earl suddenly wasn't too keen on ending Vitiello.

"Maybe you can talk to Earl, ask him when the exchange will happen, and convince him to hurry the fuck up."

Gray gave me a look as if I'd grown a second head. "You know Dad doesn't listen to me. He thinks I'm incapable. You are his favorite son."

"I'm not his son," I said firmly, surprising myself. In the past, I'd often caught myself longing for Earl to be my father, but this desire had disappeared completely after today.

"Someone has to talk to him and make him see reason. The club needs to move on like you said. And that can only happen when we finally kill Vitiello."

"Sometimes I think killing Vitiello will only be another step of the war. After that his family will seek revenge, and then we'll seek revenge on them again, and so on."

Deep down I knew Gray was probably right, but I didn't care what happened after, I just wanted to get rid of Luca. But first I'd make sure Marcella was safe. Whatever came after was irrelevant.

Chapter
Thirteen

Marcella

I woke to a fierce throbbing in my left ear. Sitting up, I winced when I touched my bandaged ear, remembering the events of yesterday. I'd passed out quickly after they'd cut off my earlobe and not experienced much of the pain, nor had I seen my cut-off earlobe. I'd only woken when Gray had awkwardly carried me up the stairs and into the bedroom. I'd dragged myself over to the bathroom where Maddox had eventually found me.

"There are painkillers on the nightstand," Maddox said. My head swiveled around to where he sat on the windowsill, only in jeans. A wave of relief over his presence followed by anger raced through me. This was his fault, and even his worried expression didn't make him less guilty.

His cut lay beside him. It was never far from him. The cut, his club, they meant the world to him.

"You have every right to give me that look. I'd hate myself too if I were you."

I didn't hate him, unfortunately. I was furious but I still didn't hate him. I shoved out of bed, swaying briefly. Maddox crossed the room in a flash, grabbing my waist.

After a moment, I pushed him away. I needed a shower, to clean myself of the dried blood in my hair and neck, and to feel more like myself again. Maddox didn't stop me as I stumbled toward the bathroom. Cowering under the streaming water, despair overwhelmed me. I was afraid of what else Earl had planned for me. I was scared for Dad, for my family. I was even scared for Maddox, which didn't even make sense. I needed to get away from here.

When I stepped out of the shower, a clean wife beater and boxers waited on the toilet lid for me. I got dressed, then took my time brushing my hair, trying to calm down and figure out what to do, but no matter how often I looked for an out, Maddox came up. He was the only one who could save me, all of us, even himself, now.

After towel-drying my hair, I returned to the bedroom. Maddox looked as if he too had racked his brain for a solution. He had to see that this was heading in the wrong direction, that it was in his hands to steer us out of the danger zone. He met my gaze and I touched my ear, wondering what he saw now.

"You're still fucking gorgeous. Knowing you, people will probably soon ask plastic surgeons to cut their earlobes off because you started a trend."

I let out a hoarse laugh. "You don't know the people I have to deal with. They'll have a blast seeing me like this."

"Didn't you hear me? You're still fucking gorgeous."

"Until Earl cuts more pieces of me off."

It was a fear I hadn't allowed more room in my brain but it lurked at the fringes all night, filled my night with horrid images.

Maddox's eyes flashed with fury. "He won't. This will be over soon. I swore to protect you."

I approached him and peered up into his hard face. "How will this end, if not badly? How will you protect me? You didn't see your uncle when he cut me. He will do it again, no matter what my father does, or you. Your club brothers stood by and watched. They too will follow your uncle down this path."

He grabbed my shoulders, looking torn and angry and desperate at once. "This club is my life, Marcella. I bleed for it. I know what you want me to do but I can't betray the club, not for you or anyone. And I won't spare your father either. He will die, but you will be safe."

"You will lose me, and then my brother or uncle or someone else will kill you to avenge my father. Is that what you want?"

I could see one thing he wanted more than anything, even if he couldn't admit it.

"The last few days were more than I ever expected to get with the spoiled princess from New York." He was good at evading the bitter truth.

"And that's enough?" I asked softly.

He growled and pulled me against his body, his lips crashing down on mine. Part of me wanted to shove him away, but the other wanted this, him. For many confusing reasons.

I raked my fingers through his hair, tugging hard, wanting him to hurt. He snarled into my mouth but only kissed me harder, his hands roaming my back.

His piercing teased my tongue, sending spikes of pleasure through every inch of my body. Kissing had never felt like this, as if lightning bolts zig-zagged through my body. The world around us and everything that had happened faded away.

He tugged down the wife beater and tongued my nipple, making sure to flick his piercing against it a few times. Then he sucked my nipple deeply into his mouth, sucking harder than I expected. My core clenched. I leaned back, watching his lips around my sensitive flesh. His hand slid down my belly, fingertips teasing my skin. I was already growing wet and desperate to feel his touch between my legs. This was our moment, and my last chance. We stumbled backward against the door.

He cupped me through the boxers, sliding his middle finger between my lower lips over the thin fabric. The additional friction of the drenched material against my sensitive flesh made me pant. He rubbed me slowly, completely ruining my underwear but I didn't care. He got down on one knee. "This is the only instance I'll ever kneel before a Vitiello," he growled, but I could only focus on his lips that were so close to my boxers. He hooked a hand under my knee and shoved my leg up. My ass banged against the door, causing the old wood to groan. Maddox slid my boxers to the side. "Dripping," he murmured. Then he buried his face in my pussy. His piercing teased my clit mercilessly.

"Mad," someone called. I didn't recognize the voice in my lust-hazy brain. He rattled against the door, almost giving me a heart attack but Maddox didn't release me. His face stayed between my legs.

"Fuck off, I'm eating out pussy," Maddox shouted before he noisily sucked at my pussy lips.

I wanted to shove him away but he flicked his piercing over my clit before he sucked it into his mouth and I exploded. My fingers tore at his hair as I ground myself against him, riding his face desperately. This was almost like an out-of-body experience, as if I could put all the weight of the past and fear of the future behind.

I knew whoever had called Maddox's name was still there but I didn't care anymore. He wouldn't live to tell the tale anyway. Once my family saved me, everyone would be dead, and they'd take whatever they'd heard or seen into the grave with them. I could only hope Maddox would see reason before he'd have to share their fate.

Maddox straightened, and the look he gave me almost felt like goodbye.

"It's too soon for goodbye," I whispered.

"Don't," he murmured. I got it. He didn't want to think or talk about this now.

He pressed into me, his expression morphing into a playful smile. "Is it true that you Italian girls have to stay virgins until your wedding night, Snow White? Or did you give your fiancé an early gift?"

I smirked, matching his forced lightheartedness. "You'll have to find out for yourself, Maddox. But a word of warning, my father will kill you for it."

"I think death will be worth it."

He ground himself against me. God, I'd never been this wet. One look from Maddox aroused me more than hours of making out with Giovanni ever had.

"I won't be gentle Snow White. Last chance to tell me what I want to know."

I didn't need gentle now. I needed him, this. I bit his lip hard in answer. He growled, his eyes becoming feral. He shoved down my boxers and lifted me off the ground so my legs wrapped around him. Then with one ferocious thrust, he shoved himself into me, or as far as my body would let him. I exhaled, my nails drawing blood on his back.

Maddox exhaled, his forehead pressed against mine, his chest heaving, lips parted as he breathed harshly. "Fuck, Snow White. Your old man will definitely kill me for this."

"Shut up, Maddox." One of them would die, but I didn't want to think about it now. Soon enough, the bloody reality would catch up with us.

He did. My inner thigh muscles trembled as I got used to the feel of him inside of me. My body bore down on him, allowing more and more of his length to slide into me. I held my breath when my pelvis settled against his and he was sheathed completely inside of me. His piercing pressed against my clit like he'd promised, but my discomfort didn't allow me to feel my G-spot.

"Why did your idiot of a fiancé not pop your cherry?"

I dug my nails even deeper into his shoulders but he didn't even flinch. "Because he was too scared of my father."

"You're worth dying for. He was a moron if he didn't realize it."

Maddox met my gaze, his blue eyes full of challenge and dark hunger. "I'm not scared of your old man. When I meet him, I'll tell him that I fucked you."

"No, you won't," I growled, but I had to admit it thrilled me to know that this man wasn't afraid to go against my father. I only wished there was a chance for us, for both of them to live.

His fingers tangled in my hair, tugging slightly until I bared my throat to him. He licked over my pulse point leisurely. "I sure as fuck will, Snow White."

He grabbed my ass and began to move. I exhaled sharply in discomfort and Maddox briefly paused, his eyes searching mine.

"Don't stop," I panted.

His fingers tightened even more on my ass and he thrust into me. I gasped at the sharp pain that was followed by a lightning bolt of pleasure as his piercing bar rubbed against my clit. Maddox began to thrust into me at a moderate pace. Sweat glistened on his forehead from holding me up and the controlled thrusts.

"Don't hold back," I got out.

He slammed into me, long hard thrusts that made my core hum with pain. He angled his thrusts so his piercing kept rubbing my clit and then he kissed me. The feel of his tongue as he claimed me only increased the pleasure. Soon it was difficult to determine where my discomfort ended and the low hum of my building orgasm began.

"So wet," he rasped as he slammed into me over and over again. My eyes rolled back. I was on the verge of coming but every time I was sure I'd topple over the cliff, pain reined me in. He stiffened, becoming so much bigger inside of me, and then he exploded with a muttered curse. His thrusts became even harder but less coordinated. My mouth fell open at the overfull sensation. I held my breath when the pain got almost too overwhelming. He bit into my shoulder as his thrusts slowed. He finally looked up, completely disheveled and sweaty. "Fuck. You were supposed to cream."

"Most girls don't come their first time."

"Bullshit," Maddox growled. He lifted me a couple more inches and pulled out. I exhaled at the stinging pain. My legs almost gave out when Maddox set me back down on the floor but he didn't allow me to fall. He pressed up to me, peering down at me with a new possessiveness and raw hunger that hadn't been there before.

"You're going to cream and scream for me, Snow White," he rasped. He rubbed me with two fingers then he slammed them into me without warning and began to thrust into me fast and hard. My eyes grew wide at the new wave of discomfort mixed with pleasure. Maddox slowed suddenly and then he added a third finger. I sucked in a sharp breath, shaking my head. "Too much?" Maddox murmured, sucking my lower lip into his mouth. "Your pretty pussy just took my entire cock. You can take three fingers. It'll be worth it, Snow White."

He moved his fingers at an excruciatingly slow pace until I began meeting his thrusts and my eyelids drooped in pleasure.

When I finally came, I clung tightly to Maddox. He wrapped his arms around me even tighter and I rested my chin on his shoulder. Slowly, the exhilaration ebbed away and I became aware of the throbbing in my ear that matched the stinging between my legs.

I pulled back slightly and met his gaze. "You have to save me. Only you can, and you know there's only one way to do it."

Maddox

Marcella lay curled up on her side beside me, her elegant back facing my way. My eyes traced the soft bumps of her spine down to her round ass with the two tantalizing dimples above her cheeks. I fought the urge to kiss every inch of her way too perfect skin.

Her words after we'd fucked repeated in my mind. I had to save her, but the option she had in mind was out of the question. I couldn't let her run. This was our only chance to get her old man. If I released her, Earl and my club brothers would never forgive me. Fuck, they'd hail me a traitor and cut my balls off and feed them to me, or the Rottweilers. I wasn't a traitor.

My eyes were drawn to the bandage over her ear. It had started bleeding again during our fuck. I still couldn't believe I'd slept with Snow White, that I had popped her cherry.

Before getting to know Marcella, I'd often fantasized about having her in my bed, but it had never been like this. I'd thought I'd feel triumphant for having touched Vitiello's precious offspring. I'd imagined taunting him with every dirty detail, imagined using Marcella as part of my revenge. Now all I could think about was that I wanted to keep her in my bed, in my life. I almost laughed at the thought of Marcella becoming my old lady. Vitiello would lose it. Yet, no matter how hard I tried, I couldn't really imagine Marcella as part of our lifestyle. She was from a very different world.

Despite the impossibility of us, I wanted to taste her every day, see lust replace the cold suspicion in her blue eyes. And the last thing I wanted to do was to share any detail of our first night together with anyone. I wanted every moment with, every inch *of* Marcella for myself. But I also wanted her safe, and she needed to be far away from the club for that, far away from me. I belonged with the club and she couldn't stay.

I raked a hand through my hair. "Stupid idiot."

Marcella stirred, twisting her head around to look at me sleepily. "Did you say something?"

"Sleep," I murmured.

She simply nodded, turned, and fell back asleep. I stretched out on my back, my arms crossed behind my head. Earl was getting suspicious. The others were getting jealous. This was all not how I'd planned it. I didn't want to let Marcella go, but I had to. I couldn't hope for Earl to hold back from hurting her further. I closed my eyes, wanting to kick my stupid ass. When had Marcella's safety become my top priority, even more important than the one thing I'd worked for all my life: revenge?

I stared up at the ceiling. Marcella had said her father would kill me for taking her virginity. Considering all I had done, he had several reasons to end my life as brutally as possible. But this, fucking his daughter, was definitely the tip of the iceberg.

But she was worth dying for. Fuck, I'd die a thousand deaths just for one more night with her.

Chapter
Fourteen

Luca

PROTECTING MY FAMILY HAD ALWAYS BEEN MY TOP PRIORITY. Nothing was more important, not even the Famiglia.

Staring down at the note from Earl White, I realized I'd failed.

Payback time, Vitiello.

Earl White

President of the Tartarus MC

"That imbecile probably doesn't know more words," Matteo muttered. I didn't react. There was a static rush in my ears, similar to the one I'd experienced years ago when I'd thought Aria was cheating on me and I had gone on a killing spree in the Tartarus clubhouse. I had lost control back then, and I was close to losing it again.

Matteo had been there back then, like he was now. And his gaze held the same concern as he watched me silently as in the past.

My body called for blood, for screams and carnage.

I could do nothing but listen to the furious beating of my heart. "How am I going to tell Aria?" I pressed out. I'd only found out four hours ago that Marcella had been kidnapped from campus. One of the men responsible for her safety had called me to tell me. The only reason why he wasn't dead yet was that I'd need every man to destroy Tartarus and trying to save his hide was a great incentive.

Matteo touched my shoulder. "I can do it."

"No," I croaked, shaking my head. I slanted a look at my boy, his face still buried in his palms. Amo had been there when the call had come in. His shock reflected my own. Despite being introduced to the Famiglia at his thirteenth birthday, I'd kept many horrid aspects of this world from him, by Aria's request.

I got up from my chair in my office where we'd returned after a futile search. There wasn't a trace of Marcella, nor of the members from Tartarus. They'd all crawled into their hiding holes, scared of what I'd do if I caught one of them. They'd sing like a canary, reveal every secret they never knew they kept. "I should go home now before word reaches Aria."

I had already called a meeting for every man of the Famiglia who was close enough to be present tonight. Some of my Underbosses and their soldiers were too far away to join in the search.

Amo stepped up to me, gripping my forearm, his eyes harsh. "Let me be a part of the search and the destruction of Tartarus. I don't want protection. I don't need to be protected. I want to save Marci and kill every fucker who hurt her. I want to smash their bodies into a bloody pulp."

He was almost my height and the fierceness in his gray eyes, *my eyes*, reminded me more of myself than ever before.

Protecting him wasn't an option anymore. I nodded and squeezed his shoulder. I hadn't been able to protect Marcella, and I could no longer protect Amo. "We'll fight side by side."

His expression filled with determination and pride. Maybe I should have let him be part of a mission before. This, his first real mission, was riskier than anything we'd been up against in a long time.

My heart rate picked up when I entered our mansion thirty minutes later. Matteo and Amo were close behind me, but this, telling Aria everything, was my burden. Valerio rushed down the steps, grinning, but one look at my face and his expression fell. "What's wrong?"

I indicated Amo and Matteo to take care of him. He was too young for the gruesome details but he, too, needed the truth. Yet, my sole focus was Aria for now.

I followed soft humming into the kitchen where I found her. She was blowing on a steaming cup of tea while reading a magazine. I hadn't expected to find her cooking. Aria was the worst cook in the world.

Her golden blonde hair was up in a messy bun, a few wayward strands framing her gorgeous face. Marcella had inherited Aria's beauty and her eyes, but my black hair.

Aria and I'd been married for twenty-four years, longer than both of us had been without the other. She was still as beautiful as on our wedding day, maybe even more so. What made her even more beautiful was that she loved more fiercely than anyone else I knew, which was why this news would break her.

"Aria," I forced out. Every fiber in my body revolted against disturbing her serenity with an ugly truth even I could hardly bear. I'd vowed to keep all harm from her and our family and failed horribly.

Aria turned with a soft smile which faded away at the look on my face. She knew me better than anyone, every twitch of my face and the meaning behind it. I could only imagine what my expression must have been like.

She set down her cup slowly, worry filling her eyes. "What's wrong?"

How could I tell her? I wanted to lie to her, to protect her at least.

I wasn't a man who shied back from an ugly truth or from anything

157

else. I'd seen and done too much to be scared, but right this moment I was fucking terrified. "Do you remember the Jersey MC?"

Her brows pulled together. "You killed them all when I was pregnant with Marcella."

My heart shriveled. Of course, she remembered. I'd acted out of sheer desperation and fury back then, not thinking about the consequences of my actions. I wanted to maim and kill, and these bikers had seemed like the perfect target. They had attacked Famiglia warehouses and killed my soldiers before so they were far from being innocent, but back then I'd have killed them even if that hadn't been the case.

My actions had gone unpunished for decades, but now Marcella was paying for my sin.

"They rebuilt their chapter in the last few years."

She nodded because I'd mentioned it to her on occasion, especially if one of their insane attacks had caused me a headache.

"Luca, you're scaring me. What's wrong? Why are you telling me all this?"

I moved toward her and touched her shoulders. "Marcella, they kidnapped—"

Aria took a step back, horror twisting her face. "No."

"Aria—"

"No," she whispered. She began to shake, backing away until her back hit the kitchen counter. Tears burst from her eyes. She put a shaking hand over her mouth, gasping for breath as her anguish stole it from her. I wanted to touch her, to console her but I wasn't sure if she wanted my touch. I was the reason for all this. Marcella had become a target because of my actions in the past. "She's alive," she said—not asked, as if her saying it would make it true.

"Yes, of course she's alive. The president probably wants to blackmail me. They won't kill her. They know I'd pulverize them and every MC in my territory and beyond in revenge." I didn't trust in Earl White's word or his honor, but I had to trust in his instinct of self-preservation. That didn't mean they wouldn't hurt her. But even if they didn't Marcella had to be terrified in the hands of those men, terrified of what they might do… I didn't want to consider the horrible options.

Aria closed her eyes, swallowing. "Oh Marci." Aria sagged against me with a choked wail, her fingers digging into my arms. I caught her and pressed her against my chest.

Her pain cut me worse than any blade ever had. "I'm sorry, love. Our daughter is paying for my sins. I'll never forgive myself and I don't expect you to ever forgive me either."

Aria pulled back slowly, wiping her eyes before she looked up at me. She clutched my hand. "These men are at fault, not you, Luca. There's nothing to forgive. When I married you, I knew of the risks of being with a Capo."

The marriage had never been her choice though, even if we'd chosen each other over and over again in the years since our wedding day.

"I'll offer to exchange myself for our daughter. It's me they want, not her."

Aria's expression became unexpectedly fierce. "Save our daughter and kill those men. They can't survive or we'll never be safe. You're the strongest man I know. Show them, and don't you dare not come back to me."

Aria's unwavering faith in me was the greatest gift I could imagine and a burden I gladly carried. I wouldn't disappoint her trust. I'd save our daughter with sheer brutality and with my life if necessary.

Amo stepped into the dining room, and his face didn't bode well. I got up at once. I hadn't been hungry anyway. The only reason why I was at the dining table was because Aria wanted to preserve a semblance of normalcy for Valerio. He knew more than she wanted, but he humored her pretending he didn't.

Aria and Valerio fell silent.

I moved closer to Amo, keeping my voice low as I asked, "What's wrong?"

Amo's face was red with anger. "The bikers posted a video of Marcella on the internet."

Aria got up and approached us. "Is Marcella all right? What happened?"

"What kind of video?"

Amo's phone beeped repeatedly with incoming messages. He slanted a look at the screen. "Fuck. I'll kill them all."

I grabbed his wrist. "Amo, what kind of video?"

My own phone began to buzz with messages.

"They posted a video of Marcella naked and tagged her on social media. It's all over Insta, TikTok and Twitter."

I balled my hands into fists, my fury so overwhelming, I had trouble reining it in. Valerio and Aria were watching me worriedly, and I needed to keep my fucking composure until I was away from home.

Aria glanced down at her cell phone and the color drained from her face.

"Mom?" Valerio asked, but she didn't react.

I went over to Aria and touched her shoulder. She lifted her head. "I want them all dead," she whispered softly. As if she had to ask. They would die, one way or another. Either by my hand or by Amo's and Matteo's after they'd killed me.

I hunched over my desk, glaring at my phone. My last call with Earl White had been yesterday. I hadn't heard from him since then and I didn't have a number to call. His last words made me fear the worst for Marcella.

Matteo paced the room. "He wants you to beg. I can't wait for the tables to have turned and to make him beg."

I'd as good as begged, not in the exact words and keeping my fury at bay had been close to impossible after the video of Marcella that the MC had posted but I had offered myself to Earl White on a silver platter, but he'd refused. If my men were closer to finding Tartarus' current hiding place, then things would be easier. I'd pulverize every biker. Fuck, I'd enjoy it more than anything I'd ever enjoyed before.

"I dream of killing the Whites every night. It's all I can think about," Amo said from his spot on my couch. He had spent every waking hour searching for Tartarus and his sister since she had been kidnapped. Even Aria who was usually so adamant about him focusing on the upcoming school year hadn't argued.

Nothing was more important than family.

Two days ago, we'd followed a lead all night but the hut we'd found had only been an abandoned storage for guns and ammo. There wasn't a trace of the current Tartarus clubhouse. If we could only get our hands on one of the bikers. They would reveal the location, but the last guy we'd followed and cornered had put a bullet in his head before we could grab him.

A knock sounded and Valerio poked his head inside my office.

"Mom just got a package. There's a hellhound print on it."

Amo jumped up from the sofa but I was already out the door, rushing after Valerio who led the way to Aria. We found her in the living room. She stared down at the package, a letter knife in her hand, but it was still closed.

"Don't open it!" I shouted. Aria jumped, her gaze darting to me. I reached her and gently pulled her away, shielding her with my body.

Amo took the knife from her hand. I shook my head. "I'll open it."

He handed me the knife and I cut through the package wrap. I doubted there was something dangerous inside, but even if there were it should be me who got hurt.

I ripped open the package and found a jar with a bloody piece of flesh inside. My pulse sped up as I read the label. "The first piece of your daughter that you get back. More will follow until you show some respect."

Matteo's eyes widened. "What is that?" he murmured. Amo still kept Aria and Valerio back.

I brought the glass closer to my face. "An earlobe."

Matteo gritted his teeth and looked away, muttering something under his breath. I wasn't sure I could speak. My fury burned too brightly.

"Luca?" Aria called, her voice ringing with panic. "What is that?"

"Take your mother and brother upstairs," I ordered Amo. Aria wouldn't have it. She shook Amo's grip off and he obviously didn't dare grab her again. I shoved the package at Matteo before I went over to Aria, stopping her from looking at the jar.

"Luca." Aria's voice trembled, her eyes filling with tears and terror as she peered up at me.

"Trust me, love. Marcella will come back to us soon."

"I'm not weak. I want to know what's happening."

I motioned at Amo to remove Valerio from the room who followed his brother under protest.

Aria clutched my arms. I couldn't find the words, couldn't tell her what was happening to Marcella and what I couldn't prevent. Even I, who had seen and done so many horrible things, couldn't bear the thought of what Marcella had gone through. The pain, the fear...

The words wouldn't pass my lips. I closed my eyes briefly. "They want to punish me, love. I won't let them hurt Marcella more."

Aria looked at Matteo who was still holding the package. She moved past me. "Show me," she ordered. Matteo glanced at me. I nodded.

Aria took the jar then dropped it back in the package. I wrapped my arms around her from behind, holding her as she cried.

Tartarus had hit me in the worst way possible, and Earl White knew it. He relished in it, and knowing men like him, he would loathe to lose this source of power. He wouldn't release Marcella. If we didn't find her soon...

Helplessness was a feeling I wasn't accustomed to, and I didn't allow it to take root. As long as I took breath, I'd search for my girl, and I'd kill every biker on my way to her.

Chapter
Fifteen

Maddox

I HAD BEEN AVOIDING EARL AS MUCH AS POSSIBLE SINCE OUR argument two days ago, but if I wanted to make sure everything finally moved in the right direction, I had to talk to him and find out what went on in his head. We had a meeting scheduled for the evening, and almost all patch-owners had agreed to come.

Marcella had been awfully quiet all day, and I wondered if she regretted our night together. She had mentioned that she'd regret me, but now I wanted her to have changed her mind.

Marcella sat on the bed and brushed her hair with a brush I'd grabbed from one of the club girls, the motion almost hypnotic. I couldn't look away. She turned her head, fixing me with those penetrating eyes. "What will you discuss at your meeting?"

"When we're going to exchange you for your father."

Marcella gave me a strange smile as if I couldn't really believe that.

"I'll convince them. They're going to listen to reason," I said, hardly believing it myself.

"What is it you want, Maddox?"

You. Ever since I met you, only you. I was half tempted to run off with her, to leave everything I'd ever known, ever wanted, behind. But I couldn't. MC life was all I knew, all I wanted. I didn't have friends or family outside of this club. I only had Tartarus.

And yet… suddenly there was Marcella, a woman, my enemy's daughter, who took up more and more of my headspace.

I didn't say anything. My thoughts were madness and betrayal. I headed over to her and bend over her. Grabbing her neck, I tilted her head back for a deep kiss. She responded at first but then she turned her mouth away, robbing me of those irresistible lips. "This will be over once your uncle hands me back to my father. Unless he decides to torture and kill me to punish my father."

She said it as if she were talking about someone else, her voice cool and controlled but her eyes reflected the fear she'd never admit to. My heart sped up at the mere mentioning of her death. "I'd never allow Earl to kill you. I'll protect you."

She smiled but it wasn't happy. "Can you? Protect me? Your club brothers want to burn me at the stake like the witch they think I am."

My club brothers wanted to stake her in a very different way. I wouldn't allow that either. As long as Marcella was under our roof, I'd make sure she wouldn't be harmed worse than she already had been. But once she was released…

The thought of letting her go, of never seeing her again, it added a heavy weight on my shoulders.

"You don't want to lose me," she whispered, pushing to her feet and grabbing my cut. Her eyes held me captive as they always did.

I considered lying, but I simply couldn't do it with her looking at me like that. I cupped her neck harder. "Of course, I don't want to lose you." I reached under my shirt that reached her thighs and shoved the boxers aside. "I'd miss that pretty pussy." I would, but it was only a small part of the reason why I couldn't imagine letting her go. Sharing details from my childhood, talking about more than drug deliveries, moonshine and guns, she was the only person I could do that.

My fingers found her clit and I began to circle it lightly, only teasing her when I really wanted to plunge into her.

"It's more than that, Maddox," Marcella said softly, her breath hitching as I kept stroking her sensitive flesh.

I leaned down and sucked her lower lip into my mouth before I kissed her. Her tongue met mine for a gentle and slow dance so very unlike our previous kisses. Her eyes stayed locked on mine and she sighed into my mouth as my fingers stroked up and down her slit, gathering her arousal to slide even more easily over her little nub.

"Whatever it is, we can't have it, not forever," I growled.

She shook her head. "We can have whatever we want. We just have to reach for it. You can have me all for yourself if you help me escape."

"Escape," I echoed. "My brothers would kill me as a traitor."

"You could come with me and ask my father for help."

I grimaced. The mere idea of asking Luca Vitiello, the man who'd slaughtered my father, for help, left a bitter taste in my mouth. "Your father would kill me for kidnapping his precious daughter."

"He won't if I ask him to spare you."

"I don't want to be at your father's mercy. He should be at mine and I definitely won't grant it to him."

Marcella's expression hardened and she tried to pull back but I held her in place by her neck and plunged my tongue into her mouth the same time as two of my fingers plunged into her wet pussy. She moaned into my mouth, her walls clenching deliciously. I thrust into her at a fast pace, relishing in her arousal and the fire burning in her eyes. Desire and anger, a beautiful combination. Eventually Marcella's grip on me turned painful as her hips rocked against my hand, chasing an orgasm.

When her walls clamped down on my fingers and her eyes widened from the force of her orgasm, I pulled away from the kiss to hear her cry of ecstasy.

"Yes, Snow White," I growled, fingering her even faster. She clung to me until finally her orgasm subsided. I lowered my hand and opened my fly.

Marcella tugged at my hair, forcing me to meet her gaze. "You can live and have me, if you leave your MC life behind and work for my father."

I scoffed. "You want me to serve under your father."

She became serious. "You can either serve under my father or you can rule over a graveyard."

"We aren't dead yet, and me and my brothers are very difficult to kill as you will see."

"My father killed Tartarus men before. He will again."

I jerked down my pants and shoved Marcella toward the bed. She gave me a challenging smile and parted her long legs. I grabbed her ankles and tugged her toward me before I slammed into her in one hard thrust. She was still tight and her face flashed with discomfort but I only waited a second for her pussy to adapt to my cock. My balls furiously slapped against her pussy and my hips against her ass until it was red. But this wasn't enough, could never be. I needed to see her face, wanted to see it every fucking morning when I woke and every night before sleep. I flipped her over and climbed on top of her.

Her eyes burned a hole into my soul and heart.

"Fuck," I growled. "I can't fucking lose you."

After our fuck, she lay in my arms, her breathing low. I'd soon have to get up to go to the meeting.

"I'm scared to die, scared they'll hurt me worse, Maddox," she whispered so softly, at first, I wasn't sure I heard her right. She had every reason to be scared.

"I'm here," I murmured, kissing her neck. Her bandaged ear taunted me with the truth.

Her breathing evened out and I got up, feeling a nervous energy take hold of my body. As I made my way downstairs, I crossed Gunnar. He touched my shoulder. "You're spending a lot of time with her. Everyone's noticed. Soon you'll have to make a choice."

"I made my choice a long time ago," I said, pointing at my cut. "Tartarus runs in my blood."

Gunnar shrugged. "Still. Some people worry. Tonight's meeting is your chance to appease them."

"Fuck 'em. I've bled more for this club than most."

"Calm down. I'm just saying."

If a man like Gunnar already started to be wary of me, I had to be careful. When Gunnar and I entered the meeting room five minutes later, most patch-holders were already seated around the table and some leaned against the walls. Most nods I received were as friendly as in the past but I could see distrust in a couple of faces. Judging by Cody's expression, he was probably the one talking shit about me. Earl sat at the head as usual. I took my seat beside him but he barely acknowledged my presence. We'd had arguments in the past, especially when I was a hot-blooded teen but it had never felt final. This time, it felt as if a rift had opened up between us that couldn't easily be bridged. I wasn't sure how to close it, wasn't sure I wanted to try.

To my surprise, Earl didn't open the meeting with the most obvious topic: the kidnapping. Instead, he wanted to discuss new routes for our weapon transports and a possible co-operation with other MCs. Considering how many we'd killed over the years, I doubted there would be many willing to talk, even if the Famiglia was a common enemy.

I was close to bursting when we were finally ready to move on to the next topic.

"How about we discuss Vitiello now?" I said, failing to mask my annoyance.

There were a few chuckles from older members who probably felt reminded of my teenage days when I constantly interrupted Earl and got banned from the table several times for my hot-blooded outburst.

Earl's eyes cut to me, full of fury. "There's nothing to discuss at this point. Vitiello fails to get off his high horse and as long as that's the case, the Italian whore stays with us."

The insult incited a new wave of rage in me which I had trouble extinguishing. I slammed my fist down on the table. "Tartarus doesn't torture women. We deal with our enemies, not their children. We want Vitiello and he offered himself to us. Let's finally get our revenge. It's time. I call for a vote."

Earl sank back in his chair, but his played calm didn't fool anyone. His eyes reflected the same fury I felt. If it wouldn't have made him look weak, he would have shouted right back at me and refused the vote.

"Then let's vote," he said with a harsh smile. "Who's voting for yes, we should keep the Vitiello whore until Luca Vitiello shows us the respect we deserve and has suffered for all the brothers he tortured and killed. Or no, if you want to end this quickly for him and his spawn."

I gritted my teeth. The way he worded it, the vote was already lost. I could see it in the expressions of my club brothers and their affirmative nods.

As expected, only three voted with no, Gunnar, Gray, and I, while the rest, more than ten men voted to keep Marcella and let Luca suffer through her. Maybe I should have seen it coming. The more moderate voices in our club had become Nomads over the years or joined smaller chapters of Tartarus in Texas or up north because they didn't want to be involved in our revenge plans. The men who remained now were absolutely loyal to Earl and in line with his radical views.

When the meeting was over, I stayed in my chair and watched how my club brothers went to the bar to celebrate a successful meeting. Gunnar touched my shoulder in passing. "You tried," he said. "Soon this will be over and then we can focus on better things than revenge."

I nodded, but I didn't believe it.

Earl spotted me and came back in, towering over me. "The whore needs to move out of your room, Mad. She's messing with your mind. It's the Vitiello gene. This is our moment of revenge, don't allow her to ruin it."

I got up and gave Earl a forced smile. "The last few weeks took a toll on me, Earl. That's all. I just want to get my hands on Vitiello before he slips away."

"He can't. Not this time. Now let's celebrate."

I followed him toward the bar and shared a couple of drinks with the club, to put their suspicions to rest and as a goodbye to those who wouldn't survive.

I'd sworn to get revenge on Luca Vitiello, to make him bleed emotionally and later, physically. I wanted him to suffer as much as I'd suffered.

Marcella had been the means to an end. She was meant to be the ransom we needed to get our hands on Vitiello. I'd despised her before I'd known her, and now this woman owned me in a way I should have never allowed. I hadn't seen it coming but I should have. Marcella Vitiello was a woman unlike any I'd encountered before.

And today I'd betray my club for her. I'd give up my life goal for her. And maybe I'd even lose my life for her. I'd never thought anything could ever be worth it, least of all a woman. Relationships come and go in a biker's life, the only lasting bond was that to your club and its brothers, but with Marcella I knew I wanted it to be an until death do us part kind of thing. Of course, death would likely do us part very soon.

She was worth it. Fuck. I knew it now. I'd die a thousand deaths for her.

Taking a last deep drag, I flicked away my cigarette. It was around ten in the morning, and I'd come out here after celebrating with my brothers last night, instead of going to bed. I couldn't sleep and also couldn't face Marcella. I needed time to think. Today Marcella was supposed to move back to the kennels, as far away from me as possible. Earl had granted me a few more hours for a fuck with her before she'd be fair game. I'd strolled the premises, had checked the fence, but it was guarded heavily.

I grabbed my phone, then stared down at it as the first sunrays of the cloudy day touched the ground beside my feet. Too many guards surrounded the perimeter for me to save Marcella alone. Fuck.

My pulse pounded when I dialed the number of Vitiello's nightclub where he had his office. I'd never talked to him before. That had always been Earl's privilege as prez.

After a few minutes, I was finally put through to the Capo's cell phone because he wasn't in the club. I wasn't surprised that he wasn't at work. He and his men probably worked 24/7 for a way to save Marcella. "What do you want?" Vitiello asked. His voice was tight with suppressed rage. I could imagine what he wanted to do to me, and I probably deserved it. But Vitiello was the last one who should judge anyone. "You better listen carefully because what I'm telling you next is where you can find Marcella."

I gave him the address, then added, "You should hurry if you want to protect your daughter from more harm."

"We both know it's a fucking trap," Vitiello growled.

"Does it matter? You'd die for her. This is your chance to prove it."

He didn't deny it, and for the first time in my life, I had something in common with my worst enemy. The funny thing was the person probably going to lose his life was me. If Vitiello attacked our clubhouse with the full force of his soldiers, none of us would survive. A quick death was all we could hope for and would probably be denied. "Be quick. Earl has more in store for your daughter."

"I'll tear you all apart," he growled, but I hung up before he could elaborate on his promise. I'd seen what he was capable of.

I sagged against the wall of the shed, staring up at the sky. It was ironic that the sun came out now that I'd decided to destroy the one thing I'd clung to all my life. Then I dragged my eyes to the tattoo of the hellhound on my upper arm. I'd been born into the club. I'd loved it with all my heart, had sworn my loyalty and life to it and my club brothers, but in only a few weeks Marcella had turned my life upside down. Her kidnapping had shown me Tartarus' ugly head, one I always tried to ignore. I'd still fight at my club brothers' side and try to kill Vitiello once Marcella was safe. I wanted to help her not spare him.

I pushed away from the wall and went in search of my half-brother. He needed to get away from here before Luca arrived. I found Gray, Gunnar, Cody, and a few others gathered around the table, playing poker, most of them looking like death warmed over from drinking too much. Some of these men were like my friends. They didn't deserve death, but if I told them about what lay ahead, they'd tell Earl, and he would evacuate everyone and bring Marcella to a new hiding place. Only this time, I wouldn't be able to protect her. I only had this one chance and I wouldn't fuck it up for anyone.

"Want to join us and stop moping around, Mad?" Gunnar asked, a cigar between his teeth. "I don't know why you have your fucking panties in a bunch anyway. If I had a gorgeous woman in my bed, I'd run around grinning from ear to ear."

"You know me. I want Vitiello's head as a trophy on our club wall. I won't be satisfied until that's the case."

This still held true. I wanted Vitiello dead. Unfortunately, that desire was at odds with my obsession for his daughter. Maybe it was for the best if Vitiello killed me, then I wouldn't be faced with that impossible problem.

"You won't have to wait much longer. Vitiello will cut his own dick off to save his daughter once we've all had a go at her," Cody said with a snicker. Even more than in the past, I felt the urge to smash his stupid face in.

"Hey Gray, I need to talk to you."

Gray shook his head. "I'm winning here. We can talk later."

My patience snapped. Vitiello was probably already on the way here with every torture device ever invented on this planet. I stalked over to him and ripped the cards from his hands. "Fold."

Gray protested then he shook his head. "What's your fucking problem?"

"My problem is that you don't follow orders. You're below me in rank, don't forget it."

"For now," he muttered, a slight slur in his voice. He must have drunk a lot to still be drunk the next morning. This kid drove me up the wall. Cody and Gunnar exchanged looks.

Gray got up. I chose to ignore his comment, even though it was probably true. His jealousy only ever showed when he was drunk. Earl would eventually favor Gray as his successor. He was his son after all. But nothing of that mattered anymore. After today, the main chapter of Tartarus MC would be dead and I was the nail in its coffin. Maybe the Nomads would come together to build a new chapter but I doubted they'd do it close to New York.

Gray followed me outside as I headed into the woods. I didn't want to risk anyone overhearing us. "What's so urgent that you ruin my Straight Flush?"

"I need you to head out now and grab a few things for me."

"No can do. Dad called the entire club in for another meeting around lunch. That's why we're all up so early. He has something planned."

My brows pulled together. Earl hadn't mentioned it to me. "What is it?"

Gray shrugged. "He usually always shares shit with you, not me."

I'd thought me celebrating with them last night had convinced Earl of my loyalty, but apparently, he was still suspicious of me. For good reason. "Whatever it is can wait. You need to go now."

Gray narrowed his eyes, suddenly not appearing drunk anymore. "Why? What's the matter?"

This discussion was wasting time we didn't have. I grabbed Gray by the collar. "Listen to me for once and get your ass away from here."

"What did you do?" he gritted out.

"Leave the clubhouse now."

He jerked free of my grip. "I'm not running off no matter what."

I might be able to live with myself if Vitiello killed my club brothers and even Earl, but I'd hate myself forever if Gray died. "Fuck, you moron, Vitiello knows our whereabouts. He's probably already on the way to kill us all."

Gray took a step back from me, horrified realization flashing across his face. "You told him?"

"I had to. Earl went too far. We all did. This was never meant to turn into a torture session of his daughter. Vitiello was supposed to pay not her."

"You're a traitor!"

He turned on his heel as if to rush back to the house and warn everyone. I didn't want them all to die but if Gray warned them, Earl might kill Marcella and probably allow every brother to have a go at her before he did. I couldn't allow it. I pulled out my gun and hit my half-brother over the head with the handle. He sagged to the ground. Grabbing him under his arms, I dragged him into the forest and hid him under a few twigs and leaves. With a little luck, he wouldn't wake before everything was over. Then at least he would survive. That was all I could do.

I hurried back to the house and paused when I noticed the tattoo machine on the bar counter. "Who's getting inked?" I asked into the round.

"The whore gets a tattoo she deserves, something really fitting," Cody said with a nasty smile, obviously enjoying that he knew more than me. He put his cards down. "Full house!"

Gunnar groaned as he put his cards down and the others muttered curses as well.

"A tattoo was never mentioned before," I said. I failed to mask my shock.

"What Vitiello did needs to be punished accordingly."

"He needs to pay, not his daughter," I muttered like a broken record, still hoping against reason that my club brothers would listen.

"It's Earl's decision, boy," Gunnar said diplomatically.

"Has her pussy clouded your judgment?" Cody asked. I gave him the finger. Then I went in search of Earl. I wasn't even sure why I was still bothering, maybe to convince myself that he hadn't lost his conscience completely.

I found him at our meeting table, lost in his thoughts, which was never a good thing. The last time he'd made that face had been when we'd found out about a mole in our rows. Only this time I was the fucking mole. "Is it true what Cody says that you want to tattoo Marcella?"

Earl snapped out of his thoughts and narrowed his eyes at me. "She gets what she deserves. I thought we agreed on that last night."

I shook my head. "This is taking things too far. Let's grab Vitiello and make him pay."

Earl shot to his feet and got in my face, and I could tell that I was losing him, his trust and what little affection he was capable of. I wanted to save him, save us, whatever bond we had, but I wasn't sure how to do it without sacrificing Marcella, and whatever conscience I still had. "I'm not sure you're still on the right side, son." For a while I'd loved hearing him call me by that name, but recently it hadn't sounded like a nice term. I doubted Earl had ever really seen me as his son. He'd appreciated my desire for revenge and that my sad story had created a stronger bond among our men. "Are you going to be a problem?" he snarled.

Cody stormed into the clubhouse. "Gray's out in the woods. Someone knocked him out."

Earl followed Cody at once but I turned on my heel and rushed toward my leather jacket thrown over one of the barstools to grab my motorcycle keys then I hurried into the armory. Before I could grab a machine gun, something was smashed against my back and I dropped to my knees with a grunt of pain. My forehead collided with the wall, making stars dance in my vision. I blinked to catch myself. Blood dripped from a cut in my forehead and ran into my left eye as I looked up. Cody stood beside me with a baseball bat in his hand. "Your uncle was right to be suspicious of you. Told me to keep an eye on you while he had a chat with Gray. If the boy tells his Pa that you knocked him out for the whore, you're dead."

I lunged at Cody, trying to rip the baseball bat out of his hand, but Earl appeared in the doorway and pointed his gun at me. "Down or I'll put a bullet in your skull, Mad."

I sank back down to my knees, my vision dancing before my eyes.

Earl towered over me with a hard smile. "Gray told me you called Vitiello so he could save his little whore."

Fuck, Gray. I'd hoped the kid would listen to reason and not blindly follow his old man's judgment, especially when Earl had lost his fucking mind.

"You went too far, Earl. I warned you."

Earl leaned down, spit flying as he snarled, "This was our revenge."

"We should leave the premises," Cody suggested, looking around nervously as if he expected Vitiello to jump out from behind a curtain any moment. It was ironic that Vitiello's appearance was my only hope right now. Who'd ever thought that day would come?

"We won't run. We have his daughter. He can't risk too much. Make sure the perimeter is safe and get Gray inside."

With a nasty smile in my direction, Cody sauntered away.

Earl's eyes settled on me. For a long time, he'd taken the spot as my father, and he was still the only family I had next to Gray and Mom. I might have lost them with my actions. Maybe I could win their trust back by helping them in their fight against Vitiello. I still wanted the man dead but not at the cost of risking Marcella's life. No matter how much I hated her father, my feelings for her were even stronger. I was a doomed fucker.

Earl shook his head with a harsh laugh. "Stupid boy." He aimed the barrel of his shotgun at my head and everything turned black.

Chapter
Sixteen

Marcella

I PEERED OUT OF THE WINDOW, THE HEAVY FEELING DEEP IN the pit of my stomach increasing with every passing moment. Maddox hadn't come to bed last night, for the first time since he'd taken me into his room. I'd tried to listen at the door for snippets of conversation that might give me a hint why, but no one had come close to the room.

Several bikers arrived on their bikes and commotion broke out in the driveway. I sat up, curious. Everyone's face was tight with worry. Hope settled in my chest. Maybe Dad had landed a hit. My hand moved to my ear, barely touching the bandage. Then I quickly jerked it away. I hadn't even seen the wound yet. I wasn't sure I had the courage to do so anytime soon.

What if something had happened to Maddox and that was why

he hadn't shown up? What if Dad was the reason behind Maddox's disappearance?

The lock turned and I stood, smiling. The smile died when Gunnar appeared in the doorway.

"No reason to smile, puppet," he said in his rough voice.

"Where's Maddox?" I asked sharply, backing away.

Gunnar shook his head. "Stupid boy." He stalked toward me and grabbed my arm. "Maddox can't help you now. You better pray your daddy sees reason."

He dragged me outside despite my struggling. My bare feet scratched over the rough floorboards. "What do you mean? What happened?" I asked over and over again but he ignored me. Nobody was in the common area when we crossed it. Where was everyone? And what was going on?

Gunnar led me down to the kennels and shoved me inside the same cage I had been in before. I whirled around just when he locked the door.

"What's going on? Please tell me, where's Maddox?"

"He'll join you soon," he said cryptically before he walked away. The dogs paced in their cages, infected by the nervous atmosphere. Satan wasn't in her cage though, and I couldn't help but worry about her, too. The familiar stench of dog piss and feces clogged my nose almost instantly. I sank down on the hut, watching as the bikers gathered guns and carried boards into the clubhouse as if to barricade the windows. Some of them walked by the kennels just to insult me and leer at my body. Only in Maddox's boxers and T I felt even more exposed.

"Get more men to the fence!" someone roared, worry swinging in their voice.

Hope flared in my veins. This could only be Dad. But where was Maddox? What was going on? What if Dad got Maddox in his hands? My mind wouldn't stop reeling. Fear battled with hope in me. I wanted to be freed but I didn't want to lose Maddox.

It was a fatal thought, and a fatal attraction.

Hugging my knees to my chest, I watched my surroundings, trying to catch up on what was going on. After the initial insults, nobody paid me any attention, but the fear I saw on many of their faces could only be because of Dad.

Movement drew my gaze back to the clubhouse.

Earl White walked out of the door, dragging an unmoving Maddox after him by the arm. I jumped off the hut and crossed the dirty kennel on my bare feet, my heart beating in my throat. The dogs in the surrounding kennels began to bark and jump against their cages. I barely flinched anymore. I had gotten used to their boisterous nature. They weren't the most dangerous beasts around.

Maddox looked lifeless, limbs dragging through the dirt, head lolling almost comically back and forth. Earl smiled darkly at me when our eyes met and immediately goose bumps rose on my skin. I tried to mask my worry but I doubted I could fool him. By now, everyone seemed to know about Maddox and me.

"Maybe this will help you clear your head and make you realize your mistake. If you apologize, I'll grant you a quick death," Earl said as he dragged Maddox into the cage beside mine. Death? What was he talking about? Maddox's left side of his face was covered with blood from a cut in his hairline. I finally noticed Maddox's chest rising and falling. At least, he wasn't dead—yet. Something was horribly wrong. Earl turned and closed the cage, then he smiled viciously at me. "And for you, I have a special surprise soon."

I didn't even want to think about what that could mean.

I eyed the dog worriedly who paced around Maddox as if he was only waiting for the perfect moment to tear into him. The second Earl and Cody were gone, I kneeled at the bars. "Maddox," I whispered then louder. "Maddox, wake up!"

His eyelids fluttered but didn't open. The dog sniffed at his wound. What if the beast started gnawing at him? Had they'd been fed today? I hadn't paid attention to the kennels while looking out of the windows.

"Shoo," I hissed, trying to scare the dog away, but it only gave me a quick glance before it continued inspecting Maddox. "Go away!" I growled, hitting the bars. When that didn't have the intended effect,

I turned around and grabbed my water bowl. I tossed the water at the dog and it jumped back. Then charged at me and jumped against the bars. I stumbled back.

Maddox let out a groan. Some of the water had hit him in the face as well. His eyes shot open and he rolled over then pushed up on his elbows. He shook his head, very dog-like before he glanced around. His gaze zeroed in on the dog trying to tear down the bars between him and me.

"Wesson, down!" he ordered in a voice as sharp as a whip. "Down!"

The beast actually listened and sank down on his belly, his pink tongue lolling about lazily. Except for Satan, I hadn't really connected with any of the other dogs.

"Are you all right?" I asked.

Maddox rubbed his head, grimacing, and pushed to his feet. He swayed slightly as he walked over to me. "Only a motherfucker of a headache."

"Your uncle was really angry at you."

"He's pissed. He thinks I chose you over the club."

I didn't say anything. "He said something about a special surprise for me today."

Maddox sighed. "That's one of the reasons why I wanted to get you out of here."

"What is it?"

"My uncle wants to tattoo something on your back."

My blood turned cold. "I don't suppose it'll be something I'll like," I said, trying to sound blasé but failing. "What is it?"

Maddox shook his head.

"Tell me."

He gripped the bars tightly, his eyes fierce. "I honestly don't know. They don't share things with me anymore."

I nodded. My fingers touched the Band-Aid over my ruined ear. "I suppose I can count myself lucky they don't choose my forehead for the tattoo. Maybe next time?"

"I can't protect you anymore," Maddox said quietly. "That's why I contacted your father and told him about our whereabouts."

My eyes widened and I pressed closer, my fingers closing over his. "You told my father?" Despite his hatred for my father—considering what he'd witnessed as a young child I could understand his reasoning even if I didn't share it—he contacted him to save me.

"He can save you. He's got the necessary manpower. He's probably already on his way. With a little luck, you'll be back home tonight."

My heart beat faster. "What about you? After that betrayal, your uncle won't forgive you."

"He won't. He'll kill me after he's done with you. He wants me to watch you getting hurt because he knows what it does to me. But I doubt he'll survive your father's attack, nor will I."

Dad would torture and kill them all, as they deserved. Unless I begged Dad to spare Maddox. That had never been the plan. I'd originally sought Maddox's trust and closeness to save myself in case Dad didn't find me in time. But things had changed even if I never meant for them to do so. I didn't want Maddox to die. My chest tightened painfully at the mere thought of his death. He wasn't innocent, far from it. He was guilty of kidnapping me, of delivering me to the hands of his uncle in the first place. Of course, his uncle would just have sent someone else if Maddox hadn't agreed but that wasn't the point. "My father won't kill you if I ask him to spare you."

Maddox leaned his forehead against the bars. "Why should you do something like that?"

"Because I want you to live," I said merely. There was more to it—nothing I wanted to consider or voice at this point.

"But at what cost? What will your father ask of me, if he listens to you at all," Maddox asked quietly.

"He'll ask you to burn your cut, to cut any ties to other bikers, and to swear loyalty—at the very least." And for that to happen, a near-miracle was necessary. Dad's hatred for bikers was limitless at this point, no doubt, and Maddox would be at the very top of his hate list.

Maddox shook his head slowly, his lips twisting with disgust, as if the mere thought of doing any of those things was impossible to him. "What's between us is one thing, but my feelings toward your father haven't changed."

"Then you have to put them to rest. It's your only chance if you want my father to spare you."

"It's better to die standing up than to live on your knees, Snow White. I'll die before I fall to my knees before your father and ask for mercy."

I rolled my eyes. "Things are always black or white for men, especially alphas. But life is full of gray areas. You can still be free and keep your precious pride if you swear loyalty to my father."

"Snow White, I'll say it a thousand times until it goes into your pretty head. Your father won't ever trust me, nor will I trust him. He and I have a past that can't be ignored. Even your charm and our feelings for you won't change that."

I pressed my forehead to his with the bars between us. "What feelings?"

Maddox smiled darkly. "I betrayed my club brothers and my own blood for you. What kind of feelings do you think?"

"Lust," I joked, but my voice was hushed. None of this had been part of the plan, not for Maddox, not for me.

"So much more."

Commotion and the snapping of twigs made me and Maddox pull apart to search the area. Cody and Earl were on their way down to us with two bikers whose names I didn't know. Earl had Satan on the leash and Cody carried some kind of machine.

"How sweet," Cody called, a nasty smile on his ugly face. Maddox's uncle, on the other hand, looked furious. "If I'd known how easily you allow pussy to cloud your judgment, I would have made sure you stay away from her."

Maddox eyed his uncle with contempt and wariness. "It's time to end this game. Vitiello was our target, Earl."

His uncle ignored him in favor of hovering in front of my cage and eyeing me with an unsettling glint in his eyes. "Cody has a knack for ink. I hope you'll appreciate it."

He unlocked the cage door. I resisted the urge to back away even if every fiber of my body screamed to flee. I was a Vitiello. I couldn't appear weak even if I was terrified of what lay ahead. I'd felt the same terror when I'd first been kidnapped, ready to break under the force of my fear, but I hadn't broken down, and I wouldn't now either.

Cody carried the tattoo machine, I realized now, into the cage before he grabbed my upper arm in a crushing grip as two more bikers crowded into the narrow cage. They set a generator down beside me and attached the tattoo machine to it.

"Let her go," Maddox seethed, his eyes brimming with fury as he gripped the bars, looking ready to tear them down.

"Your word means dick, asshole," Cody said. Would they torture and kill us before my father arrived?

I believed in a higher power but I'd never been much of a prayer. Still, I begged whoever was listening to let my father arrive in time. In time to spare me more pain and whatever Cody was going to ink into my skin. To save Maddox too.

Cody shoved me against the dog hut and I fell forward, bracing myself on the dirty surface. Another man gripped my neck and held me down. A rip sounded and air touched my skin as my back was exposed. I struggled but I didn't stand a chance against the three men in the cage with me.

"Earl, be reasonable, for fuck's sake. Vitiello will be here any moment. Don't waste your time on this," Maddox tried to reason with his uncle but his voice didn't sound like someone who wanted to negotiate. It sounded like murder.

"Vitiello wants to screw us over? His daughter pays the price."

I rolled my eyes so far to the side until I caught Maddox's gaze. The buzz of a tattoo needle sounded. I dug my teeth into my lower lip. The moment the needle touched my back, pain radiated down my spine. I squeezed my eyes shut, against Maddox's desperate expression and the world as a whole. Cody was probably making sure it was particularly painful but except for a few sharp intakes of breath, I didn't give any of them the satisfaction of a scream or my begging. They would all pay tenfold. Even if it took my last breath, I'd make sure of it.

Eventually the pain turned into a fiery burn and throbbing that I eventually got used to. I wasn't sure how long the ordeal took but when I was finally released, I felt too weak to straighten. I pretended I had passed out. My eyes burned with tears ready to fall and so I forced my lids shut.

"Not as tough as her father now?" Earl said.

I didn't react. I should have given a comeback but right this moment, I couldn't do it. I needed my energy for the fight that lay ahead. I needed my strength for the reunion with my family so they didn't have to worry more than they already had. I wouldn't waste any of it on Earl or Cody or any other ugly biker.

"You're dead," Maddox growled.

I wasn't sure whom he was talking to. Probably Cody. His bond to his uncle was still too strong.

A warm breath ghosted over my ear, raising goose bumps all over my body and sending a shiver down my spine, which sent a new wave of pain down my back. "This is what you get for messing with us. And soon I'll fuck your ass right before your father's eyes. Maybe I'll force him to fuck you as well to save you," Earl rasped.

I wanted nothing more than to kick him in the balls but I remained motionless. I still wasn't sure if my legs would have carried me if I'd tried. I felt shaky and my back was throbbing. Worse than the pain, though, was the uncertainty about the tattoo. It had to be something nasty. Earl seemed way too smug.

"Now to you, Mad. I was thinking what to do to you, if I should have you watch the whore getting fucked by each of us before killing you, but I realized keeping you alive at this point is a risk I just can't take."

I turned my head to the side until I could see everything. Earl unlocked the cage door and Cody removed the other dog from the cage.

Earl unleashed Satan. "I think we both know it has to end like this." Earl's smile was cruel. He locked Satan in the cage with Maddox, who slowly turned around so his back was pressed against the bars.

My blood turned cold, realizing what Earl was about to do. But Maddox knew the dogs… Satan wouldn't attack him… right?

"Satan, kill," Earl shouted.

I pushed up despite the pain in my back. Satan hesitated a moment before she charged at Maddox and lunged at him. Maddox brought up his arms to protect his face and throat. Satan barked and bared her teeth but didn't bite Maddox yet.

"Kill him!" Earl growled.

I stumbled to my feet and toward the bars, clutching them. "No, Satan, stop!"

"Release!" Maddox screamed. "No!"

Satan dropped back on her paws and turned around herself, obviously confused by the myriad of orders. Earl might have been her owner but he'd never treated her how a dog was supposed to be treated. Maybe that would bite him in the ass now.

"Stupid bitch," Cody hissed. Earl stalked toward another cage with a big male Rottweiler and grabbed him by the neck, dragging him toward Maddox's cage.

"No," I whispered. Blood rushed in my ears. I was starting to feel nauseous from fear and the inking, but I clung to the bars despite my wobbly legs.

Earl unlocked the door again and thrust the other dog inside. Satan whirled around, baring her teeth. These dogs were trained to fight against each other.

"Kill," Earl ordered, pointing at Maddox, and the male dog didn't hesitate. He charged at Maddox but Satan obviously wanted to defend her territory and collided with him.

Earl shrugged. "He's got twenty-five pounds on her. When he's killed her, he can chew off your face, Mad. Enjoy the show, whore."

Cody and Earl turned around and left.

The bigger dog was on top of Satan, but it was difficult to follow their vicious fight as they snarled and bit and struggled.

Satan yelped in pain.

"Maddox!"

"Fuck," Maddox muttered. He removed his belt and wrapped it around his hand so the buckle covered his knuckles then he stalked toward the fighting dogs, grabbed the bigger male by the collar and jerked him back. The animal was heavy so it didn't fly very far and quickly turned back on Maddox who aimed a punch with the buckle at the dog's snout. With a loud whine, the dog jumped away, shaking its head. Maddox towered over it. "Down, now!" The dog laid down, panting heavily, its muzzle covered in blood. Probably Satan's. She laid on her side, breathing heavily.

I sank down on my knees, feeling shaky. My back throbbed and I was terrified. For myself, for Maddox, even for Satan. It was too much to stomach. Everything caught up with me in that moment and part of me wanted to curl up in the corner.

"Snow White?" Maddox murmured, his voice laced with concern. "Marcella?"

I lifted my head too quickly and regretted it almost instantly as a sharp pain shot through my back. My skin felt as if it was too small for my body and might tear at any moment. Ignoring this, I straightened fully again then perched on the edge of the hut. When my vertigo had disappeared, I locked gazes with Maddox.

"Is Satan injured badly?"

He shook his head. "Don't think about it now. We have to get you out of here alive."

His gaze darted to my exposed back. Guilt and fury created a potent combination in his eyes.

"What does the tattoo say?" I asked, surprised at how raw and dry my voice sounded.

"Don't think about it now. There are more important things to worry about."

"Don't tell me what to worry about, Maddox. I want to know." I needed to know. Everything was better than this soul-crushing uncertainty. My mind would conjure the worst scenarios.

"Marcella," he rasped, his eyes urging me to let it drop.

"Tell me," I growled. "I'm not breakable, so don't treat me like that!"

"Vitiello whore."

I nodded, then shoved to my feet and briefly turned my back on Maddox to hide my expression from him. I was so mad at him. This was his fault.

"I'm fucking sorry. This was never supposed to happen. I swear. If I'd known—"

"Then what?" I asked harshly, whirling on him. "You wouldn't have kidnapped me?"

Maddox dropped his forehead against the bars. "Yes. And I would have done everything in my power to stop Earl from letting anyone else kidnap you either."

I gave him a disbelieving look. "You hate my father more than anything in the world. You said it yourself. You would have done anything to get revenge on him. What do you care about a lost earlobe and an insulting tattoo for the daughter of your worst enemy?"

"Sometimes priorities shift. You don't have to believe me but it is the goddamn truth."

I walked closer to him. The wind picked up, touching my aching back. "And what are your priorities now, Maddox?"

Maddox stretched out a tattooed arm, his palm upward, waiting for me to take it.

I didn't budge.

"I betrayed my brothers for you. Maybe I'll die for you once your father gets his hands on me."

"You brought this upon yourself, not me."

"If someone had killed your father right before your eyes, wouldn't your brother have wanted revenge?"

"Not just my brother," I admitted.

Maddox nodded grimly.

I put my hand in his and his fingers closed around mine. "You want to kill my father. As long as that's the case, we're lost."

"I've lived for revenge for so long, it's difficult to let go of something like that. But if there's anyone I'd do it for, then it's you, Snow White. I'd do anything for you."

I wanted to believe him. But after everything that had happened, I wasn't willing to give him the benefit of the doubt.

"Attack!" someone screamed.

Maddox's hand around mine tightened. "Your father is here to save you and kill me, Snow White."

"Unless one of your biker brothers kills me first," I said.

He tugged me toward him, his eyes burning with emotion. "I'm going to make sure you'll get to your father safely. Now give a dying man his last kiss."

I allowed him to pull me even closer until my lips touched his through the bars. He deepened the kiss, filling it with longing and desire. I sunk into him even as more screams rang out, as the world around us exploded into war. Shots cut through the yelling. The quick-fire of machine guns. Like a drowning man coming up for air, Maddox ripped away from me and released me. "Press against the wall until I tell you to move or you see your father. Now!"

I did what he asked and stumbled toward the back of the kennel.

Maddox and I looked at each other again, and this felt like a goodbye. One of us would likely die, maybe even the both of us. My heart clenched thinking this was the end for us, for a love that was never meant to be, a love without a chance at a happy end.

Chapter
Seventeen

Maddox

I NEEDED TO MAKE SURE MARCELLA GOT OUT OF THIS ALIVE. I'D die either way, either by the hands of my club brothers or by her father. There was a strange sense of relief in the knowledge of certain death.

I scanned our surroundings, hoping for Gray to dash past. He was our only hope. None of the other men, not even Gunnar would help me escape. I wasn't even sure if Gray would do it. The rift between us had grown in the past weeks. Gunfire sounded down at the fence. Our gun power would keep Vitiello and his army back for a while. I wouldn't wait here like a mouse in the trap.

I tried not to glance at Marcella who was pressed to the wall of her kennel. I wanted her out of harm's way. The chances of being hit by a stray bullet were just way too high. Not to mention that Earl might still kill her to punish Vitiello.

I cast a cautious glance at the dog. It hadn't moved from its place, but it was watching me. I hoped it had forgotten Earl's orders. Being torn apart by teeth wasn't my wish for death. Not that death at Luca's hands would be much better. Satan was still breathing but blood had gathered under her hind leg. I doubted she'd make it.

And then I spotted a flash of bright blond hair and the matching cut. "Gray!" I shouted.

His eyes darted to me, wide with disorientation and anxiety. He bowed down to escape the bullets.

"Gray! Come here!"

He glanced my way once more, conflict reflecting on his face. When Earl had been off with his club brothers, getting drunk or pussy, and Mom had been down with a bout of depression, I had taken care of him, had held him at night when he'd been scared of the monsters of the dark.

Then he dashed toward me, his head low. I wasn't sure if Luca and his men had breached the fence yet, but I suspected they had. A wire-mesh fence wouldn't hold them back for long but getting past our armed guards would take longer.

When Gray finally arrived in front of my cage, I breathed a sigh of relief.

"What happened to the dogs?"

"You've got to help me, Gray. I'll die if I stay locked in here."

Gray's gaze flitted to Marcella and he narrowed his eyes. "You are the reason why we're under attack. If I release you, you'll only fight against us."

"Gray," I said imploringly, pressing tightly against the bars. "Earl set the dogs on me so they could tear me apart."

Gray shook his head as if he couldn't believe it. "He wouldn't—"

"Do it? Come on, we both know that's not true."

Gray didn't say anything, only watched Satan.

"We're brothers. Do you really want me defenseless in a dog cage so Vitiello can tear me apart? You know what he did to my father. And he'll do the same to me, no matter if I helped his daughter, which is all I did. You saw what Earl did to her. It's not right. This has nothing to do with Vitiello. I still want him dead and won't hesitate to kill him if given the chance."

I needed to get through to Gray quickly before Earl spotted us, or my brother was hit by a Famiglia bullet.

He glanced back to the clubhouse then to me. "I don't know if I can trust you."

"You can," I said fiercely, but I wasn't sure he could. Right in this moment, my sole priority was to get Marcella to safety. Once that was taken care of, I'd do my best to help Gray. If something happened to him because of my betrayal, I'd never be able to forgive myself. I wanted him safe. I wanted a different life for him.

Gray took out his key chain, and I had to resist the urge to rip it out of his hand. Instead, I waited for him to unlock my cage. The moment the familiar click sounded, I shoved open the door and rushed to Marcella's kennel.

"Now her."

"No," Gray growled. "I don't care what happens to her. She ruined everything."

"It wasn't her fucking choice to be kidnapped by us."

"But it was her choice to seduce you and mess with your mind. Before her, the club always came first. You lived for the club, for revenge, and now look at you."

"You were never for kidnapping her. Look at her back!" I turned to Marcella. "Show him."

She presented her naked, tattooed back to us. The sight still set my blood aflame with rage. The place between her shoulders was red and bloody, and *Vitiello whore* was written in ugly black letters across her skin.

Gray's eyes widened and he swallowed.

"Gray, help me. Do you want an innocent woman's death on your conscience?"

Screams rang out.

Gray turned back to the fights but I couldn't allow him to leave with the keys. I lunged at him and grabbed his arm. "Give me the keys."

He turned to me with a disbelieving expression. "I knew it!"

"You know nothing, Gray. Don't be a sheep that blindly follows the herd into death. Leave while you still have the chance."

"I won't leave the club."

I pulled him even closer. "Gray. Our club took a wrong turn when we kidnapped Marcella, but we sure as fuck went straight into hellfire territory when Earl started torturing her. Don't tell me you're suddenly okay with what happened?"

"No," he growled. "I was against the kidnapping from the start but Earl's the president of this club and it's our job to follow his orders."

Gray shook off my grip and stumbled away. I hoped he'd get on his bike and save his own ass. He was a good guy and didn't deserve to go down with this club. If Vitiello got his hands on him, he wouldn't show him mercy, even if he was still pretty much a kid.

I whirled around to Marcella's cage. She stumbled toward the door when I unlocked it and fell into my arms. I kissed her fiercely, not caring about the bullets and screams. I needed another taste of her before I might never see her again. She briefly relaxed against me and time seemed to stand still. Nothing mattered but her lips, her body, the fire burning in her eyes. "We need to get you to your father," I rasped.

"What about Satan?"

"Marcella, we can't help her now. She's too heavy for us to carry." I linked our hands and guided her away from the cages. The other dogs had quieted and hidden in their huts. The vision in my left eye was still impaired. Maybe blood had dried on my eyeball, or the hit to my head had left lasting damage, I wasn't sure. Marcella had trouble keeping up with my steps but she didn't complain.

I spotted Gunnar and a couple of prospects storming out of the clubhouse and toward the fence, probably to defend our borders but knowing Vitiello's numbers, I doubted they stood any chance. He would barrel right through us and would leave nothing in his wake.

An explosion sounded, blasting splinters of wood and fence all around us. I shoved Marcella down and shielded her with my body. My back burned but I didn't move until a new wave of screams and shots rang out. The sound of shotguns made my head swivel up. As I'd feared, Earl and several bikers stormed out of the clubhouse and in the direction of the kennels.

I jerked Marcella up onto her feet. She, too, had seen the bikers heading our way. I dragged her away but running toward the fence line where the majority of the fighting was happening posed the risk of being hit by a bullet from either side. Vitiello was on his way, I only needed to make sure Marcella stayed alive until then. Nothing else mattered.

I stormed to the most unlikely place, to the clubhouse. As expected, it was empty except for one terrified looking prospect. He fumbled with his gun but didn't manage to loosen the safety pin. I released Marcella's hand and lunged at him, ripping the gun out of his hand before I hit him over the head with the barrel. I grabbed another gun and his knife, then I dragged Marcella behind the bar. It had been enforced with wooden boards and could hold off a few bullets. Of course, the shotguns would eventually tear through it, but I had to trust that Vitiello would find us.

The shooting and screaming came closer. It sounded as if World War III had broken out. Marcella peered at me with wide eyes, panting softly.

"Everything will be okay. Your father will be here any moment and I'll keep you safe until then." And then all hell broke loose around us. The shelf behind us exploded. Alcohol and glass shards catapulted our way. My back lit up with new pain, but I only focused on Marcella who cowered in front of me. I touched her cheek briefly, wanting to burn the image of her face into my mind so I could recall it in my last moments.

Marcella

Steps rang out and a door was thrown shut. "Barricade the door!" Earl screamed and I held my breath, realizing he was in the house and judging from the myriad of voices several men were with him. Maddox and I were trapped.

"Earl!" Dad roared. "I give you five seconds to hand over my daughter before I tear down the fucking house and chop you and your fucking family into pieces."

My heart swelled with relief hearing Dad's voice.

"Fuck you! I'll send her head out to you, that's all you get. We'll keep her cold pussy to keep us entertained."

Maddox's muscles tautened as he raised the guns. "Stay down," he mouthed.

Another explosion sounded and splinters flew through the room. A man staggered toward us, probably to seek cover. "Prez, they are—"

Maddox shot him in the head before he could finish the sentence and all hell broke loose. My ears rang from the gunfire. Maddox jumped up, raising his guns. "Earl, don't be stupid. Everyone's going to die because of your ego." Maddox ducked and a bullet burst through another of the liquor bottles.

"Damn dogs, I'll drown them all."

"For fuck's sake! Be reasonable and hand Marcella over!"

More gunfire sounded followed by the sound of breaking wood. A moment later something hit the ground with a loud bang.

"Door down!" someone yelled.

Maddox jerked to his feet when Gunnar showed up, holding a knife in his hands. They began grappling. It was obvious that Maddox didn't want to kill the older man. Eventually he managed to land a hard hit to the man's temple. Gunnar crumpled on the floor and didn't stir again.

The next biker who lunged at Maddox wasn't as lucky. Maddox impaled his knife in the guy's chest.

I began shaking, my ears ringing from the gunfire and wounded men screaming in pain. Maybe I'd die right in front of Dad.

Blood splatters covered the wooden boards and the walls. Maddox stepped out from the cover and fired. I crawled forward, peering out from behind the bar. Brutal carnage reigned around me. Blood and body parts lay on the ground.

And amid it all stood Dad, Matteo and Amo and several Famiglia soldiers, right before the front door while Earl and his men hid behind the overturned pool table. It took me a moment to recognize Amo. His eyes were wild and in his right hand, he held an ax, covered in blood and flesh. I didn't know how many of the savagely killed bikers were his fault. This wasn't the Amo I remembered.

The brother I'd left behind had seen fights as a fun game. Becoming a Capo had been a distant goal, one he hadn't been prepared for yet. He'd been a cocky, thrill-seeking boy who liked to impress girls with his future title and looks. His induction had been proforma. Up until this point, Dad had kept him away from the worst of the business by Mom's request. Amo had always had a penchant for violence. It ran in his blood, like it ran in mine, albeit not as strong. But it had lain dormant. Now as I saw his blood sprinkled face and the raw hunger for revenge in his eyes, matching Dad's, I realized his true nature had been awakened.

Maddox pushed me back when another biker jumped at us and rammed a knife into the man, killing another one of his MC brothers to save me. Behind the couch on the right, I spotted Gray. Maddox would be devastated when he realized his brother hadn't fled but stayed for the fight.

More Famiglia men pushed into the house until Earl and a few other bikers made a dash for the stairs to seek safety on the second floor.

Maddox grabbed my arm and helped me to my feet, dragging me across the room and shielding me with his body. "Go to your family." He pushed me forward, away from his warmth and I stumbled a few steps, disoriented. Matteo caught me in his arms but I gasped in pain when he touched my back. He briefly looked at my exposed back, and his expression twisted with disbelief then fury. "I'll have a blast killing them."

"Take Marci to safety," Dad growled. Marci, the name no longer seemed fitting for the girl I had become.

Matteo began to drag me away from the scene but I turned in his hold to address Dad. "Don't kill him!" I pointed at Maddox, but I couldn't say more because Matteo tightened his hold on me and dragged me away. My gaze brushed over Maddox and his parting smile as he stood covered in blood amid his dead club brothers. He had made peace with death. The last thing I saw was how he jumped behind the sofa beside his brother Gray to fight at his side.

"No!" I screamed.

"Come on, Marcella. Let's get you to a doctor."

I peered up at my uncle. "Tell Dad he can't kill Maddox."

"Let your dad and me handle those assholes. And don't worry, your dad wants to keep as many of them as possible alive for questioning and thorough payback."

I glanced back at the clubhouse as I stumbled along with my uncle. Two armed guards were by our sides and didn't leave even when we got into a black van. Inside, the Famiglia doc was already waiting. Dad had thought of everything.

"Why didn't Amo take me to safety?" I asked, surprised Dad had allowed him to stay.

Matteo twisted his knife in his hand, obviously eager to use it on someone. "Your brother insisted he was allowed to fight and your dad prefers to keep an eye on him so he doesn't do something stupid. But I'll keep you safe." His mouth pulled into a smile that looked completely wrong. Matteo was easy going for a mobster but today his darker side had come out to play.

His expression twisted again when he regarded my back. I could only imagine what it looked like. I faced him. "Can't you go to Dad and tell him not to kill Maddox? I won't let the doc treat me otherwise."

Matteo scanned my face curiously. "The plan is to keep Earl, Maddox, and Gray White as well as the sergeant at arms alive so we can deal with them thoroughly in the next few days." Excitement swung in his voice, reminding me of the stories about Matteo's penchant for torture that I'd heard. It was always difficult to imagine considering how funny he often was.

"Is everyone else safe? Mom? Valerio? What about Isabella and Gianna? Lily and the kids?" I was rambling but my lips moved on their own accord.

"Romero and Growl are responsible for their safety. Don't worry. Soon everything will be over, and the men who hurt you will be dog food."

Maddox.

I knew what my family had planned, but it gave me time to figure out what to do with Maddox and how to convince Dad not to slice him into bite-sized pieces. I could only pray that Maddox didn't get himself killed today.

"Do you have any injuries?" the doc asked calmly as he sat down on the bench beside me.

I gingerly touched my ear, which Maddox had covered with a fresh bandage yesterday. "My ear and my back."

"Let's start with your back, shall we?"

I nodded numbly. The doc had free access to my back due to my ripped-apart shirt. After a few minutes of careful prodding, he said, "I'm going to disinfect everything and refresh your tetanus shot. And just to cover all our bases, I'll get some bloodwork done to check for possible infections the needle might have carried." What he didn't dare to say: possible diseases through intercourse.

My heart skipped a beat and I stared at him in horror.

"What kind of infections?" Matteo asked before I could utter a word.

"Hepatitis, HIV to name a few."

I could feel the blood slowly leave my face. I hadn't even considered that the needle might be contaminated. The ugliness of the tattoo had been my only concern so far.

Matteo squatted before me, giving me a reassuring look. "You'll be fine, Marcella."

"What about a possible pregnancy?" the doc asked in a very quiet voice.

Matteo's expression shifted to fury but then his gaze darted to me.

I shook my head vigorously but I couldn't be sure I wasn't pregnant. I'd been on the pill for over a year when Maddox kidnapped me. Of course, I didn't have them with me. But I didn't want to consider it now. I'd take care of this problem when I was home.

The relief in Matteo's face was overwhelming. He touched my arm. "Soon you'll be home and forget this ever happened."

I nodded, but I felt shaky and cold. Up until this point, I'd managed to put up a mask of control but it was slipping quickly. I barely registered as the doctor removed the bandage to check on my ear. "There's the option to reconstruct your earlobe. I know one of the best plastic surgeons in New York who'll gladly treat you."

"As if your dad and I will give him a choice," Matteo muttered, hitting his palm with the blade of his favorite knife.

I shook my head. "It stays the way it is. Only make sure it doesn't get infected."

Matteo met my gaze, obviously confused. Maybe he worried I suffered from PTSD, but I didn't think that was the case.

"I want a reminder."

"I hope you don't consider keeping the tattoo as well," he joked in a dry voice.

I shrugged. "How bad is it?"

"Bad," he said.

"There are options to remove a tattoo."

"I know," I said. I hadn't even dared to peer over my shoulder yet. Later would be time to face the horror.

The doc covered the tattoo with bandages and Matteo threw a blanket over my shoulders then we sat in silence, waiting for the fight to be over. I could see in Matteo's face that he wanted to return and be part of the bloodshed. I was thankful he stayed with me. I didn't want to be alone right now.

My mind drifted to Maddox, who'd risked everything to save me. Calling my father and tell him about the clubhouse was suicidal. He'd told me he loved me. I didn't trust my own feelings. Could true love be born in captivity?

Chapter
Eighteen

Maddox

I watched Marcella being dragged away by Vitiello's brother, the knife lover. Her eyes flashed with panic as they settled on me, and she shouted at her father to spare me.

I smiled wryly. The look I saw on Luca Vitiello's face was one I'd seen many years ago, He'd come to maim and kill, not spare anyone. Certainly not me, and not Gray either. I didn't deserve mercy, and I never wanted it. My gaze darted to my brother hunched behind a sofa. I didn't care for my life, but I'd get Gray out of here alive even if I had to kill Luca and his men.

I made a mad dash for the sofa and landed on the floor beside Gray. He was bleeding from a bullet wound in his upper arm but otherwise looked unharmed. I checked the wound, ignoring his wince as I prodded around in his torn-apart flesh. The bullet was lodged inside, which wasn't a bad thing considering it prevented worse bleeding. There would be time to remove it later.

Gray held a gun in his left hand but knowing he strongly favored his right, now injured arm, he might as well be unarmed.

"You got ammo?"

He nodded. "Four more shots."

That wasn't nearly enough against the army we were up against. It wasn't even enough against Luca fucking Vitiello out for blood.

"Okay, listen to me, Gray. I'll try to distract them and fire every bullet I have on them so you can save your sorry ass."

His eyes widened. "I won't run off like a coward. Dad needs my help."

"Earl ran off upstairs to save his own ass, leaving you here to deal with Vitiello and his army. He doesn't deserve your worry."

Gray shook his head. "I'm not a coward."

"No, you're not. But you aren't a fool either, and staying here is foolish. We can't get out of this alive, not with the numbers against us. But you know all the secret pathways out of the woods. If anyone can get away from here, it's you." Gray kept shaking his head. I grabbed his cut. "Fuck. Mom needs you. If Earl and I die, then she needs you."

That seemed to get through his thick skull.

"Get out of there, White," Luca called. I assumed he meant me, considering that Earl had run upstairs to hide.

I gave a nod toward Gray. "You run toward the back door as fast as your legs carry you when I give you the sign, understood?" I wouldn't be responsible for his death.

"Understood," Gray muttered.

"Good." I pushed to my feet and began firing at everything that moved. Luca and another man I didn't know sought cover outside but kept firing at me. Amo Vitiello hid behind the overturned pool table but he too shot at me. I ducked behind the sofa, glad for the metal sheets Gunnar had attached to the underside a few weeks ago in preparation for a possible attack.

By Sin I *Rise*

I jumped back up just when Luca and two men stepped in again. I raised my gun, ready to blast holes into everyone.

Luca was distracted by his son making a crazy-ass dash upstairs, probably to kill the remaining bikers by himself. I knew that invincible feeling of my teenage days. "Follow Amo!" he roared at his men. They didn't hesitate and rushed after the younger Vitiello, leaving their Capo alone with me.

"Run," I screamed at Gray as I used this once-in-a-lifetime moment and lunged. Vitiello reacted too late and I barreled into him, sending us both flying to the floor. He grabbed me by the throat, cutting off my air supply, but I only tightened my hold on the knife and rammed it into his leg, the only place I could reach. The fucker hardly winced but his hold on my throat loosened enough for me to suck in a deep breath. In his eyes, I saw the same hatred I felt.

His son let out a roar upstairs, followed by shots, screams, and more gunfire. Outside, the gunfire ceased, which meant soon the rest of Vitiello's soldiers would arrive. Their Capo would be dead by then.

Vitiello tightened his hold on my throat once more, his eyes burning with rage. I rammed my knife into his thigh again. My head began to swim from lack of oxygen. I tried to shove away from him but his fingers around my throat were like a fucking vise. I brought up the knife and his other hand shot up, grasping my wrist to stop me from plunging the blade into his head and split his skull.

A scream rang out upstairs and for an instant Vitiello's attention shifted, full of worry, and I ripped from his hold and brought the knife down, aiming for his eye. This was the moment I'd been waiting for all my life.

Marcella's face flashed before my mind, and I jerked my arm to the side in the last moment, grazing the side of his head and ramming the knife into the wooden board. I couldn't do this to her. Fuck. What had this woman done to me?

Vitiello's eyes locked on mine, furious and questioning. He didn't understand why I hadn't killed him. I hardly did myself.

"This is for Marcella, only for her, you murdering bastard."

His eyes moved to something behind me but before I could react, pain radiated through my skull and my vision went black.

Marcella

The door of the van opened and Dad climbed in, limping badly. A long gash on the side of his head was bleeding profusely, dripping blood all over his shirt, face and arm. He immediately pulled me into a tight hug which he loosened when I winced. He stank of blood and even less appealing bodily fluids but his closeness still felt like a balm on my tumultuous soul. He pulled back and cupped my cheeks, searching my eyes as if he worried I wasn't the same daughter he remembered. I'd certainly changed but I was still me, the version of me that had never surfaced because my cozy life had never required it. Behind Dad, still outside of the van waited Amo. He wiped blood and flesh off his arms. I marveled at the harsh lines of his face that hadn't been there before. He briefly looked up and forced a smile that looked grotesque on his bloody face. I could still see the violence and wrath in his eyes.

For some reason, I couldn't bear seeing him like that. The kidnapping had changed me. How could it not? But I'd hoped it hadn't done lasting damage to the people I loved. Seeing them now, I realized my wish hadn't been granted.

"What happened to your leg?" I asked Dad, looking away from Amo.

"Nothing. We'll take you home now," he said in a gruff voice. I'd never seen Dad like this, covered in blood and at the edge of control.

"What about Maddox?" I asked, couldn't help it. I needed to know. Maybe his death would have made things easier, but my heart clenched agonizingly at the mere thought. He was the reason why I was here today, in more than one sense. He was guilty of my kidnapping and responsible for my freedom. I hated and... maybe loved him—if love could even bloom in a situation like ours.

Dad thrust his fist against the side of the van, expression twisting with rage.

My heart thudded harder. "Dad?"

Dad's face darkened. "He's alive like a few others and will be taken to a location where they can be questioned."

Relief washed through me. I knew what questioning meant in mafia terms but as long as he hadn't been killed yet, there was still hope for him, for us. If I should even hope for us or him. My thoughts were confusing and too unsteady to grasp hold of. Every new thought slipped away like quicksand before I could finish it.

Matteo grabbed his phone and jumped out of the van. "I'll call Gianna. She'll rip me a new one if I don't tell her we're fine."

So many people had worried for their loved ones who risked their life for me. I couldn't imagine what Gianna and Isabella had gone through while Matteo fought against mad bikers to save me.

Dad picked up his phone. His expression told me he was calling Mom. "She's safe," he said first thing.

I could hear Mom's shuddering sigh. Then Dad held the phone out to me. I took it with shaking fingers.

"Mom," I said. "I'm fine."

"Oh, Marci, I'm so happy to hear your voice. I can't wait to hold you in my arms."

"We'll be home in about an hour," Dad called.

"Hurry," Mom said softly.

Dad wrapped his arm around my shoulder as he led me into the house, trying to hide his limp but it must have been bad if he couldn't hide it even around Mom. And even Amo hovered close by as if I needed constant surveillance now. Some of the violence had left his expression but not all of it.

"Get a grip," Dad murmured. "Your mom doesn't need to see you like this."

Amo nodded and briefly closed his eyes. I could see his face morphing to something gentler and more boyish, but it was an obvious struggle, and his eyes, when he opened them, still felt off.

The moment I stepped into the house, Mom jumped off the couch. Valerio was with her and so were my aunts Gianna and Liliana, and my cousins, Isabella, Flavio, Sara, and Inessa. Romero and Growl kept watch like Matteo had said. Mom rushed over to me and Dad finally released me, only for Mom to take his place.

Mom hugged me so tightly I could barely breathe. I winced when her palms brushed the fresh tattoo on my upper back. She pulled back with tear-filled eyes full of worry. Her gaze flitted over my ruined ear before she forced it back to my eyes. Her palm still lightly rested on the bandage over my back. "What happened to your back?"

I didn't want to tell her. Not because I was ashamed. I wasn't. I was furious and scared. Furious because Earl had done this to me and scared that I'd always have to carry his judgment of me on my skin. When I didn't say anything, she looked to Dad. The man who'd slaughtered several bikers in an act of fury and strength looked tired in that moment. His guilt over what had happened to me was unmistakable in every line of his face, but worst of all in his eyes. Amo made sure to look anywhere but at Mom, which was probably for the best, considering he still had that madman gleam in his eyes.

I didn't want to put the burden of telling Mom about the tattoo on Dad. She didn't look at him as if she blamed him for what happened, but I still worried that their relationship had suffered because of my kidnapping. My parents were absolute relationship goals in my mind and the thought that something might change that was almost worse than what had happened to me in the last few weeks.

"They tattooed me," I said, trying to sound blasé.

The color drained from Mom's face and Dad's lips tightened in an effort to restrain his fury for the men who'd done this to me.

Mom glanced at Dad questioningly, but she didn't ask what the tattoo was.

"We'll have it removed as soon as you feel up to it," Dad said firmly. "I told the doc to make all necessary arrangements."

"Thanks, Dad."

Valerio came up to me and hugged me too. "Next time I'll kick biker ass too when they kidnap you."

I choked on laughter. "I sure hope this was the last kidnapping, and you aren't supposed to curse."

He rolled his eyes and I tousled his blond mane before he could duck away. After more hugging from Gianna and Isabella, Aunt Liliana, Romero, and my cousins, I finally went upstairs, bone tired. I quickly excused myself, overwhelmed by the wave of emotions I felt.

Alone in my bedroom after the first shower in what felt like days, I peeled the bandage off my back and turned toward the long mirror. I sucked in a sharp breath. Maddox had told me what the tattoo said but seeing it with my own eyes still felt like a punch in the stomach.

The black letters looked almost smudged and were thin. They reminded me of tattoos that prisoners got behind bars. The words Vitiello whore glared back at me. They sat right between my shoulder blades below my neck. A whore stamp how Earl had called it. I swallowed once, then I turned away from the mirror. Once people found out about what went on between Maddox and me, I would hear the insult often.

A knock sounded and I jumped, my heart rate picking up immediately.

I grabbed a bathrobe and threw it over before I went to the door, trying to banish my unreasonable anxiety. This was my home. I was safe here.

When I opened the door, Mom smiled at me. "I just wanted to check on you."

I let her in. "Is Dad home?"

"Yes, he's downstairs with your uncles, discussing their plans for tomorrow. He wants to tell you good night later."

I smiled, feeling reminded of all the times he did it when I was younger.

Mom hesitated then touched my shoulder. "Is there anything you want to talk to me about?"

I shook my head. "Not yet. I'm fine for now." There were so many things I was confused about, I needed time to sort through them before I could talk to anyone.

"Will you be all right alone tonight? I could stay with you."

I kissed Mom's cheek. "I'll be fine, Mom. I'm not scared of the dark."

Mom nodded, but I could tell she still worried about me. "Good night then." After she left, I put on one of my favorite nightgowns to feel more like myself again and slipped under the covers. As I lay awake, I made the decision to transform the tattoo on my back into something that proved I was stronger than Earl thought I could ever be. I wouldn't hide or back down. I'd attack.

I picked up my phone and began searching tattoo artists. I wouldn't let anyone's judgment determine who I was. Not now, not ever.

Despite my words, horrible images haunted me the moment I turned off the lights. Crude tattoos, cut-off pieces of me, torn-apart bodies, and fighting dogs. My stomach churned.

A knock made me jerk up in bed. "Yes?" I called, sounding shaky.

Dad stepped in, brows puckering. "Are you all right, Princess?"

"Can you not call me that?" I asked, remembering the many times Earl or Cody had used the term to make me feel dirty.

Dad stiffened but nodded. He remained by the door as if he suddenly wasn't sure how to act around me. I could tell he had many questions he wanted to ask, but he didn't. "I came to wish you a good night."

"Thanks," I said quietly. He turned to leave.

"Dad?"

He faced me again.

"I'm coming with you tomorrow when you question the captives."

"Marci—"

"Please."

He nodded, but his expression still said no. "I don't think it's a good idea, but I won't stop you. Amo and I are going to head over to the prison very early. You should sleep in and come over later with Matteo."

Once he'd left, I tossed in bed for another hour, but the dark brought up bad memories and I couldn't sleep with my lights on. In the last few weeks, Maddox had been by my side at night, and no matter how ridiculous it was, I'd felt safe by his side. Now all alone, anxiety got the better of me.

I got out of bed, threw on my bathrobe, and crossed the corridor to Amo's room. I knocked.

"Come in," Amo called.

I slipped in and closed the door. Amo sat at his desk in front of his computer, only in sweats. "Playing Fortnite?" I asked, relieved he was back to his routine.

"That's for kids and losers," he muttered. "I'm doing research on interrogation methods used by the Mossad and KGB."

"Oh," I whispered. I felt a strange sense of loss. My little brother was gone. His sixteenth birthday was still two months away but he had grown up in the weeks I had been gone.

Amo looked up from the screen, frowning. "Do you need help?"

I shook my head. "Can I sleep in here tonight?" I couldn't remember the last time Amo and I had slept in the same room together. We were too old for sleepovers, but I didn't know where else to go.

"Sure," he said slowly, eyeing me critically.

I crawled under the covers. "I'll sleep at the edge."

"Don't worry. I can't sleep anyway. Too much adrenaline."

I nodded. "You should play video games again like you used to, you know?"

"I'm going to rip the bikers to shreds tomorrow. That's the only entertainment I need," he muttered.

I closed my eyes, hoping Amo would be back to his old self soon, but deep down I knew neither of us could retrieve what was lost.

I didn't sleep much, so I was already awake and back in my room when Mom knocked at my door early the next morning. My thoughts had revolved around Maddox and my family most of the night.

"Come in," I said, sitting up in bed. The night had been filled with pain in my back and uncertainty in my heart.

Mom was already dressed in a thin knit dress, and unlike yesterday, her eyes were clear. No sign of tears. She looked resolute as if she'd come to save our whole family single-handedly. She held something in her hand as she headed toward me and perched on the edge of my bed. "I have something for you," she said. I was glad that she didn't ask how my night had been. She could probably guess that I'd barely slept. I hoped Amo wouldn't tell her or Dad that I'd been too scared to sleep in my own room. Tonight I'd stay strong no matter what.

She stroked my hair like she had done when I was a little girl then she opened her hand, presenting a half-moon-shaped, white-gold ear climber studded with diamonds.

My eyes widened. "It's beautiful." I gingerly touched my ear. It was still tender but I avoided touching it.

"Until you decide to have it fixed, you can cover it with beautiful jewelry."

I picked up the earpiece. "I don't think I'll get it fixed. It's a good reminder that I shouldn't take anything for granted." I held up the ear climber. "Can you help me put it on?"

I still hadn't looked at the wound but I would have to if I put it on by myself.

Mom scooted closer, then very gently attached the earpiece to my ear. I bit back a wince as the jewelry touched my still tender ear. "It's a good thing that you have more holes in your ear."

I laughed. I still remembered how Dad had disapproved of me getting my ear pierced, but I always only wore elegant small diamonds so he made peace with it eventually.

"How does it look?" I asked.

Mom beamed. "Absolutely stunning. Go, see for yourself."

I climbed out of bed and checked out my reflection. The earpiece perfectly covered up my missing earlobe. I touched it and smiled. This way I could keep the reminder but choose when I wanted to present it to the world.

I turned to Mom. "How did you get this done so quickly? Please don't tell me Dad threatened every jeweler in New York last night to get it as soon as possible."

Mom giggled. "No, no. I actually started looking for an earpiece like that when... when we found out that your ear got hurt." She made it sound as if I'd had an accident that cost me my earlobe, and not that vengeful bikers had cut it off and sent it to my family. "But your dad would have threatened them all for you if necessary. He'd do anything for us."

"I know," I said. "I don't blame him, you know. Please don't tell me you and Dad fought because of me."

Mom got up and came over to me. She touched my cheek. "I was terrified for you. And your dad blamed himself. I could see how much he hated himself for it. But I didn't fight with him. We're all part of this world. Your dad tries to protect us from it to the best of his abilities."

"I always knew he'd save me. I never doubted it."

"He barely slept. He and every soldier in his command searched for you day and night."

Tears shot into my eyes but I didn't allow them to fall. I didn't like to cry, not even in front of Mom.

Mom, too, fought tears. She touched my arm. "Your dad said one of the bikers revealed the clubhouse whereabouts to him."

I nodded. "Maddox."

Silence spread between us as Mom searched my eyes. My voice had been off, even I could tell. I cleared my throat. "He and I got closer during my captivity."

Mom didn't show her shock if she felt any. It felt good to tell her. If anyone would understand then it was her. Mom believed in love against all odds, in true love. She'd taught me to believe in it as well. I'd clung to Giovanni, desperately hoping what we had would magically turn into the kind of all-consuming love Mom and Dad lived before my eyes every day.

I feared I'd now found it: the kind of love that left you breathless, that hurt almost as much as it made you feel good. It was a love I wasn't sure I should pursue.

"Oh Marci," Mom said, as if she could see all my thoughts.

"I wanted to use him so he'd help me escape and he basically did..."

"But you fell for him?"

Falling in love. I'd never really understood the term—as if love was something as inevitable as the force of gravity. As if it grabbed you and dragged you down with it. With Giovanni, it had been a logical choice. But what Maddox and I had defied logic. It went against everything he and I had believed in. It went against reason, against my family's beliefs.

"Dad would never allow it. Not with a biker. Not after what Maddox did."

Mom tilted her head in consideration. "I think the latter is the bigger problem. What about you? Can you forgive Maddox for what he did? For kidnapping you? For allowing others to hurt you?"

It was a question I'd often asked myself, already during my captivity and all the more in the hours since my escape. My heart and mind were at odds. I didn't want to forgive him, but my heart already had. But I wasn't someone who acted on impulse. I thought things through, weighed the pros against the cons.

Love didn't work that way. But if Maddox's love for me, or my love for him was toxic, I'd rather find the antidote as quickly as possible.

"If you have to think about it this long, he really has to mean a lot to you. But please don't forget that trust is the base of a working marriage."

My eyes widened. "Mom, I never said anything about marrying Maddox." Then I realized that it would be expected to do just that— marry him. My dating Giovanni was tolerated because he was my fiancé and our wedding date had been set. The ensuing scandal after our breakup was nothing in comparison to the waves a relationship with

Maddox would create. Even if I didn't care about the backlash for my reputation, I had to consider what it would do to my family. But even a relationship with Maddox seemed impossible at this point. I couldn't see how we could make a future work.

"You don't have much time to make up your mind, love," Mom said softly. "You know what your dad has planned for the bikers he caught."

"I know," I said. "Uncle Matteo will pick me up and take me to the Famiglia prison."

Mom pursed her lips. "Your dad mentioned it. I don't think it's a good idea to confront the man who did this to you."

I smiled. "Don't worry, Mom. The tables have turned. I'm no longer in their hands. I won't break down now, not after surviving weeks of captivity."

"I don't doubt it. I marvel at your strength." She paused. "If you ever want to talk about what happened between Maddox and you, then I'm here, you know that, right?"

I nodded. "Did everyone see the video of me?"

"Many did," Mom said honestly. "Your dad tried everything to have it removed and eventually he did it."

"The internet never forgets," I said.

To think that I'd spent hours agonizing over the perfect image to post on Instagram. Eventually I'd have to watch the video and face the resulting scandal on my social media accounts. But not yet.

"You have nothing to be ashamed of. They forced you, and you looked proud and gorgeous despite the situation."

"That wasn't my choice," I agreed. "But I slept with Maddox. Not because he forced me and not even because I hoped he'd help me escape if I did, but only because in that moment I wanted to."

I wanted to get it off my chest.

For a second, Mom was unable to hide her shock but then she nodded. "I thought that might be the case, but I'd hoped I was wrong."

I pursed my lips. "Because I was supposed to stay a virgin for marriage."

Mom shook her head. "I don't care about that, Marci."

I wasn't sure if Mom really meant it. Few things had changed over the years. Dad may have abolished the bloody sheets tradition once I got closer to marriage age, but many people still followed the old ways. Now it was made out to be the bride's choice and not a duty she had to succumb to. But few girls had the guts to decide against the bloody sheets tradition and those who did were often seen as sluts who didn't want to risk revealing their wanton ways. Sometimes a choice wasn't one as long as society only regarded one decision as the valid one.

"But Dad does."

"Your dad would prefer if you'd go to a nunnery and never get involved with boys at all."

I bit back a smile. "But he accepted Giovanni."

"Dad knew he'd have to let you go and allow you to grow up. When you chose Giovanni, he tolerated him because he was someone he knew and…"

"Could control."

Mom shrugged. "Your father is controlling."

"Maddox isn't as easy to control. Will Dad ever accept him?"

"I don't know. Maybe, but it'll take time and a lot of work on Maddox's part. Maybe you shouldn't yet tell your dad that you slept with Maddox. It'll only complicate things."

"Do you really think he doesn't suspect something?"

"Oh, I'm sure he does. But your dad is blind when it comes to you becoming a woman."

"Men."

Mom touched my hand. "Did you use protection?"

It took me a moment to realize what she meant and heat rose into my cheeks. "No," I admitted.

Mom nodded, swallowing. "I'll grab a pregnancy test for you today, then you can take it in case you don't get your period."

My period was due any day now. I didn't have a regular cycle so it was difficult to say. "Thanks, Mom."

By Sin I *Rise*

My life had always been a carefully planned construct, an intricate entity I'd spent years structuring and building. It was nothing but a house of cards, I realized now. I always thought I had enough safety measures built into my plan of my future that even a few missing cards wouldn't bring my house of cards to fall. Of course, I had never considered someone to barrel into my life and smash my house of cards to bits and pieces. All my cleverly laid ahead plans, suddenly on the verge of falling apart.

I loved Maddox, loved him as much as I'd always dreamed of loving someone, desired him as fiercely as I'd hoped for. My thoughts revolved around him in a way I'd never experienced before, certainly not with Giovanni. I loved him, but I also loved my family. How can you compare one love to another? How can you weigh it against each other? I couldn't do it. I couldn't give up Maddox. I couldn't give up my family.

I stared back down at the earrings.

I'd give Maddox a choice today, the impossible choice, one that would determine if we even had a chance, a choice that could rip my heart in two.

Chapter
Nineteen

Maddox

MY HEAD THROBBED WITH A HEADACHE WHEN I CAME TO myself. I wasn't sure what time it was. I could hear shuffling around me and raspy breathing. With a groan, I forced my eyes open despite the agony this caused.

Dank gray walls. Stench of humidity and mold, piss and blood. I was in a basement, in Vitiello's torture chamber, no doubt.

"Finally awake, eh?" Cody muttered.

I turned my head and realized I was tied to a chair. I tried to topple it over, but its legs were attached to the floor. Of course, Vitiello would think of everything.

"This is your fault," Earl growled.

He and Cody were on chairs to my left and beside them was Smith, a prospect. He looked pretty bad off, bleeding from two wounds in his leg and side. But I was only glad it wasn't Gray in his stead. "How long have we been here?"

Cody spit in my direction but it landed a few inches from my boots. "Long enough that I pissed my pants twice, you asshole."

Earl watched me with ferocious eyes.

"If you'd listened to me and exchanged Marcella for Vitiello, we would be the ones doing the torturing. But you couldn't get enough," I growled.

"Don't mention that whore's name!"

I shook my head. "I hope Vitiello starts torturing us soon. Nothing can be worse than being in a room with you two assholes."

"He'll kill me last, so I get to watch you die slowly and painfully," Earl said with a nasty grin.

"What about Gray? Have you seen him?"

"Coward ran off. He's dead to me. Won't survive on his own for long anyway. Vitiello will catch him soon enough."

"It's your job to keep him safe. Instead, you saved your own ass and ran upstairs."

The heavy door groaned.

"Oh shit," Cody said. "Please God, save me."

I sent him an amused look. "You really think God looks kindly upon you?"

Amo and Luca Vitiello entered the room. One look at them and I knew I wouldn't die today, even if I begged for it.

I'd been shot, stabbed, burned, had broken countless bones in accidents. I wasn't scared of pain or death, but I knew Vitiello had ways to make even hardened men cry for their mommy.

"Is Marcella all right?" I asked.

Earl snorted.

Amo strolled over to me and punched me in the ribs and stomach. "Never mention her again."

I coughed then grinned. "So you're taking over from Daddy as the head-torturer now?"

"No," Luca said in a low voice that might have made me shit my pants if I hadn't heard it before. "I will make sure to deal with each of you. But we have plenty of time for Amo and my brother to get their turn as well."

Amo went over to a table with instruments that I hadn't noticed before.

"Oh God," Cody whimpered when Amo picked up prongs.

I steeled myself, praying that I'd be strong enough not to beg for mercy. Maybe I had the guts to bite my own tongue off. Closing my eyes, I recalled Marcella. An image worthy of my last moments.

Marcella

I'd rarely put as much effort into my appearance for a party or social event as I did now to watch Earl White die a cruel death. I'd bought the black leather pants and the red silk blouse after my breakup with Giovanni but had never gotten the chance to wear either. Today was the day.

My hands shook when I slipped on my black patent leather Louboutins. I flexed my fingers, willing them to cease the tremor. Sucking in a deep breath, I opened my door and headed out.

Mom waited in the lobby for me. Her eyes swam with unshed tears and worry. She took my hand, searching my eyes. "Are you sure?"

She hadn't tried to talk me out of visiting my captors, but I could see that she was almost sick with worry. Yet, I needed this to really make peace with everything that had happened. Valerio was over at Aunt Liliana's place, so he didn't witness too much of our turmoil. I bet he and our cousin Flavio would talk about nothing else but the kidnapping and what would happen to my kidnappers anyway. Our parents always thought we were oblivious and that they could protect us.

"Absolutely. I want to be there. I want to show them before they die that I'm stronger than before."

"You are. I'm so proud of you, Marci. You are a true warrior. You have your father's strength."

"And yours. I know the stories of how you risked your life for Dad, how you went into enemy territory to help your little brother. Your fierceness is more subtle than Dad's but it's there all the same."

Mom swallowed hard, but the tears fell anyway. "Show them your true colors."

I nodded with a firm smile before I headed outside.

Uncle Matteo waited for me in his car in the driveway and I sank down in the passenger seat beside him. He also owned a bike, which he usually rode over to our house when he came without Gianna and Isabella. It was one thing he and Maddox had in common. And even Amo who only did dirt racing on occasion. I caught myself imagining how they might one day do a bike trip together and immediately wanted to slap myself. These men were mortal enemies. Nothing had changed.

Matteo scanned my face. I wished makeup could cover up my turmoil like it did blemishes, but Matteo could probably see them plainly.

"Are you good to go?" Matteo asked carefully. He, like so many others, hadn't hesitated to risk their life for me. I could only imagine how scared Isabella had been for her dad, how worried Aunt Gianna must have been. I had trouble expressing the amount of gratefulness I felt for them, and also for the soldiers I didn't even know.

"I am. This is my battle and I won't shy back from it," I said firmly.

Matteo grinned. "That's my tough niece."

I smiled but slowly another question formed in my mind, one I hadn't had time to consider fully yet. "How many died in their attempt to save me?"

Matteo gave me a careful look. "You should talk to your dad about it."

"Matteo," I said in exasperation. "I'm not a young child anymore. I can handle the truth and I need it."

Matteo nodded. He, unlike Dad with me, allowed his daughter Isabella more freedom and told her things Dad always tried to keep from me. "Three men died."

I swallowed. My life wasn't worth more than theirs but they had put it down for me.

"They know of the risk when they become Made Men, and our fights with the bikers have cost far more men their lives. This isn't your fault."

Maybe it wasn't, but I felt guilt anyway. "I want to send my condolences to the families. They need to know that I'm sorry for their loss and understand their sorrow."

"You've grown."

"I think that's natural."

"No, I mean, while you were gone."

"Something like that changes your outlook on life," I said quietly.

"It does."

Matteo pulled up in front of a warehouse in an industrial area. I had never been there, but before today I'd never been allowed to be present at any kind of Famiglia business, much less a torture session.

Matteo got out of the car but I remained sitting for a moment longer. This would be a challenge for two reasons. Earl White.

...and Maddox.

Less than twenty-four hours had passed since I'd last seen him. My first night in freedom, one filled with little sleep and more nightmares. I'd lived a privileged life until the day Maddox ripped me out of my comfort zone. Now I had changed. Because of the pain and humiliation I'd suffered, but also because of my feelings for Maddox. Feelings I was terrified of. My life would be easier if I forgot them, *forgot him*. If I allowed Dad and Amo to kill Maddox. That way the choice would be taken out of my hands.

Matteo gave me a worried look. I'd remained frozen in the car, staring up at the huge building as if it meant my doom.

Not my doom.

This would be my ultimate liberation. My palms became clammy as I followed Matteo toward the steel door. Before he opened it, he turned to me once more. "Maddox White, do you want him dead?"

I was taken aback by Matteo's directness but I shouldn't have been surprised.

"No," I said, a truth I couldn't even admit to myself so far.

"Your dad won't like it, and me neither. He means trouble."

"You always say Gianna is trouble and that you like trouble. Why can't I?"

Matteo chuckled. "You shouldn't use me as an example for your life choices."

I shrugged then my eyes wandered back to the steel door. My pulse picked up, a strange mix of fear and excitement. "I haven't made up my mind about Maddox yet."

"You should do it quickly. Your dad will kill him soon."

Matteo finally opened the door for me and we headed toward another steel door at the end of the vast hall. My heels clicked on the bare stone floor and with every step I took, my pulse quickened. Matteo touched my shoulder. "Wait here and let me check if we can enter."

I nodded and didn't point out that I knew what Dad and Amo would be doing with the bikers. Matteo poked his head in, then he opened the door wider and motioned me in. Taking a deep breath to steel myself, I entered, followed by Matteo. With a bone-chilling clang, the heavy steel door fell shut behind me. A shudder raced down my spine as I scanned the barren room.

Four men were tied to chairs, one of them Maddox. His gaze hit me, blue eyes that awakened my emotions all over again. The left side of his face was swollen and bluish, but apart from that Dad and Amo hadn't laid a hand on him yet. The other men hadn't been as lucky—one of them the man who was responsible for everything.

Earl White had suffered a broken arm and his ear didn't look good either. Cody hung limply in his chair. I didn't know the name of the fourth man. I'd thought one of the captives might be Gray. That he wasn't here worried me for Maddox. It was obvious how protective he was of his half-brother. If he was dead, that would break Maddox's heart and definitely wouldn't improve his relationship with my father.

Dad immediately came toward me, shielding me from the men. "Marci, you know I don't think you should be here. There's nothing these men have to say that you should hear, and they aren't worthy to hear a single word from your lips."

"You said you wouldn't stop me," I reminded him. I wasn't surprised he'd changed his mind. He still thought he could protect me from evil.

My gaze sought Maddox once more. His penetrating stare hadn't left me for a moment.

Dad followed my gaze and sighed quietly. "Don't go too close." Then he faced the prisoners. "If any of you try anything, I'm going to make you regret it."

The promise of violence in Dad's voice made me shiver but I gave him a small smile before I moved farther into the room.

"Come to join in the fun?" Earl asked with a grim smile, revealing a bloody mouth that was missing a couple of teeth. That explained the bloody pliers on one of the tables. "Share your daddy's bloodlust?"

I'd wanted a last confrontation but I hadn't made up my mind if I could watch the torture Dad, Amo and Matteo certainly had in mind for the bikers. "Your dirty blood will never touch me," I said simply, satisfied by the coldness of my voice.

Seeing Maddox tied up to the chair, I had to resist the urge to rush over to him and free him. He wasn't innocent, and I needed to make sure I could really trust him. Maybe he regretted his decision to help me escape already. Yet, in his eyes, I could see the same longing I felt and desperately tried to hide.

"Letting Daddy and your brother do the dirty work, whore?" Earl said, bursting through my thoughts, obviously growing frustrated at my lack of reaction. I tensed, remembering the ugly words tattooed on my back. Similar words would probably quickly make the rounds if people found out I'd slept with Maddox. If I was pregnant... I didn't feel pregnant, and I didn't want to consider the option. Right now I could only focus on one thing, if Maddox and I had a chance, if it even made sense to give us a chance.

Dad grabbed Earl by the throat, looking less human than I'd ever seen him. Amo was at his side. No trace of the little brother left I'd last seen before my kidnapping. These men would have scared me if they weren't my blood, my protectors. If their unabashed rage and vengefulness weren't emotions that simmered deep inside of me as well.

"No," I said firmly, as much to Earl as to Dad and Amo. Dad didn't loosen his hold on Earl, who was slowly turning red, spluttering as he fought for breath.

"Dad, don't."

Dad looked at me, obviously unsure of what I wanted. "Let us give him what he deserves. He'll suffer more than any man has ever suffered."

Did he think I wanted him to spare my tormentor? That was the last thing on my mind. Mom was the forgiving type, but even she would probably have Earl die a painful death at Dad's hands if he asked her for her opinion. Of course, he'd never do such a thing because he didn't want her to have blood on her hands.

"Let me dig his goddamn balls out with an ice cream spoon," Amo growled, motioning at the assortment of knives, pliers, and other tools for torture spread out on a small wooden table.

My stomach turned at the display and blood pooling beneath it, and I dragged my eyes away. I wasn't like Dad and Amo. I wasn't like Mom either. I was somewhere in between. Capable of a certain amount of cruelness if driven to the brink but not capable of executing it myself. Maybe this was weakness, but I no longer strive for perfection.

A nasty smile rushed over Earl's face at my brief show of hesitation. I swallowed and stiffened my shoulders before I headed for the table and picked up a knife. The handle felt unfamiliar in my palm. Dad had always made sure I didn't handle weapons. My protection had been the task of others. I'd accepted it, certain nothing could touch me as long as Dad was there. But I had realized that no matter how strong your protectors are, you need to be capable to survive on your own.

"He will suffer but not by your hands, Dad," I said firmly, forcing a smile, and turned to Maddox. His gaze moved from the gleaming blade to my eyes. As it always did, my heart skipped a beat as I met his gaze. This was our moment of truth, the moment that would prove his loyalty or end what was never meant to be. I wasn't sure my heart would survive the latter.

Earl nodded at my ear. Another mark he'd left. Sometimes I wondered what else he would have done to me if Maddox hadn't revealed my whereabouts to Dad. Earl White had enjoyed torturing me and not just because I was my father's daughter. "You can cover up your ruined ear with expensive jewelry but that tattoo…"

"Will soon be covered by a beautiful tattoo designed by the best tattoo artist in the States," I interrupted him. I wasn't going to let him make me feel small for even a second.

He grunted. "There are things you won't ever be able to cover up. We left our mark inside of you. You'll fear the dark until the day you die."

I wished he wasn't right. Maybe last night had been the exception but I worried it would take me a while to be comfortable in the dark again, to not flinch when someone knocked and not look over my shoulder. But eventually I'd overcome this.

I stepped closer to him, smiling darkly. "I have darkness running in my veins. I am my father's daughter, don't ever underestimate me because I'm a woman. Being a woman doesn't mean I'm not strong. And trust me when I say that nothing you did will leave a scar. Your name and family will long be forgotten while mine will rule over the East and hunt down every biker affiliated to Tartarus."

I moved toward Maddox, following the invisible pull I'd felt from the very first moment I'd seen him. He never took his eyes off me. He looked like a man ready to die. Maybe I should let him. It would be easier for my family, easier for me if you didn't take my heart into account, and maybe it would even be easier for him, because I wasn't sure if he could handle the choice I would soon be giving him.

I walked around him until I was at his back and bent down to cut through his bindings. Dad and Amo rocked forward but I shook my head. "No."

They stopped but I could tell they were both ready to lunge if Maddox moved the wrong way. Maddox was clever enough to leave his arms at his side after I'd freed him from his bindings. I walked back to the front and met his gaze. I could see the questions in his blue eyes.

Flipping the knife around, I held out the handle to him.

"Marci," Dad growled.

I shook my head again. This was my moment of truth with Maddox, the defining decision in our relationship. I needed the truth even if it killed me.

"Maddox," I said, leaning down to him despite Dad's warning. He couldn't understand the bond that Maddox and I shared. "Take this knife and kill your uncle. Do it for me."

His blue eyes held mine, one of them bloodshot. His lips were busted and his upper body was littered with cuts and bruises, only the beginning if I allowed it. "Kill your uncle with this knife. Make him bleed. Do it for me. Let him feel every ounce of pain I felt, let him feel it tenfold. Make him beg me for mercy, for death even. Do it if you love me."

Love. A word I'd been terrified to use, a word that still ripped open a chasm in my chest, one only Maddox might be able to close. I'd hardly slept the night, debating if I could, if I should burden Maddox with this choice, but it was the only option to heal some of the wounds the kidnapping had ripped open.

I wouldn't let Dad or Amo kill another father figure of Maddox's. I needed him to do it. There was no place in this world for the man who'd cut off my earlobe and tattooed me. The man who would have killed me and even Maddox because he was so blinded by his need for revenge that he couldn't stop, no matter the price.

Maddox didn't take his eyes off mine as he slowly moved his arms to the front. They were cut where the ties had been and he flexed his fingers as if they were stiff from the awkward position they'd been forced into. The seconds seemed to drag on in excruciating slowness until he finally took the knife from my hand.

"Marci," Amo growled, stalking toward me with his own knife

drawn, but I raised my palm and he stopped in his tracks. His confusion was palpable, but how could I explain what I myself hardly understood?

"Step back," Dad ordered me.

I didn't. Instead, I grabbed Maddox's neck and kissed him harshly before whispering against his lips, "Make him bleed for what he did to me." I pulled my earring off to remind him, then lifted my hair to reveal the ugly tattoo.

Maddox leaned forward, pressing a hot kiss to the tattoo. "You are truly your father's daughter, Snow White, and a true queen if there ever was one. And if this is what it takes to prove my love and loyalty to you, then I'll do it."

My heart swelled with relief. I stepped back as Maddox stumbled to his feet, swaying slightly from the torture he'd suffered at my father's and brother's hand. My own legs felt unsteady as I backed away. His lips were chapped from dehydration but he held his head high as he staggered toward his uncle.

Dad grabbed my arm, looking into my eyes with concern.

"Trust me," I said. "Maddox will make him bleed for me."

Dad shook his head as if I was being delusional. "And what if he frees him?"

"He won't," I said and felt it deep in my heart. Maddox had made his choice and it was me. His uncle had lost Maddox along the way because he chose a way Maddox couldn't follow, not just because of his love for me, but also because he was decent deep inside his heart.

I turned to Earl once more with a hard smile. "Some people think women can't be cruel. I think we're just more creative when it comes to cruelty. Enjoy the pain at the hands of your own flesh and blood."

I'd practiced these words several times last night until they sounded effortlessly cruel, as if this was everyday business for me, even if it wasn't.

"You can have all the cunts in the world, son. Don't let the whore play you with her magic pussy."

Amo jerked forward and thrust his fist into Earl's face. His head snapped back and for a moment I was worried that Amo had actually broken Earl's neck and messed with my plan. But Earl sagged forward and shook his head dizzily.

He slowly dragged his gaze back up. "She's using you. She manipulated you from the start so you'd help her. I didn't see it soon enough or I would have kept her in my bedroom and fucked her three holes bloody until she knew her place."

Maddox's hand shot forward, impaling the blade in his uncle's abdomen. I sucked in a sharp breath, sure he'd killed him. I was torn between relief that it was over and Maddox had really ended his uncle for me, and disappointment because the man hadn't suffered enough yet. It was a horrible thing to think, but one I couldn't suppress.

Earl's eyes widened grotesquely and he let out a choked moan. Maddox's face was only inches from his uncle's and the look in his eyes banished the last tiny flicker of doubt in my mind. He would avenge me and prove his love to me.

"You won't ever get the chance to touch Marcella. And today I'll make you regret every second of pain you made her feel. You'll beg her for forgiveness and call her queen when I'm done with you."

From the corner of my eye, I saw Amo and Dad exchange stunned looks. My chest swelled even more.

His first scream rocketed off the walls. Goose bumps rose on my skin. A few months ago, I couldn't have stayed but my own screams of pain not too long ago had made me numb to the sound. I'd stay until the bitter end and watch.

Crossing my arms, I leaned against the wall and clipped my diamond earring back on my ruined ear. Another scream, even louder than the one before, rang out. Amo leaned beside me, regarding me as if he saw me in a new light.

"You changed," he said quietly.

"So did you."

He nodded. Dad looked at us, regret passing over his face. He'd dedicated his life to protect us, but this life left nothing untouched. It was only a matter of time before we'd be dragged into the darkness.

Chapter
Twenty

Maddox

"GRAY WILL HATE YOU FOR THIS," EARL CROAKED, HIS breathing ragged. I didn't say anything, only watched the life drain out of him as the blood left his body. He hadn't mentioned Mom. I would have to tell her about his death myself. I owed it to her, even if she'd never talk to me again. And Gray? I could only hope he was far away. He was still young. He had a future ahead of him. I hoped he'd try to find something he was good at and not go looking for the next MC.

Earl's chest rose once more before he sagged into himself. I felt a pang in my chest, a strange mix of guilt and wistfulness.

My breathing was shallow and quick, still nothing in comparison to the pounding of my pulse. Earl lay lifeless at my feet, his eyes locked on mine. There was hatred but also disappointment in them. Maybe I imagined both. He'd never been a good man, and definitely not a good father, even less to Gray than to me. Still, I'd have never thought I'd kill him. He'd been my guidance on my path to revenge. He'd fired up my hatred whenever it threatened to extinguish. He'd been my idol when it came to women, school, and every other life choice. Many of them had been shitty, but I doubted my choices would have been better on my own. With my old man's blood running through my veins, a messed-up life had always been my destiny. Falling for a mafia princess was the cherry on top.

That wasn't why we were here now, why I'd killed the only father figure I'd known since I was a little boy. I hadn't wanted to see his bad sides, and I had enough bad sides myself so I'd never dared to cast my judgment over another human being. Yet, Earl had gone too far. He'd crossed a barrier that had always been in place, a barrier that took him and our club down a road where there was no coming back from. We should have realized it when more and more members became Nomads, many good men the club could have used during votings.

I was guilty of kidnapping an innocent woman, and even allowing Earl to lock her in a kennel and video-recording her naked. All of these made me feel fucking guilty and like a major dick. We should have stuck with Vitiello and his men. We should have attacked him directly, but at the very least we should have kept Marcella safe from pain. That Earl had begun torturing her, that he had wanted to keep doing it, I couldn't accept it. I'd seen the look in his eyes. I had been as lost to him as he was to me. He wanted to kill me and he would have done it if Vitiello hadn't smashed our clubhouse to the ground. He would probably have killed Marcella first and made me watch. I had been a traitor in his eyes, when *he* had betrayed everything we'd always wanted the club to stand for. Honor and a free lifestyle. A home for all those who didn't fit inside the confines of society. Brotherhood, friendship. We lost all those along the way and what remained was bitterness and hunger for revenge and money.

Still, Earl's death had been merciful in comparison to the end Luca would have given him.

Cora Reilly

I finally dragged my eyes away from Earl. My fingers cramped around the handle of the knife and my skin was sticky with sweat and blood. Some of it my own, but most of it was Earl's. I met Marcella's gaze. I wasn't sure how much of the torture she had watched. She was pale as she leaned against the wall, her arms hugging herself and her knuckles white from the grip her fingers had on her elbows. She swallowed, her eyes searching mine before she straightened and cleared her throat. "Thank you," she said simply.

I nodded, lost for words.

"The knife," Luca said in a voice like a whip. He was probably pissed that Earl had only suffered a brief time. He'd no doubt make sure I suffered twice as much to make up for it.

I unfurled my fingers and let the knife tumble to the ground with a clang. This might have been my last chance to ram a knife into Luca's chest, but the hunger for revenge had been replaced by my need to guarantee Marcella's wellbeing. Once I was dead, and I had absolutely no doubt that her father would soon kill me, Marcella needed her entire family to get past the events of the kidnapping. Even if she'd told Earl that his actions—our actions—didn't leave scars, I'd heard the slightest tremor in her voice, seen the brief flare of pain in her eyes.

Amo moved forward and picked up the knife, his eyes never leaving me. Hatred simmered in them. I would have felt the same if I were in his place.

"It's time to go now, Marcella," Luca said firmly. He motioned at his brother who'd watched everything with a calculating look.

She nodded, but instead of leaving, she headed toward him. He lowered his head so she could whisper in his ear. He shook his head at first but she gripped his arm, her fingers turning white again, and whispered some more. Eventually he pulled back and gave one sharp nod, but he didn't look happy about whatever he'd agreed on.

Her eyes darted to me, and I felt a fucking pang in my heart, knowing that this was the last time I'd see her. I wanted more time with her. I wanted another kiss, another whiff of her scent. I needed more seconds,

228

minutes, hours, days with her, but even then, it would never be enough. I had a feeling that even a lifetime with Marcella wouldn't sate my longing for her. It was an insatiable hunger, a burning need. I didn't have a lifetime, not even a few seconds.

She turned and left the room. The heavy steel door fell closed with a harrowing bang.

Earl was dead. Cody was as good as dead, and Smith was a simpering mess. I supposed I would be next. Maybe Marcella had asked her father to give me a quick death, a trickle of mercy. Maybe he'd agreed. Maybe she trusted his promise. But she wasn't here now, and I knew the kind of hatred Luca must feel for me. It was one I was painfully familiar with. I'd given up mine for Marcella.

I sank down in my chair, waiting for them to do what they wanted. I met Luca's gaze. I wasn't scared of him, and I'd die with my head held high. Amo shook his head and staggered toward me. Would he kill me with the same knife I'd used on Earl? It would be a fitting end.

Amo gripped my arm, and I had to resist the urge to smash my fist into his face. These were my enemies. My feelings for Marcella hadn't changed that.

"You're lucky my sister has a heart," Amo snarled as he jerked me to my feet. "If it were up to me, you'd choke on your blood." He shoved me toward the door where Luca was waiting. My body bristled at his closeness. Two decades of hatred flared up.

"Because of Marcella, you'll live, even if you don't deserve it," Luca growled.

I smiled coldly. "Ditto."

His eyes flashed with fury. He wanted to kill me. I could see the desire burning him up. But Marcella's influence was too strong. This woman held more power in her elegant hands than she realized.

"Take him to the other cell, Growl," he barked at a big guy with tattoos all over. The guy looked as if he wasn't sure he heard his boss right, but he didn't protest, only grabbed my upper arm and led me down the dark hallway. He unlocked another steel door and shoved me inside.

My legs almost gave out, but I caught myself against the wall. Growl regarded me a second longer.

"Nice tattoos," I said dryly.

He nodded but didn't deign me with a reply. Without a word, he closed the door. I sank to the cold stone floor, suddenly feeling every cut and bruise and broken bone in my body. When I'd expected death, nothing had mattered. Now I wondered if I'd be left to rot in this place. Maybe death would have been kinder than being locked in the underground with only the memory of Marcella while she found a new guy, probably some Famiglia asshole, to marry. Eventually I closed my eyes, waiting for death or whatever else Vitiello had in store for me.

Marcella

When the steel door fell shut behind my back with a chilling bang, I leaned against it and took a shuddering breath. "Marcella?" Matteo asked. He was supposed to take me home.

"Give me a moment."

I closed my eyes. Maddox had really killed his uncle. I hoped he wouldn't feel guilty for it. He must realize that his uncle had been a dead man the second my family had captured him. Dad would have made his end far more excruciating.

"Watching something like this takes some getting used to," Matteo said gently.

I opened my eyes. "I don't think I want to get used to something like that."

Matteo smiled. "You don't have to. After today, you can leave all this behind you."

"You really think I can?"

Matteo shrugged. "Not if you don't try. Some things always stay with you. You just learn to ignore them. Let's get you home now. Aria is probably already worried sick. I don't want her to kick my ass."

I didn't laugh despite the humor in his voice. "I'll stay. I'm going to wait for Dad and Amo to be done. I want to be there when they come out. They do this for me. I owe it to them," I said firmly.

"Torturing bikers isn't a huge sacrifice for them, trust me. Go home and think of something else. Let today be a new start for you," Matteo said imploringly.

It was a new start, but not in a way Matteo meant.

"I'm staying."

Matteo sighed. "You tell your mother."

I took out my new phone and sent her a quick text before I followed Matteo toward a table and chairs beside a rundown kitchenette. He sat down, but I was too agitated.

I paced the warehouse, my stilettos loud in the huge building. I gave Matteo a look. "Why aren't you in there, helping Dad and Amo torture and kill the two bikers?"

"Two bikers aren't enough for all of us, especially since you took care of the two Whites we really wanted to get our hands on."

"You want Maddox dead."

"All of us want him dead and he wants us dead."

"Maddox killed his uncle for me, and Dad promised to spare Maddox's life."

Matteo chuckled, shaking his head. "That's not the outcome I expected."

It wasn't the outcome he'd wanted was what he really meant. I didn't expect their hatred to evaporate but I wanted there to be the chance for it to wane eventually. "Where did Growl take Maddox?"

"Don't even think about going there now. Talk to your dad and your mom, and sleep over whatever you think you want right now. All right?"

I nodded. Matteo was right. I sank down beside him on a chair. A couple of guards crossed the warehouse and threw me curious glances. I nodded a greeting at them.

Two hours passed before Dad and Amo finally showed up. They had changed clothes but the darkness still clung to them, especially Dad looked worn out. He was impossibly strong but his guilt ate away at him. I could see it every second I was with him.

He glanced at Matteo. "What's she still doing here?"

"I refused to leave," I said before he could reprimand Matteo.

"You should forget all this, Marci. Live the life you used to have. I'll make sure nothing ever happens to you again. I'll triple your guards and kill every man who means a danger to you."

I smiled sadly. "This world means danger. You can't shield me from it." I loved that he still thought he could.

He shook his head. "This was never meant to happen."

He looked like he wished he could torture himself to death. Guilt wasn't an emotion he was very familiar with. That probably made it harder to deal with. I walked over to him and hugged his middle tightly, my cheek pressed against his chest.

"I'm my father's daughter, Dad," I whispered thickly. "And if that means I'll have to bleed for our family then that's what I'll do. I'll do it gladly."

"You paid for my sins," he rasped, and I had to look up. His eyes were so full of darkness even Mom's light wouldn't be able to penetrate it.

"What is the sin but a manmade phantasm?"

"Too clever and beautiful for this world."

"This world doesn't scare me, Dad. I'm thankful for your protection, but ultimately freedom always comes with a certain risk, and I'd rather have the freedom to walk around and do things I like than being locked in a mansion. I don't expect you to guarantee my safety, but I love you for trying."

Dad touched my cheek. "I could send you to a university in England where you'd be safer."

"Dad, no matter where I go, I'll always be a Vitiello and I don't want to be anyone else." I paused, knowing what I'd say next would be even a harder pill to swallow for Dad.

"I want to be part of the business."

Dad tensed, already beginning to shake his head. I'd expected this reaction and in the past, it would have made me retreat, but I'd gone through hell.

I pulled back from him. Hugging him like a small kid wouldn't increase my chances.

"Don't say you want to protect me from this side of our world, Dad. I deserve to reap the rewards of my suffering."

Dad glanced at Amo, who'd been listening with a deep frown, still cleaning his hands with a towel. Amo met my gaze. Amo was alpha. He was born to be Capo. He carried natural authority. He'd be a good Capo one day. I'd never take that from him. I could see that both he and Dad thought I was asking to become the head of the Famiglia, the first woman to ever lead an Italian American family. But like Dad had said, I was clever and knew how our men ticked. They'd never accept me, no matter what I'd do. I'd have to rule with utmost brutality and still they'd never admire and love me like they did Dad and would one day Amo.

My family was more important than being number one.

"You are older," Amo said quietly. "It's your birthright." I could see how much it cost him to give me this, and I couldn't believe what he was offering, that he was really willing to step back from the position he'd been groomed for from birth.

I swallowed, overcome by unwelcome emotionality. I stalked toward him and hugged him, my face pressed against his chest, feeling his heart pound against my cheek.

"No one deserves it more than you," he murmured.

"You do," I croaked. "And I won't take that from you. Never."

I pulled back and stared at Amo. Darkness and anger still simmered in his gray eyes and I worried they'd never go away.

He nodded, obviously fighting with himself.

I turned to Dad, who looked honestly confused. "I don't know what place I want in the Famiglia yet. For now, I want to lead a group of enforcers who'll hunt down every single member of the Tartarus MC in our territory who sympathizes with Earl White, and if Remo Falcone allows it, even beyond our borders. They can die or they can fall to their knees and swear loyalty to us. Once that's taken care of, I could handle logistics or negotiate new co-operations."

Admiration flickered in Dad's eyes, but at the same time, his hesitancy remained. What I had to say next wouldn't make it easier for him.

"I want Maddox at my side."

Dad's expression hardened, and Amo scoffed. "He's not one of us."

"Sparing his life is one thing, which I still consider a mistake, but allowing him to work for us and be near you? That's out of the question, Marci. I won't ever allow it."

I straightened my shoulders, prepared for the battle. "He could be one of us. He saved me."

"After he kidnapped you," Amo growled. "Those pieces of MC shit aren't loyal."

"He's loyal to me."

Dad glowered. "Marci, don't mistake him leaving the sinking ship for anything but what it is: fear of losing his life."

I narrowed my eyes. "I'm not a child and I'm not a fool. Maddox isn't scared of death. Were you even close to finding their clubhouse when he called you?"

Dad and Amo exchanged a look. "We would have found it eventually," Dad said carefully.

"That would have been too late. Earl enjoyed torturing me. He wanted to pass me around like a trophy."

I could see the battle in Dad's eyes. "Your mom told me you weren't…" He swallowed hard, torn between fury and despair.

"I wasn't raped, no, Dad. Maddox kept me safe. He risked his life to save me. He killed his uncle to avenge me."

"Then why did he do it?" Amo asked.

"Because he loves me."

Amo laughed as if I'd lost my mind, but Dad only regarded me with worry. "How do you know?"

"He told me, and I can see it in his eyes. I just know it deep down." Dad looked away.

"Let him prove himself, to you, to me, to our family."

"I won't allow him near you or your mother or Valerio without supervision."

I touched Dad's arm. "Trust me on this, Dad."

"I trust you, Marci, but after what he did, I can't see myself trusting that man. And I doubt your mom would want your kidnapper near you or our family."

"I talked to Mom about Maddox. She knows how love can change everything. It changed you."

Amo grimaced as if the whole love discussion made him sick. "If love turns you into an idiot, I'd rather not fall in love. It's a waste of time and energy. We are enemies, Marci. That won't change."

Dad ignored him. He had only eyes for me, and he looked almost scared as he asked, "If you talk about love, you mean his possible feelings for you."

"His feelings for me, yes, and my feelings for him."

Dad released a harsh breath. "What are you saying, Marci? That you love him?"

I swallowed hard. "I think so, yes."

Amo cursed in Italian, and Dad shook his head, looking full of despair. "Thinking isn't enough in this case. He's the reason why you got that horrible tattoo. He's the reason why you lost your ear, and you tell me you like that bastard?"

"Maddox isn't the reason. He wanted to stop his uncle."

"But he didn't."

"He couldn't."

Dad shook his head. "He's the enemy."

"He doesn't have to be."

"He can't be part of our world. Our men would never accept him."

"I know it'll be a hard battle, but it's one I'm willing to fight."

"And Maddox, do you really think he wants to work for me, follow my orders?" Dad motioned at the cut on the side of his head then at his leg. "He stabbed me. He wanted to kill me. He probably still wants to kill me and your brother."

"But he didn't?"

Dad chuckled darkly. "Did you ask him if he wants to be part of our world?"

I swallowed, trying to come to terms with the fact that Maddox had attacked Dad. Maybe his desire for revenge was still too strong. But what would become of us then? I wouldn't leave my family. "I have to talk to him."

"We can give him a quick death if that's what you want after the talk," Amo said.

I gave him a hard look. "That's not funny."

"No, it's not," Amo agreed. "It's fucking bullshit that you think you love our enemy."

Dad wrapped an arm around me. "Wait a day or two before you talk to him. Give yourself time to bring distance between yourself and the kidnapping. Talk to your mom again."

"Okay," I said. Dad was right. I needed a clear head for my conversation with Maddox. Too much was at stake. Not just my happiness and his life, but also my family's wellbeing. I couldn't be selfish with this.

Dad and Amo exchanged a look with Matteo. It wasn't difficult to read their expressions. They all hoped I'd change my mind and let them kill Maddox.

"If we let him live, maybe even let him go, he might try to kill your father and brother again. You really want to risk it?" Matteo asked quietly as we headed to the car outside.

Chapter
Twenty-One

Maddox

I T WAS DARK IN THE WINDOWLESS ROOM THEY HAD DRAGGED me into after I'd killed my uncle. The stench of piss and blood culminated in an overwhelming odor of despair. I wondered how many had died inside these walls, broken apart by Vitiello's capable hands. Now there were two Vitiellos, and I couldn't tell who was worse, the father or the son.

My hands were still sticky with my uncle's blood. I had killed him on Marcella's request without hesitation. I'd do it again, even if it had brought me here into this hopeless prison and not into the arms of the woman I couldn't stop thinking about. Maybe I should have known she wouldn't forgive me as easily. Even killing my uncle didn't change the fact that I'd kidnapped her and had been unable to protect her from my uncle's cruelty. She'd carry the marks of my sins all her life.

I lost all sense of time, not that it mattered. I often caught myself wishing for death.

The door creaked open and the light from the corridor hit my face, momentarily blinding me. I squinted against the brightness to see who'd come to see me. Marcella to say goodbye before her father ended it? But the form that took shape was too ginormous to belong to anyone but Luca Vitiello himself. It took several seconds before he came into focus.

His expression was pure steel, his eyes the merciless pools I remembered from many years ago. He didn't say anything. Maybe he hoped to see me beg for mercy, but it would have been a waste of both our times. He didn't grant mercy and I'd cut my own dick off before I'd ever ask him for it. Maybe I had killed my uncle and helped Vitiello save Marcella, but I sure as fuck hadn't done it for him. Everything I'd done had been for Snow White.

I still wanted him dead. Maybe that would always be the case.

"Is it time?" I croaked. My throat scratchy from too many hours without something to drink.

Luca's face didn't so much as twitch. He was probably imagining all the ways he'd dismember and torture me. He hated my fucking guts, for what I'd done to Marcella—and I whole-heartedly agreed with him on that point—but also for who I was, a biker, my father's son, the man who'd touched his daughter. If Marcella told him how I'd taken her precious virginity, he'd probably kill me just for that transgression.

Fuck, dying with that memory in my mind might be worth dying over and over again.

"You kidnapped my daughter, risked her wellbeing and safety, only to save her weeks later. I wonder why you did it? Maybe you realized the Famiglia and I would catch up eventually and you saw it as your only chance to save your fucking hide."

I shoved to my feet but regretted it as a wave of dizziness overcame me, so I sat back down on the ground. Vitiello regarded me without emotion. I was less than dirt in his eyes.

"The same reason why I didn't ram my knife into your eye. For Marcella."

"Because you feel guilty?" he scoffed.

I felt guilty, but would that have propelled me to destroy the club? "Guilt is only a tiny part of it."

"Then why?" Luca growled.

"Because I love her." I laughed, realizing the absurdity of the situation. "I love the daughter of the man who destroyed my life."

Luca waved me off. "Many people lose someone. That's part of our world."

"I'm sure many kids watch their father's bowels being strewn about like fucking confetti," I muttered. "What I've been wondering since you slaughtered my club is if you noticed me that day?"

Luca stared me down as if I'd grown a second head. "What the fuck are you talking about?"

I pushed to my feet, even if they felt like rubber. I couldn't have this conversation sitting at Vitiello's feet like a dog. "I'm asking if you noticed that terrified five-year-old boy cowering under the couch while you maimed the people he considered his family?"

Luca's face remained the impassive, harsh mask I knew. Marcella too had a chilling poker face but it was nothing in comparison to that of her old man. "I didn't see a boy that day."

"Would it have changed things or would you have killed me alongside my father and his men?"

"I don't kill children or innocent women," Vitiello said.

It was difficult to believe he could spare anyone. Marcella's story of her father simply didn't fit the image of the man that I had.

"So you would have turned on your heel and left if you'd known I was there?"

It was a rhetorical question. The look in Vitiello's eyes hadn't been that of a man capable of turning his back on bloodshed. He'd thirsted for violence and rampage. Nothing, not even a little boy could have stopped him.

His penetrating stare gave me the answer I'd expected.

"What would you have done to me then?"

"Locked you in my car so you wouldn't have to watch in an ideal world."

"Your kind of ideal world includes locking a young boy in your car so you can slaughter his father and his men?"

"I doubt your ideal world is filled with sunshine and rainbows." He narrowed his eyes. "And you kidnapped an innocent girl, so you certainly don't have a right to judge me. My only judge will be God."

"You believe in God?"

He didn't reply.

"You're forgetting the law authorities. They might one day judge you too."

"Unlikely. But that's not the point. You kidnapped my daughter."

"Which would have never happened if you hadn't slaughtered my father and his club!"

I breathed harshly, losing myself to the anger of the past again. Fuck. I still wanted to kill him.

"You deserve death and I want nothing more than to kill you, but I can't because I love your daughter!"

Luca took a step closer, glaring. "You deserve death as much as I do, and I want to kill you more than anything for what you let happen to Marcella, but I can't because I love my daughter."

We stared at each other, trapped with our hatred and reined in by our love for one girl.

"And now, here we are," I said wryly. "You could let one of your men kill me and stage a suicide scene. Tell Marcella guilt wrecked me over getting my club brothers killed."

"That's an option," Luca said. "Are you feeling guilty about it?"

"Most of them had to die for Marcella to be safe."

Luca didn't say anything for a long time. Maybe he really considered the suicide plan. "My daughter thinks you are loyal to her."

"I am," I said. "I'd do anything for her."

Luca smiled darkly. "I think she'll test both our love for her. I don't know if I should hope you fail or not. Either way, Marcella will face obstacles I never wanted for her." He tilted his head in consideration. "I don't have to tell you what I'll do if I think you're messing with her."

"I'd have put my life down for her. I won't ever hurt her."

"If that's the case, you should leave and never come back. Go to Texas and ride into the fucking sunset with your brother but allow Marcella to have the future she deserves and had always planned for herself before you destroyed everything." He tossed a book at me that read bullet journal. "Look at the first page."

I opened the book and squinted down at the paper. It was a sort of bullet journal and Marcella had listed her plan for the next five years. Get a degree at twenty-two, marry the same year, create marketing plans for Famiglia businesses, first child at twenty-five…

"Life can't be planned like that," I muttered, but seeing Marcella's hopes for her future hit home. Her life plans weren't in line with my life choices so far. "You sure those aren't the things you wanted for her?"

"She wrote them down. You really think you and her could ever be together? Marcella is educated and socially adept. She thrives on social events. She's always been careful to protect her public image. If news got out that she's with you, everything she's built for herself will crumble. Do you really want to ruin her?"

I couldn't believe he was paying the guilt card, and I couldn't believe he was actually making an impact on me. "Would you have let the woman you love go?"

Luca smiled darkly. "I'm selfish. Maybe you want to be better than me."

"You're not doing this for her."

He grabbed me by the throat and in my weakened state, I couldn't fight him off. My back collided with the wall. His eyes burned with pure fury. "Don't tell me that I'm not doing this for Marcella. I'd die for her. I only want the best for her and that's sure as fuck not you." He released me and stepped back, breathing harshly.

I rubbed my throat. "Marcella isn't a child. She can make her own life choices."

For a moment, I was sure Luca would kill me right on the spot but then he turned on his heel and left. I wasn't surprised that he didn't approve of me being with Marcella. We came from different worlds, there was no denying it. I wanted nothing more than to be with her, but I wasn't sure how our worlds could ever merge.

A few hours later, Marcella came in, followed by her brother, who looked at me as if he wanted to smash my face in. The feelings were mutual. She looked like the girl from before the kidnapping. High heels, tight leather pants, silky blouse, and a diamond earring over her missing earlobe that probably cost more than my Harley.

I wondered why she was here. Her expression was pure control, beautiful perfection that taunted and tantalized me as I sat in my own stink, waiting for the end.

Marcella turned to Amo. "I want to talk to Maddox alone."

"I'm supposed to keep an eye on you."

"Don't be ridiculous, Amo. Maddox killed his uncle and biker brothers for me. He won't hurt me."

Amo gave me a look that made it perfectly clear what would happen if I touched her.

"Can you get Maddox something to drink and eat?"

My last meal?

Amo gave a terse nod, then he left. Marcella closed the door after him before she turned fully to me.

I shoved to my feet, trying to hide the fact that I was dehydrated and starving. I didn't want her to remember me as a weakling.

"Is this goodbye?" I asked.

"My father doesn't trust you. He doesn't think you are loyal."

I moved closer, every step sent a twinge through my body. I was fairly sure I had several broken bones that needed treatment. "Didn't I prove it when I betrayed the club for you?"

I would have given anything for this woman, for a taste of her lips, to hear a declaration of love from those red lips.

"I thought so, yes, but then you tried to kill my father. I saw the stab wound in his leg and the cut on his head where you missed."

"Missed?" I echoed, then laughed. "I didn't miss anything, Snow White. I chose not to kill him because I couldn't do it to you, and that's exactly what I told him. I suppose he didn't mention that detail?"

She narrowed her eyes thoughtfully but didn't say anything, still not willing to stab her father in the back. "You gave up revenge for me?"

"I did." But after my conversation with Luca today, I wished I'd gone through with it.

"What about the next time you get the chance to stab my father? How will you choose then?"

I wanted to kill him, no doubt, but going through with it? I chuckled. "I think you don't understand. There's always only one choice, and that's you. Unless you want me to kill your old man, which probably will only happen in my dreams, I won't try to kill him again. I'm not sure he can say the same."

"So you want to kill him and he wants to kill you, but you both don't go through with it for me."

"More powerful than any queen I know."

Marcella sighed and touched her elbows with newly manicured fingers. Fuck. I wanted her in my arms. It was physically painful to have her so close and not touch her. "What do you want, Maddox?"

"You."

"But I come with baggage. I'm a Vitiello. I'll always be a part of my family and I'll even join the business. If you want me, you have to figure out a way to become part of them too."

I laughed, couldn't help it. "Look, I'm all for dreaming and setting high goals, but your old man won't ever accept me as part of the business." I paused, realizing what else she had said. "You want me as part of your family?"

"My family is part of me, so if you love me, you'll have to try loving them as well."

I shook my head, sagging against the wall. "I only recently gave up revenge for you. Going from hating your father's guts to love is a far leap that might take several lifetimes. Even if I'm lithe like one, I'm not a cat."

Marcella rolled her eyes and moved closer until she was right in front of me. I wasn't sure how she could stand the stink, but I was glad for her closeness. "What my dad did to you as a child was horrible, and I understand your hatred. Forgiveness takes time. I'm just asking you to try to overcome your anger."

I wasn't sure that was an option, for either Luca or me. "What about you? How long will it take for you to forgive me?"

"I forgive you," she said quietly.

"You do?"

"But I don't trust you fully yet. I can't, not after what happened."

"If you don't trust me, your father definitely won't." I smiled wryly. "Then this is goodbye after all."

"No," she said firmly. She peered up at me, fixing me with those blue eyes that haunted me. Eyes that made me want to believe in the impossible. "I didn't tell him. That's between you and me. I want you in my life. Now it's up to you to decide whether you want that too."

I didn't want to lose her. "Forgiving your father is torture," I murmured and Marcella's face flickered with disappointment. "But I'll gladly suffer for you. I'm going to prove my loyalty to you a million times if I have to, Snow White. I'll earn your trust. I'll bleed for you. I'll kill for you. I'll do anything until you trust me absolutely."

"Absolute trust is a rare thing."

I wanted nothing more than to kiss her, but I could only imagine how vile I looked.

"What we have is a rare thing too."

"For you to win my trust, you'll have to make peace with my father, with my family. You'll have to let go of your hunger for vengeance. You need to be on my father's side because it's the side I'm on, and that won't change. Can you really do that?"

"For you, yes." I was willing to try. I wasn't sure I could succeed.

Amo returned, eyeing us critically. He really carried a tray with food and water, though I was wary of the contents. "Time to head home," he said.

Marcella nodded slowly but didn't move.

"You look like a million dollars," I murmured.

"More than you can afford," Amo growled.

"Amo," Marcella hissed before she turned to me again. "Make the right decision."

She turned, every move full of elegance, and left. Amo shook his head at me before he too left and threw the door shut.

"If only I knew what that was."

Chapter
Twenty-Two

Maddox

ANOTHER DAY PASSED, IN WHICH SOMEONE BROUGHT ME food and water. Despite my worry that they'd spit into my provisions, I was just too thirsty and hungry to be choosy. My thoughts became more and more confusing.

When Luca opened the door the next time, his expression didn't give anything away. "What now?" I asked.

"I don't trust you. But I trust my daughter, and she wants your freedom."

I perked up. I couldn't believe Marcella had really convinced her old man. "I have to say I'm surprised."

Luca's mouth thinned. "I still believe you deserve death for what you did, but Marcella suffered and it's her decision."

I got up. "You're really going to let me go? How's that supposed to work? And what about your soldiers, won't they be pissed you release their enemy?"

"If you had killed one of my soldiers during the fight, I would have killed you, no matter what Marcella says, but you didn't. You even killed another biker. My men want the Famiglia strong and if I tell them that having you on our side makes us stronger, they'll eventually grow used to you."

"I doubt it," I muttered. The fights between our MC and the Famiglia had become increasingly ugly in the last few years. There was too much bad blood between us. It would take years to get past it, if at all.

Luca narrowed his eyes. "Marcella said you'd be willing to cooperate, to recruit bikers willing to work with us, and eliminate those who still pose a risk for Marcella."

"That's right. But I sure as hell am not going to swear an oath to you, Vitiello. I'm doing this because of Marcella, but I still have my pride."

"You really think you're in a position to negotiate?"

I met his gaze square on. "If you don't like it, kill me. I love your daughter. The man she met and fell in love with had a backbone and pride. I won't become someone else so you decide to spare me. I'll work with you, not for you, and I'll do it gladly because it'll make Marcella's position in the Famiglia stronger. That's all. If you don't like it, put a bullet in my head now and spare us both the chitchat."

Luca nodded. Maybe he'd just agreed to end me. The guy was impossible to read. "You aren't a coward. And I don't give a fuck what you call it as long as you don't do anything that hurts the Famiglia, and especially Marcella. I don't even give a fuck if you have your own side business as long as it doesn't interfere with my business. The Famiglia earns enough money to spare a bit."

I gritted my teeth against his condescending tone, even if I was relieved that he'd given me that option. I would have tried to make money with old contacts anyway. I wasn't going to accept Vitiello's paycheck.

"You weren't that gracious when it came to Tartarus trying to sell drugs and guns in your territory."

"Your club flooded my clubs and streets with shitty drugs, even pretending it was Famiglia stuff. Not to mention that you tried to mess with my business and burned down one of my warehouses." He paused, glaring. "Maybe you don't remember, but when your father was the president of the Jersey chapter, your club was still into sex trafficking. The police fished several dead prostitutes out of the Hudson and began asking me questions. I warned your father to stop the shit but he was trying to fund his weapons with the sex slaves."

Earl had mentioned something along the lines. Back then, the main chapter in Texas had still been involved in sex trafficking as well, but eventually, they got too much heat from the Russians and Mexicans, so they stopped. Luckily that happened years before I became a part of the club. "Don't pretend you killed my father because you felt sorry for the poor sex slaves. You were out for blood that day. You just wanted to kill and my father and his club brothers were a convenient target."

"I don't deny it. And I sure as hell won't apologize for it. Your father deserved to die and he wouldn't have hesitated to kill me either. In hindsight, I would have made sure you weren't there to watch."

I supposed that was as close to an apology as Luca Vitiello ever got. Marcella had mentioned that her father wasn't in the habit of apologizing. We fell silent and just stared at each other. His eyes reflected the same distrust and loathing I felt. "Fuck, this feels wrong."

"I don't need a fucking oath from you, but I want your word that you won't hurt Marcella and will help us with other bikers."

"You have my word. I'm surprised you care for it. Is a biker's word worth anything in your eyes?"

Luca shrugged. "If you don't stand by your word, I can still hunt down your brother Gray."

I got in his face. "He's off-limits, Vitiello. He's minding his own business and that won't change." I sure as hell hoped that was really the case. Gray needed a strong support system, and I worried he'd seek it in another MC, or maybe in a rebuilt Tartarus.

Luca only smiled coldly. Fuck, Marcella, how am I supposed to do this?

"Where's Marcella?"

A muscle in Luca's cheek tautened. "At home. She knows I'm here to talk to you but I didn't think it was a good idea to have her around while we still needed to settle things."

"In case you'll have to shoot me."

He didn't say anything.

"If you let me go, I'll have to take care of a few things first, especially talk to my mother, then I'd like to talk to Marcella. How can I contact her?"

"Come by the Sphere and I'll arrange a meeting."

I had to bite back a comment. This was a bitter pill to swallow for Vitiello, so I cut him some slack, but I sure as fuck wouldn't ask him every time I was going to meet his daughter.

"Are you sure none of your men are accidentally going to shoot me because they thought I was on the run?"

"My men do as I say."

"I bet," I said. "Your reputation keeps them in line."

"It's more than that. The Famiglia is based on loyalty. That's not something you'd understand."

"Loyalty should never be given blindly. Loyalty must be earned, and my uncle and many of my club brothers chose a path I couldn't support."

"What about the rest? We didn't kill every member."

"Like I said, my brother is off-limits. He's a kid and he won't cause trouble without Earl. Knowing him, he'll become a mechanic and mind his own business in the middle of nowhere Texas with my mom. She's off-limits too."

Luca smiled grimly. "I'm not sure I trust your assessment of your brother's harmlessness. But Marcella asked me to spare him and your mother, so for her, I'll do it, until your brother gives me reason to see him as a danger to my family."

"He won't be. Gray isn't vindictive."

"Are you sure he won't mind you killing his father?"

I hadn't seen Gray since he'd managed to escape. I wasn't sure how much he knew, definitely not that I had killed Earl. "Unless you've spread the word, no one knows that I killed Earl."

"So you don't plan on telling him." .

Gray deserved the truth, but I worried it would set him off, not to mention that it would make my work of looking for rogue bikers out to kill Marcella all the more difficult. Though, word about me becoming a traitor was probably already making the rounds, so it was only a matter of time before there'd be a bounty on my head.

Luca motioned at the door. "You're free to leave."

Surprise washed through me. I'd still thought he wouldn't go through with it. I still wasn't one-hundred percent sure I wouldn't end with a bullet in the back of my head the moment I turned my back on him.

"I suppose my bike's ash, right?"

"We burned down everything."

I nodded, not really surprised. "What about the dogs?"

They weren't my dogs and I'd never quite trusted them, but it really wasn't their fault that Earl had turned them into fighting machines. They deserved better.

"One of our enforcers, Growl, took one in and found a place in a shelter for the rest. Don't ask me where. He's the one who has a heart for beasts like that."

He turned and left the cell. Showing me his back was supposed to show me he didn't fear me. But he was still limping slightly even if he was trying to hide it. I followed him cautiously, still wary of his motives. Outside in the long corridor, waited the tall, tattooed man who'd taken me to the cell.

Luca gave him a nod, and I half expected Growl to pull a gun and put a bullet through my head. Instead, he motioned for me to follow him. He carried a bunch of clothes under one arm. I looked around but didn't see anyone else. Luca still watched me with an assessing expression. He thought I wasn't good enough for his daughter but I'd prove him wrong, but more than that, I was going to prove to Marcella that she could trust me.

The guy, Growl, stopped inside a washroom and put the clothes down on a bench in front of a row of lockers. The shower stalls were clean and fairly modern. Luca and his men probably showered here after they were done torturing their enemies. I still carried Earl's and also my blood on my skin, mixed with sweat and grime and dirt. I began to peel off my shirt when I realized Growl leaned against the wall, not really watching me, focused on the screen of his phone.

"Are you going to keep an eye on me so I don't do anything stupid?" I asked wryly.

He nodded.

I winced. A part of the shirt had gotten stuck to a wound under my ribs. With a tug, it came off. "Fuck," I muttered when blood began to trickle out.

"Should get stitches," Growl murmured.

I cocked an eyebrow. "Yeah, thanks. I was busy rotting in my cell."

Again a nod.

"So you took care of the dogs?"

"They deserve a better life."

"Thanks."

Growl nodded. "Luca's trust must be earned. I used to be the enemy. Now I'm not."

I got out of my remaining clothes. "Not sure he really wants to try."

"If he wanted you dead, you'd be dead, so he gives you a chance that few people get. Don't mess up."

I stepped into the shower with a groan.

Thirty minutes later, I followed Growl outside. The jeans and shirt were a bit too small for my tall frame. They obviously weren't Growl's.

To my surprise, Matteo Vitiello waited in the driveway beside a bike. A sleek black Kawasaki.

"Don't mess this up," Growl said as way of goodbye.

I headed for Matteo who was apparently waiting for me. "Growl's not the most communicative guy, is he?"

Matteo's grin became challenging. "I suppose you'll be seeing more of Growl once you start working with us."

It was obvious he didn't think I would.

"Looks like it. Maybe you can call a cab for me since my phone and bike are ashes."

"Where are you heading?" he asked, still with that smile that made me want to knock him out.

"I need to take care of business and check on my mother."

"What kind of business? Meeting old friends?"

"My old friends are dead or out for my blood," I said with a harsh smile. "But there are a few old funds I'd like to save before someone else does. I'm all out of dimes right now. And I sure as fuck won't borrow it from the Famiglia."

The calculation and distrust in Matteo's eyes really set me off. After days in a stinking cell with hardly any food and water, I wasn't in the mood for bullshit talk. He didn't have to like me or trust me. All that mattered was that Marcella did.

Matteo motioned at the Kawasaki. "You know what, why don't you take my bike. It's not a Harley but it'll take you wherever you need to go."

I raised my eyebrows. "You're giving me your bike."

"I'm sure you'll bring it back once you've taken care of business." His voice made it clear he thought I'd run off and never come back. I took the keys that he held out.

"Thanks. I'll take good care of it," I said with a forced smile. "Do you need me to call you a cab?"

Matteo flashed me a grin. "Oh, don't worry. I'll catch a ride with Luca."

Of course, the Capo was still around somewhere. They'd probably have a meeting once I was gone to discuss me, maybe even send someone after me to check if I was doing anything against the Famiglia.

"Once you're back, there's a lot to discuss. If you want to be with Marcella, we have to make arrangements for the engagement and wedding, change your wardrobe and give you a few lessons in etiquette so you can become part of her social circles."

He was baiting me, the asshole. As if he or Luca wanted me to marry Marcella. Unfortunately, his words had the intended effect. My body bristled at the mere idea of what he'd said. I didn't want to be groomed into someone else. Fuck, marriage had always seemed unnecessary in my mind.

I put on the helmet and started the bike. Matteo stepped back. With a salute, I drove away. I resisted the urge to look over my back. Turning my back on a Vitiello still gave me the chills. Riding the Kawasaki was an entirely new feeling for me. I preferred the steady rumble of the Harley and felt a pang when I thought of my now burned Harley. Still, the familiar feeling of freedom that always overwhelmed me on a bike grabbed me.

Could I really give up my freedom, my lifestyle, even part of myself for Marcella?

Marcella

Mom regarded me with worry as we sat at the dining table. Maddox had been released in the morning and Matteo had even given him his bike because Maddox had a few errands to run. I suspected he was looking for his brother and mother to make sure they were all right. Still, I'd hoped he'd figure out a way to contact me by now.

"Matteo shouldn't have given him his bike. I asked him for the thing for months and he just gifts it to our enemy," Amo muttered.

"It wasn't a gift. It's borrowed until he returns it when he comes back," I said firmly.

Amo shook his head. "*Right.*"

"Marcella," Dad began, obviously trying to deliver a blow as gently as possible. I knew what they all thought.

"Maddox hasn't run off. He's taking care of a few things and then he'll return to New York to prove himself."

Dad looked at Mom.

"Marcella knows him better than we do," she said in her usual diplomatic way. "If she puts her trust in him, I'm sure she has her reasons."

"Thanks, Mom."

"But I really want to meet him in person as soon as possible."

I stifled a smile at the sudden steel in her voice. "I'll introduce him to you." I didn't miss the look of wariness on Dad's face. He'd probably stand guard every second while Mom met Maddox. It was strange. Despite his radio silence and my family's doubts about his return, I believed he'd come back. After what he'd risked to save me, I was certain about his feelings for me.

When there hadn't been word about Maddox the next morning, I really began to get nervous. But I didn't want to waste time fretting. Maddox would return, and if he didn't... then he never deserved me to begin with. Still, my heart ached thinking about it.

I decided to distract myself with something I'd been meaning to do for a couple of days now. I called Growl and asked if he could pick me up and take me to the shelter that he'd built with Cara to help abused fight dogs. Dad had mentioned that they'd taken the Rottweilers there.

Thirty minutes later, he pulled up in front of our mansion. Two bodyguards waited in front of the door when I stepped outside. They accompanied me to Growl's car then got into a second car and followed us. "Thanks for coming so quickly," I said.

"I was surprised you want to see the dogs."

"I was terrified of them at first but I kind of bonded with the dog that was beside my cage. Her name is Satan, but she was badly injured. Do you know if she survived?"

"I don't know their names. I still need to name them."

"Don't name any dog Satan please."

Growl nodded.

"I have to admit seeing the dogs again isn't the only reason why I asked you to pick me up."

"I figured," Growl rasped. "Your father told me you'll join the business."

"I want to lead our Enforcer team, to coordinate the hits on MCs who're giving us trouble and also to find the remaining Tartarus bikers who pose a risk."

Growl merely nodded but I really wanted him to say something.

"I want to know if we'll have a problem because I'm a woman or because you wanted to be in charge of the enforcers."

"I don't have trouble serving you, and I never wanted to lead anyone. I'm happy with the job I'm doing every day."

"What about the other enforcers? Have they said something to you?"

"Most of them know better than to badmouth you."

They feared my dad but didn't respect me. I'd do my best to change it.

After almost one hour, we arrived at a farm building with several huge fenced-in areas. We got out and a lanky guy in his teens came out. "Troubled teens run the shelter under your guidance, right?"

"It gives them and the dogs a new home."

Growl led me around to a smaller area where ten Rottweilers in total were kept. "They don't get along with the other dogs yet so we have to keep them separate."

It didn't take me long to spot Satan, and relief rushed through me. Her side was bandaged and she had to wear a cone so she didn't lick the wound, but otherwise she looked good.

"She's alone in the cage because the other dogs wouldn't accept her while she's injured."

To my surprise, she trotted toward the fence the moment she spotted me. Considering our first encounter, we'd come a long way. "Hey girl," I said. She huffed and wagged her tail. Properly fed and with a big yard to run in, she seemed so much more relaxed than the dog I remembered.

Seeing her also brought back many memories from my captivity that I didn't want to recall. I still felt caught in a sort of limbo, back at home physically, but with my mind still lost in the clubhouse. I patted her gently through the bars. "Will you find a good home for her?"

"It won't be easy, given their upbringing."

"I wish I could take her in but Dad would never allow it."

"Your father wants to protect you."

"I know," I said. "From everything. Maddox, dogs…"

"Maddox needs to earn your father's trust. That's not an easy thing to do, but I was your father's enemy once and he gave me the benefit of the doubt. Maddox can do the same."

I smiled. "Thanks, Growl." I glanced at Satan who watched me. "Can you do me a favor and call her Santana? That's still close to her name but much better."

"Sure. You want to spend more time with her?"

"Yes." I stayed for another hour to pat her before Growl took me back home. I went up to my room to research possible tattoos so I wouldn't constantly think about Maddox.

In the early evening, a bike engine rumbled outside. My eyes widened and I jumped up from the sofa in my room. I stormed downstairs and toward the front door, my heart galloping wildly. I opened it and deflated when I saw Matteo on his bike—the bike he'd given to Maddox.

He ran a hand through his hair and gave me a small smile.

Steps sounded behind me, and Dad appeared beside me. His expression didn't bode well.

"What's wrong? Where's Maddox?"

Matteo came up the stairs, exchanging another secretive look with Dad.

"Dad," I said angrily. "Where's Maddox?"

Amo and Mom were in the foyer by now.

Dad touched my shoulder. "He showed up at Growl's shelter this afternoon and dropped off two more dogs and Matteo's bike."

We must have missed each other by an hour. "But where is he now?"

"He ran off like we all knew he would," Amo said.

I whirled on him to lash out, but Mom's compassionate expression told me Amo's words were true. "What?" I whispered, shocked. "He wouldn't just run off. He saved me, he betrayed his club for me…"

"Maybe he's come to regret his decision," Matteo said gently.

Dad touched my shoulder. "Maddox only knows his biker lifestyle. He doesn't want to be bound by a woman or social conventions. The call of the road, of freedom, was too strong."

"You think he chose freedom over me?"

"What he considers freedom at least."

"That's what he told Growl?"

Matteo nodded. "I talked to Growl when I picked up my bike. Maddox didn't stay long. He made sure to run off as quickly as he could. He's probably heading out of our territory now. The men who followed him yesterday saw him picking up a bag full of cash."

I swallowed hard. "He could have been free by my side."

"Good choice. If he builds up his fucking club again, I'll kill him, and this time Marci won't stop us," Amo muttered.

I ignored him. Mom wrapped an arm around me. "You have a wonderful future ahead of you, Marci. You don't need him. You have us."

I didn't need him, but I wanted him by my side. I'd wanted him to become part of my life, of my family. I'd thought we could overcome the chasm between our backgrounds.

But our bond had been fatal from the very beginning. Maddox had saved me, and I had saved him. That was all there was.

Now I just had to convince my heart of it.

To be continued in
By Sin I Rise - Part Two...

Please consider leaving a review.
Readers like you help other readers discover new books!

If you want to be among the first to get updates on books, please join
my Facebook group: Cora's Flamingo Squad
www.facebook.com/groups/172463493660891

More Mafia books by me:

Read about the first generation of mobsters in....

Born in Blood Mafia Chronicles:

Bound by Honor
(Aria & Luca)

Bound by Duty
(Valentina & Dante)

Bound by Hatred
(Gianna & Matteo)

Bound By Temptation
(Liliana & Romero)

Bound By Vengeance
(Growl & Cara)

Bound By Love
(Luca & Aria)

Bound By The Past
(Valentina & Dante)

Bound By Blood
(Anthology)

Luca Vitiello (Luca's POV of Bound by Honor)

The Camorra Chronicles:

Twisted Loyalties (#1)
Fabiano

Twisted Emotions (#2)
Nino

Twisted Pride (#3)
Remo

Twisted Bonds (#4)
Nino

Twisted Hearts (#5)
Savio

Twisted Cravings (#6)
Adamo

Standalone mafia romances

Fragile Longing
Sweet Temptation

Contemporary Romances

Only Work, No Play
Not Meant To Be Broken

About the Author

Cora is the author of the Born in Blood Mafia Series, the Camorra Chronicles and many other books, most of them featuring dangerously sexy bad boys. She likes her men like her martinis—dirty and strong.

Cora lives in Germany with a cute but crazy Bearded Collie, as well as the cute but crazy man at her side. In 2021, she gave birth to a wonderful daughter. When she doesn't spend her days dreaming up sexy books, she plans her next travel adventure or cooks too spicy dishes from all over the world.

Made in the USA
Las Vegas, NV
25 September 2023

78111832R00159